Advance Praise for *Tomorrow We Die*

Shawn Grady writes like an insider, with scenes pulsing with the real language and gritty drama of medicine. This novel has all the elements: endearing characters, the hope of love, and the ever present shadow of the grim reaper. Don't start this after supper if you want to sleep tonight.

—HARRY KRAUS, MD
bestselling author of *The Six-Liter Club* and *Salty Like Blood*

Packed with adrenaline and heart-drumming action, laced with unforgettable characters and humor, *Tomorrow We Die* pulses with authenticity that can only come from someone who knows his stuff—as a paramedic as well as a writer. Discover one of Shawn's books and you'll want to read them all.

—TOSCA LEE
author of *Demon: A Memoir* and *Havah: The Story of Eve*

With lights flashing and sirens blaring, Shawn Grady rushes the reader into the world of the emergency medical technician, with all its tension, triumph, and tragedy. Well-written and carefully crafted, this novel will keep you on the edge of your seat, so buckle up for a great ride.

—RICHARD L. MABRY, MD
author of *Code Blue*

Shawn Grady fills his literary syringe with potent storytelling, flawless research, and snappy dialogue, then injects them into the reader's bloodstream. *Tomorrow We Die* is a wild ambulance ride of a novel that races toward a suspenseful conclusion.

—ERIC WILSON
NY Times bestselling author of *Fireproof* and *Valley of Bones*

BOOKS BY SHAWN GRADY

Through the Fire
Tomorrow We Die

TOMORROW
WE
DIE

SHAWN GRADY

BETHANY HOUSE
MINNEAPOLIS, MINNESOTA

Tomorrow We Die
Copyright © 2010
Shawn Peter Grady

3 2210 00341 4569

Cover design by Lookout Design, Inc.

Published by Bethany House Publishers
11400 Hampshire Avenue South
Bloomington, Minnesota 55438

Bethany House Publishers is a division of
Baker Publishing Group, Grand Rapids, Michigan.

Printed in the United States of America

Library of Congress Cataloging-in-Publication Data

Grady, Shawn.
    Tomorrow we die / Shawn Grady.
        p.   cm.
    ISBN 978-0-7642-0596-5 (pbk.)
    1. Emergency medical technicians—Fiction. I. Title.
    PS3607.R3285T66   2010
    813'.6—dc22

                                                            2010005988

For
Sarah Beth

"If the dead do not rise, 'Let us eat and drink, for tomorrow we die.'"

—Saul of Tarsus

CHAPTER 01

I spent the day chasing the Angel of Death.

Being a paramedic can be a hard life, living in an ambulance for twelve hours a day, parked on street corners, inhaling reheated 7-Eleven burritos and Red Bull. There are shifts that wear on you, when no matter what you do, even if you run calls as smoothly as possible and do everything just right, that despite all the king's horses and all the king's men . . .

Death walks in without remorse.

I've seen people's spirits leave them before my eyes. And there is always something different in the room right then, something transcendental, as if unseen ushers are escorting a soul from this world. The entire week had been like that for my partner and me—always one step behind the Reaper.

So you can imagine my surprise when we actually caught him.

The harder my partner pushed on the gas pedal, the longer 395 northbound grew.

I pounded on the dashboard. "Come on, you pig."

"That's all she's got. Governor's kicked in." Bones hunched over the steering wheel, bouncing his head to an inaudible rhythm.

I felt our momentum level out at seventy-five miles per hour. The management made sure to keep our speed under control, among other things.

I sat back in my seat, placing my right foot up against the dash and the door. "Is this our third cardiac arrest?"

He nodded. "Just sifting with his scythe. Folks better break off a hyssop branch, if you know what I'm saying."

I had no idea what he was saying.

But that wasn't unusual.

My partner, Thaddeus McCoy, had been called Bones for as long as I'd known him. The nickname seemed especially fitting, even beyond his surname, given that he wore black medic pants—not the dark navy blue like everyone else—and a black leather belt that wrapped around his front with no visible buckle on it. His pants tapered down near the top of his boots, giving his uniform a 1960s *Star Trek* appearance. He sported a wiry body frame with pale Germanic skin, closely cropped straw-colored hair, and a well-groomed moustache that, were it shaved any smaller above his lip, would bestow upon him a Charlie Chaplin–like countenance.

Our call had come in as an "unknown man down on the sidewalk at First and West, in front of the church—unknown if conscious or breathing." Which, at the risk of sounding jaded, was generally code for "drunk guy on the street corner." But one thing I'd learned as a medic was to never judge too early. And based on the updated report we'd received from dispatch, this sounded like the real thing. A couple minutes into our response the dispatcher advised us that per an off-duty park ranger on scene, our patient was pulseless and apneic, and bystander CPR had been initiated. She also mentioned that the Reno Fire Department had a working structure fire just north of downtown and their next-in unit would likely arrive several minutes after us. If this guy had a chance, we were it.

"Look, Jonathan," Bones squealed in a high Mr. Bill voice, holding the radio microphone up by his side window, light posts and cars whizzing past, "I'm the fastest mic in the world."

I refused to respond to his impromptu puppet, knowing that if I so much as acknowledged it, I would find myself talking to a derisive plastic microphone for the rest of the shift. I turned my focus to the map book in my lap. "So you want to take Mill downtown and then jog over to First and West."

This time Bones spoke in the guttural voice he uses for our ambulance, Medic Two, which through the outpouring of his hyperactive imagination has also grown a sentient, albeit simpleton, personality. "Yes, Jonathan. That sounds good. . . . And I love you."

"That's great." I cringed with the realization that I'd just validated his anthropomorphic creation.

"Jonathan," in Medic Two's deep, gravelly voice he continued, "I love you."

I patted the vinyl on the dashboard as if it were a horse's neck. "Thanks, Medic Two."

"Jonathan?"

"Yes?"

"Do you love me too?"

There was no escaping this now.

"Yes, yes I do, Medic Two."

"More than Medic Seven?"

"Yes, more than Medic Seven."

"Good. I love you too. . . . Jonathan?"

I looked up at the ceiling of the cab. "Yes?"

"I'm not a pig. I'm really fast."

"You're right, Medic Two. My bad."

Bones greeted other vehicles in Medic Two's voice as we wailed passed them on the freeway. "Hello. Hi. I love you."

At the Mill Street exit, we hit heavy traffic. Most cars pulled to the right, but one older model GMC pickup skidded to a stop in front of us. Bones locked up our brakes and laid on the air horn. I lurched forward in my seat, held tight by the shoulder belt.

"Pull to the right!" Bones motioned with his hands, mouthing his words with exaggeration. "Pull. To. The. Right."

Getting impatient, I picked up the PA mic. "Pull to the right. Yes, you. Pull to the right."

The driver turned his wheel and rolled right, giving us just enough room to squeeze by on the shoulder to the left. Bones shot a friendly glance his direction as we passed. Already five minutes into our response, the chances of our patient surviving decreased exponentially with every second lost. With permanent brain death occurring after six minutes in cardiac arrest, time was running out.

We shot past County Hospital and screamed west into the heart of downtown Reno. We wove between and around taxicabs and shuttle busses and passed weekly motels. The snow-covered Sierras disappeared behind the towering casinos. We swung over to First Street, and Bones killed the siren save for a couple *whoop-whoops* as he brought the box to a stop in front of the church. There on the sidewalk, in the shadow of a hundred-year-old vine-covered Methodist sanctuary, knelt a balding park ranger doing chest compressions on a pale man in a long black overcoat.

"Medic Two's on scene—no fire department," I reported to dispatch and opened the door. The spring air felt brisk. I grabbed the defibrillator off the gurney in back and brought it to the patient's side, kneeling by the park ranger. "Go ahead and stop compressions."

The patient looked to be in his sixties, sporting a scraggly gray beard and wispy hair. Yellowish vomit oozed down the side of his face. His eyes were in a fixed and dilated stare. Bones cut off his shirt. I placed the defibrillator patches on his chest and looked at the monitor to examine his heart rhythm.

"Coarse V-fib, Bones. Charging to one-twenty. I'm clear— everyone clear." The park ranger held his hands up and glanced at his knees.

I delivered the first biphasic electrical shock and watched the man's body arch in tension and then relax again flat upon the concrete.

"Still fib. Charging to one-fifty. Everyone clear."

I delivered a second shock. No change.

"Charging to two hundred. Clear."

The Shock button glowed a fiery red, the air taut with the high-pitched whining of potential energy.

God, just let me have this one back.

My finger met the button. The man's body surged upward.

What followed was silence—and the long flat line of asystole.

I exhaled and nodded to the park ranger. "All right. Let's resume compressions. Bones, you want me to bag him while you set up to intubate?"

"Yes, sir, I do."

I inserted a curved piece of plastic to hold back the man's tongue from his throat. And after placing a mask over his mouth and nose, I squeezed the purple bag attached to it to inflate his lungs and breathe for him. "As soon as we get that tube, let's drop some epi down—"

The monitor beeped.

I waved off the park ranger. "Hold up."

The angled complexes of an organized heart rhythm graced the screen's black background—like a repetitive drawing of a small foothill leading to a mountain peak that dropped into a valley on the opposite side. Slow at first, then more rapid.

"Sinus tach. We got pulses with that?"

Bones reached for a carotid pulse at the neck. "I got one here."

I felt the patient's wrist. "Yeah, me too. I've got radials."

We'd gotten him back. Hope sprang forth in me. Only time would tell if we'd saved his heart but not his brain.

He was still unconscious, so Bones zipped open the intubation kit and prepared to place a breathing tube down the patient's throat.

I wrapped a tourniquet tight around his arm. The only vein I could feel popped up in the crook of his elbow. I swabbed it with alcohol and inserted the needle. A burgundy flash of blood filled the needle hub. I advanced it just a tad more before threading the plastic catheter into the vein.

"Sharp out." I placed the bare needle flat on the sidewalk and hooked up IV tubing connected to a bag of saline.

Blanket protocol for a patient on the streets like this involved a medication called Narcan to reverse the effects of possible heroin overdose. I administered the standard dose and squeezed the IV bag to flush it into his bloodstream.

Bones clicked into place a curved steel blade on a cylindrical handle. He twirled the sickle-shaped laryngoscope in his left hand and pulled out the short piece of plastic that held back the patient's tongue. He positioned the head and shined the light from the end of the laryngoscope blade down the man's throat. With his opposite hand, he angled an endotracheal tube in toward the vocal cords.

The park ranger stood wide-eyed, staring at the twisted progression of it all.

I picked up the needle from the pavement and plunged a drop of blood onto a glucometer to check our patient's blood-sugar level. The display flashed a normal reading.

Bones withdrew the laryngoscope blade and picked up the bag mask. He seated it over the man's mouth and squeezed. "I'm having a hard time seeing down there. I'll give it another go."

He set the bag mask down and positioned himself for a second attempt. He squinted down the man's gullet, his fist straining to keep the handle in position.

Our patient bolted upright.

Bones flipped on his back, the laryngoscope skidding away like a hockey stick on ice.

The man flashed wild eyes, found me, and grabbed my shirt collar. He labored to breathe, staring with constricted pupils and sweat beading on his brow. His mouth trembled, trying to form a sentence.

He found words with a winded, raspy voice. "Arepo . . . Arepo the Sower."

"Hey, it's okay. We're the paramedics. Here, let's lay you—"

"Listen." He grabbed the back of my neck, struggling to keep himself upright. His hands felt dirty and rough. "Arepo the Sower . . . holds the wheels at work."

I shook my head and lifted his arm away. "He's delirious. Here, you need oxygen."

He slipped back toward the concrete.

"Here, yeah, lie back. Bones, let's throw him on some O's."

Bones reached for an oxygen mask. The man tensed and winced, his heart rhythm oscillating on the heart monitor.

Bones shifted the screen to see it. "He's throwing runs of V-tach."

The man reached inside his coat and, with a trembling hand, produced a folded piece of notebook paper. He grasped my forearm and forced it into my palm.

"Martin." His eyes locked with mine. "Give this to Martin."

CHAPTER 02

The defib alarmed.

Color drained from his face.

I squeezed his shoulders. "Wait. What? Who's Martin?"

Bones picked up the laryngoscope. "He's bradying down."

The man slumped to the sidewalk. On instinct I rolled him away from me. It wasn't five seconds later that he spewed yellow chunks all over the park ranger's shoes.

Bones cleared the man's mouth with the portable suction catheter.

A vigorous sternal rub didn't wake him.

Bones reset his intubation equipment and talked to himself. "GCS less than eight. Intubate."

A fire engine siren blared a couple blocks out.

Things moved too fast to process.

Slow down . . . stick with ABCs.

Airway.

His respirations were shallow and slow. His skin felt cool and sweaty. I held his wrist but couldn't find a radial pulse anymore, only a thready carotid on the neck at thirty beats per minute. Bones placed his stethoscope in his ears one-handed, the other hand holding an inserted tube at the man's lips. He listened to lung sounds to make sure his tube was good.

Airway secured. Progress. The rumble of a fire engine exhaust brake sounded behind me, followed by the squeak and hiss of an air brake.

We needed to get our patient's heart rate up before it stopped beating again. "Bones, I'm gonna try to pace him."

I set the defib to deliver sequential minishocks of electricity to our patient's heart. The pectoral muscles in his chest twitched. Heartbeats flicked faster on the display. "Okay, we've got electrical capture."

Bones nodded. "And I've got radials with that."

A firefighter walked up. "Where you guys at?"

"Let's grab a quick blood pressure and then load and go."

The fire captain clipped a radio mic to his shirt. "Saint Mary's?"

"Yeah, that'll be closest. Mind if we take two of your guys?"

"Not at all."

One firefighter moved to the man's head to squeeze the bag now attached to the breathing tube. The other pumped the handle of a blood-pressure cuff with a stethoscope in his ears.

He bled off the air. "Eighty-two over fifty."

"Okay." I blew out a quick breath. "Let's roll him on the flat and get him loaded onto the gurney."

We buckled the patient on the bed. My eyes met the park ranger's. "Thank you."

He gave a nod.

I climbed into the back of the ambulance.

Bones looked back through the doghouse, the small opening between the cab and the patient area. "All set?"

"Let's roll."

He flicked on the siren and set off for the ER. I found myself wishing I had gathered more history on scene. Had our patient been complaining of anything before he passed out? Did he simply go into spontaneous cardiac arrest? Had the Narcan helped at all?

I turned my focus to a vial of amiodarone and inserted a needled syringe to draw it up. The medication would deter his heart from going back into a lethal rhythm. I flicked the bubbles to the top of the syringe and injected the contents into a second IV bag I'd hung from the gurney pole.

The siren shut off and the ambulance jostled into the parking lot. It turned, the back-up alarm sounded, and through the back windows the emergency room doors drew closer. The firefighter across from me reported another blood pressure similar to the first.

Questions about the patient abounded in my mind.

What happened to you?

What were you trying to tell me?

I took a last listen to lung sounds to ensure the breathing tube was still in place, then stood up and organized the myriad wires and IV tubing aboard the gurney.

"All right. Monitor, O² bottle, tube's secure, IV bags and tubing . . . we're all set."

The ambulance shut off. Bones came around back and swung open the doors. He raised his arms, grinning with televangelist grandeur. "Thou, unknown man down. Come forth."

We got off work an hour late after cleaning and restocking the ambulance and finishing paperwork. The Sierras stood dark and majestic, silhouetted by the day's crimson farewell. What was it they said in the navy? *Red at night, sailors delight. Red in the morn', sailors mourn.*

Norah Jones escorted me home, her sultry, smoky voice enticing

"Come Away With Me" through the car speakers. The black leather of my VW Passat presented a comfortable contrast to the gritty chaos of the workday. I longed to shed my uniform, to be free of the sublime stench of the ambulance.

A paper crinkled in the side pocket of my pants. And I heard my patient's raspy voice. . . . *"Arepo the Sower holds the wheels at work."*

I pulled out the note and unfolded it atop the steering wheel. A series of markings littered both sides of the sheet—straight and curved lines, dashes and slashes.

Chicken scratches.

I tossed it onto the passenger-side floor.

Streetlights glowed along the sidewalks. The lengthening day disappeared in the west. Blue and red lights illumined my dash.

That look in his eyes . . .

"Give this to Martin."

I shrugged it off, watching the road zip beneath me. Norah finished. The Byrds came on. *"To everything . . . turn, turn, turn."*

I laughed and shook my head. The man had been obviously low on oxygen and perhaps delusional. A paper full of scribbles meant nothing. I was going home. I was going to relax and get away from work and have my own life for at least the next ten hours.

The notepaper sat on the floor.

I couldn't see throwing it away in good conscience. That left me one option . . .

I hit the blinker at the next intersection. I'd turn around, take a half hour to go back to Saint Mary's, and give the piece of paper to the man—or at least to his nurse—and be done with it. The sooner I found him, the sooner I could drop it off and be home in a hot shower.

Night had fallen by the time I pulled into the hospital parking lot. The fatigue in my muscles made it feel later than it was. The evening air bit sharp with the reminder that winter had yet to fully loosen its grip.

At the ER doors I punched in the key code to enter. By now they probably would have moved our patient to the cardiac intensive care unit, but I decided to stop and ask to be sure. A multitasking middle-aged nurse with long, frizzy brown hair gave me three seconds, time enough for her to say, "CIC, 'bout an hour ago," before trading the clipboard chart she was holding with a new one from a shelf. I don't think she even heard me thank her as she set off for the next patient room.

I made my way down the long corridor that led to the elevators. The entire hospital buzzed in a constant state of movement, someone always going somewhere and doing something. The extent of my interaction was limited to a polite smile as I shifted with the sea of changing faces.

In the elevator I ran my fingers over the folds on the paper. I placed it in my jacket pocket, and at the fifth floor exited and walked toward a tall reception counter in the cardiac intensive care unit. Behind it sat a young nurse with straight black hair just long enough to be pulled into a ponytail. She reclined in a cheap office chair, staring blank-faced at the surrounding rows of flat-panel monitors coursing with electrical heart rhythms. I recognized her from the ER.

She grinned with straight white teeth. "Uh-oh. Here comes trouble."

I smiled and scoured the back of my mind for her name.

Sherri . . . Brandi . . . no, something more androgynous . . .

"Bobbi," I said in stride. "Hey."

"How have you been, Jonathan?" She almost succeeded in concealing a glance at the name sewn on my work jacket.

"I'm all right. Tired. It's been a busy week. We ran three cardiac arrests in a row today."

"So you're the one who's been sending us so much business."

"I wish I could say that. Only one made it to the hospital."

"Oh yeah? What's the name?" She leaned forward and pulled a scrunchy out of her hair.

"I actually don't know it. We found him on the street, and he didn't have any ID."

"Hmm." She sifted through a stack of charts on the desk. "We did get a John Doe from the ER about an hour ago. This says he was a field save, came in intubated. Male, in his sixties."

"That sounds like him."

"Wow." She stared at the chart. "You're not going to believe this."

"What?" I leaned forward on the counter.

"According to this he just AMA'd outta here."

Against Medical Advice. "He just up and walked out?"

Bobbi twirled her scrunchy and looked aside. "So that's what all the commotion was about . . ."

"What commotion?"

"You know, being stuck out here I am so out of the loop. I swear, I feel like all I do is stare at ectopy and hit Silence buttons."

"Bobbi, what commotion?"

"What? Oh. Well, a tall, disheveled-looking man stormed past the front here. And I thought I heard a couple of the other nurses saying that he was lucky he didn't yank his vocal cords out."

"He pulled his tube."

"Yeah." She glanced at the chart. "And his IVs too."

"That must've been him." I nodded at a small brass key with a plastic ring tag clipped to the top of the chart. "What's that?"

She picked it up off of the clipboard and read a small sticky note beneath it. "'Patient belonging left behind.'" She twirled the key between her fingers and thumb.

"What does it say on the tag there?"

She held it close to her nose. "River Crown Motel." Then flipped it over.

I huffed. "The River Crown. No doubt."

"You know it?"

"Too well. East Fourth Street." I scratched the back of my neck. "I just can't believe that he left already."

"Maybe you should check on him."

"This day is never going to end."

"What's that?"

I've come this far. . . . "You know, you're probably right. He could be really sick somewhere."

"Yeah." She made a face of joking concern. "Or at the very least locked out." Bobbi looked around and then took my hand in both of hers on the countertop. A cool metal shape dropped in my palm. "You really are so sweet to go the extra mile. Poor guy, he might not even be able to get into his room." She ran her fingers along my knuckles.

Were I less tired and less consumed by the growing cloud of mystery surrounding this patient and his absurd statements and the ridiculous piece of paper that I couldn't seem to throw away, I may have capitalized on that moment and scored a date with a hot young nurse. But instead, half considering myself a fool, I simply patted her hand and smiled. "Thanks, Bobbi." I turned and made my way to the elevators.

"Don't be a stranger, Jonathan."

Back in my car, I hunched over the wheel and exhaled. The steam from my breath climbed over the windshield and retreated. I held up the key in the fluorescent parking lot light.

All right, Jonathan, let's get this done.

CHAPTER 03

I waited at a red light for no one.

Across the intersection sat my destination, marked by a dilapi-
dated neon sign that read *River Crow Mo el*. With the green light I
pulled forward and parked in a lot that over time had become more
gravel than intact concrete. The motel was two-story, L-shaped,
probably built in the sixties during the heyday of Highway 40.
Construction of the interstate years ago dropped a slow poison
into the old artery, prompting the appearance of strip clubs, bars,
and boarded-up businesses. The River Crown's rectangular pool
now brimmed with pebbles, adorned at the edges by dead junipers
in terra-cotta basins. The room doors sported custom number-
ing by hand with what appeared to be black permanent marker.
A dull amber light loomed at the corner office. I found the door
unlocked.

The small reception room reeked of smoke and dust and sweat-
gland-excreted alcohol. Fifty years of shag-carpet collective odor.
The walls, infested with faint yellow orange patches of bacterial
growth, were in desperate need of cleaning or painting—or both.
Behind the front desk, the light and shadows of a television danced
from a dark room at the end of a hallway. Save for the muffled din
of the TV set, it was silent.

I sounded the ringer.

A short and stocky man waddled to the front. His scruffy gray beard failed to mask the folds of his double chin. He looked me over. "What do *you* want?"

He obviously did not in any way assume that I was looking for a room. I remembered I was still in uniform.

"I am . . ." I didn't know how to phrase it. I decided I'd keep it simple. "I'm looking for a man."

I paused, not knowing quite how else to proceed since I knew so little about my patient. But then I realized what my pause could imply after my curt statement and became immediately embarrassed, knowing that I had to say something quickly, regardless of its pertinence.

I cleared my throat. "That is . . . a specific person I need to find."

His eyebrows relaxed from the raised position they had been in.

"Right." I drummed my hands on my thighs. "Perhaps you would recognize him if I described him?"

"You don't know his name?"

"No, see, I'm a paramedic."

He gave me an impatient look, as if I was patronizing him.

This was supposed to be easy. "He's tall, slim, with sort of thin, wispy, light-colored hair and a beard. He wears a black overcoat—"

"Yeah, yeah. That's Simon Letell." The man ran his finger down a guest list. "He's in 210. Real quiet guy, a little off his nut, keeps to himself mostly."

"He's been here for a while, then?"

"At least a month."

"Thank you. I appreciate the help."

He gave a wry half smile and shuffled back to the hole of

a room he had come from. I turned and made my way out the door.

The chill fresh air was a relief. I shifted my gaze to the upper floor and wasn't able to make out room 210, so I walked to the stairwell at the inside corner of the motel. It smelled like urine, and the soles of my shoes stuck to the steps. At the top of the stairs a row of pale lights shone, illuminating a balcony bordered by a four-foot wooden sidewall with chipping blue paint. The first door was numbered 218, with 216 beyond it, so I made my way down toward 210.

My legs locked in place.

Adrenaline welled up in my chest. My lips parted as I squinted my eyes to bring into better focus the dark mass lying on the balcony floor—directly in front of room 210.

Not again.

Simon Letell's feet pointed toward me, his long dark overcoat enshrouding him as he lay on his side, one hand tucked in toward his chest, and his other arm bent up by his head, quasi-fetal position. His face was ghastly white. The pupils of his wide-open eyes were fixed, dilated, and gelled over. His mouth hung agape, his yellowish teeth apart. The side of his face that lay upon the concrete was livid purple. I placed my fingers upon his wrist and tried to move his arm. Rigor mortis had already set in. He lay frozen in the position in which he had died, his skin waxen cold.

An icy wind swirled through the upper walkway.

I pulled my phone from my pocket and called dispatch. I told them to send a coroner. No need for medics.

I took a few steps back and leaned against the balcony wall.

My one save was now beyond saving. The Reaper had the last laugh after all.

I exhaled and, through the wafting steam, read the numbers on Simon Letell's door—

Two ... One ... Zero.

CHAPTER 04

I didn't tell the police about the notepaper.

I explained my presence as a simple welfare-check, doing a favor for the nurses on the fifth floor of Saint Mary's. I recognized the cops, and they me, though not one of us knew the others' names. But they made little of it. There wasn't any trauma or sign of struggle on Simon's body. They took down my personal info for their report and dismissed me with a "Have a nice night. See you on the streets," and I set off with the blessing of their professional courtesy.

Sitting back in the driver's seat of the Passat, I felt overcome with a sudden weighted exhaustion and wondered if I would be able to make the drive home. One look out of my window served as the catalyst for pressing onward. I longed for the comfort of the house I rented in old southwest Reno, where the world felt normal and beautiful. Where tree roots took precedence over sidewalks, and the mountains beyond stood as silent sentries. I shifted into gear, my thoughts free-floating with visions of sheltering oaks, mystical cottonwoods, and the peeling white bark of aspen trunks.

My phone vibrated. I fished it out. "Hello?"

"Jonathan?"

"Yeah?"

"It's Joseph Kurtz."

I should have recognized his voice. It was *Doctor* Joseph Kurtz, dean of the University of Nevada, Reno, Medical School. It was he who had first convinced me to pursue paramedic school—and more recently, med school. He'd coached me in my preparations for the MCATs.

With his ponytail and round spectacles, he'd always struck me as something of a misplaced beatnik. Decades ago he'd traded his beret for a stethoscope and in recent years had become the medical-school dean, bringing an out-of-the-box style of leadership that had garnered national recognition for the med school's programs. He also happened to sit on the board that was considering my application for scholarship.

"Hey, Doc. Good to hear your voice."

"You too, Jonathan. What've you been up to?"

"Oh, just happened to be checking up on a patient."

"Right, right. That's my good medic. Well, I won't keep you, but I do have some very good news."

My heart hopscotched.

"The board reviewed your MCAT scores, and they were very impressed. I am not sure if you're aware of how few people in the country actually score in the ninety-eighth percentile. We examined your financial application, and I am happy to tell you that you've been approved for a full-ride scholarship."

I held the phone out and looked at it in disbelief. Yep, Dr. Kurtz's number. There was no way I could afford med school on the $11.70 an hour I was bringing home as a paramedic. My hopes had rested entirely on scholarship applications.

A full ride. "I can't believe it. Out of all the applicants?"

"You outshined them all, bud. Congratulations."

"Wow. That . . . that makes my year."

"Just thought I'd pass on the good news."

"Thank you so much."

"Hey, you earned it. Made my personal recommendation easy.

But, look, the scholarship is provisional, based on an ongoing evaluation."

"Like with grades?" I glanced out my side window and merged into a lane.

"That . . . and the board wants to make sure that its scholarship recipients are examples of the professional caliber that the med school produces."

"How do they measure that?"

"It's difficult to quantify. But for starters, I'd recommend that you enroll in the summer prep courses."

"That's all stuff I've pretty much taken."

"I know. I know. But it shows the board that you're serious and committed. This is a huge gift, and you don't want to do anything to jeopardize it, right?"

Summer prep was a full-time commitment. I doubted that I could even keep up per diem hours on the ambulance. "What about meals and lodging? The scholarship program only covers that during the main school year."

"We discussed that and have decided to make an exception for you."

That only gave me a month. I'd have to give notice on my lease, move everything out, put some stuff in storage. And my dad—

"Jonathan?"

"Yeah? Sorry. Just taking it all in. I'm definitely on board."

"That's what I like to hear. Well done, bud."

"Thanks again."

After hanging up, I went on autopilot for the next couple of miles, blinking out of my reverie when I pulled onto my driveway. The glow I felt inside dampened a bit as I parked in the cave-like garage. The walls of my house had been built with stones that came out of the hole the original builder dug for the basement back in the thirties. *My* house only because it had come to feel that way after renting for the past four years. My dad lived there too. And I always had to qualify this—no, I didn't live with my dad. Yes, I did live with him. He rented a room from me. In the house that I rented.

Street light stretched through open blinds, lending the only light inside. I sat in the dining room and stared out the back window. Closer than in winter, Orion ran up from the mountains into the night sky, Ursa Major still eluding him at an angle.

The day had kept me moving, doing, talking. As the high waned from the scholarship news, the inevitable quiet of evening crept in. It made it impossible to ignore the shadowy plane of hurt that lay just beneath the surface of my consciousness, ever present and waiting for me to slow down. The memory of that day . . . the long lingering wound that refused to mend.

Was I fooling myself? Was I foolish to think that med school and becoming an ER physician would make things any different, that it would somehow enable me to overcome the pain?

To outwit death?

The rain from that day didn't stop, nor did the images of that shattered windshield.

I traced a finger over the small scar at my hairline.

My father ambled in wearing boxers and a collared button-up shirt. "Hey, Jonner." He held an empty gin glass that he took to the kitchen.

He rarely drank in front of me. As though that would somehow cross a line. It would actually admit that he was doing it. That he was an alcoholic. And it would set a bad example for his son. Didn't matter that I was twenty-six and doing more of the caring and providing for him than the other way around. Only God knew how he'd fare if I left him alone.

But I would leave him—in a month's time. "Hey, Dad."

Tap water echoed in his glass. "How was the day?" He said the words as if they were lyrics to a song. I knew by then that he wasn't inquiring so much as delivering a requisite greeting, like saying the pledge of allegiance.

I counted the stars in Orion's Belt. The moonlight iced blue the peaks of Mount Rose.

I took a deep breath. "I got the call today. I made it. A full-ride scholarship to UNR Med School."

Red lights from an airplane diminished as it ascended from the valley. The bare limbs of our oak shook with a sudden breeze.

I turned. The kitchen was empty. The flickers of my father's television illuminated the hallway.

The thin façade of normalcy fell away, and the dark ocean of pain churned inside of me.

I grimaced and pushed my lips together.

"Good night, Dad."

CHAPTER 05

I jolted awake with my alarm clock at 5:20 Saturday morning.
I opened the blinds and stared at the sliver of dawn over the eastern
hills. In the kitchen I flicked on my iPod at its docking station.
Charlie Parker bebopped from the speakers as I brought the paper
in from the front doorstep.

I used to be in the habit of reading a chapter from the Bible each
morning. A "quiet time." Silence, however, had become increasingly
unpalatable, and subsequently, minutes that should have been spent
conversing with God were now filled with distractions and noise,
the modern panacea for a troubled soul.

I stared into the pantry. A box of Alpha-Bits remained the last
cereal selection. Yeah, Alpha-Bits. Shopping when I was hungry
was always a bad idea. I'd go to buy the staples and come home
with Fruity Pebbles and beef jerky.

I sat with my bowl and glanced down the hallway. The door
to my dad's room hung ajar, his snoring rhythmic and hard to
ignore. My head felt cloudy and unfocused. I was about to take
a bite of cereal when a grouping of letters in the milk caught my
attention.

R E P A

I used my spoon to move the A to the front and guided an O
to the end.

AREPO

"Arepo . . ."

"Arepo the Sower holds the wheels at work . . ."

I brought my hands away from the bowl, as though it had become a crystal ball. I took a glance at the ingredients on the side of the cereal box.

I need coffee.

After a quick shower, I changed into my medic uniform and threw a lunch into a collapsible cooler. I was out the door before six and arrived at the ambulance headquarters fifteen minutes before shift, meeting up with Bones in the ambulance bay.

Sitting in the back of Medic Two, he ran his fingers over medication vials bedded in foam inside a plastic drug container.

He looked up. "Greetings, visitor from planet Sleep. How goes your journey to the land of waking?"

I stowed my cooler in a front cabinet. "I think I want to return to my home planet."

"Nonsense! You must check in with the system status authorities at once. Henceforth we will secure caffeinated beverages."

He'd no doubt already had a couple cups. "It's early, so let me translate. . . . Are you saying you want me to get the radios and drug keys?"

"Of course."

I stepped out of the ambulance and walked down the hall that led to dispatch.

"That's why you're the best partner in the world, Jonathan. But don't let that inflate your noggin."

I started the engine and dropped the ambulance into gear.

Bones put us in service with dispatch. "Medic Two, McCoy and Trestle, oh-six-thirty to eighteen-thirty."

"Copy," dispatch said. "Post Rock Boulevard and Victorian Avenue."

I looked over at Bones. "Starbucks?"

Bones, ever the connoisseur, said, "Never. No finer brew can be found than that which flows from the 7-Eleven."

"How can you drink that stuff?"

"Nectar of the gods, Jonny-boy."

"Try nectar of the broke."

"And . . . that would be us."

Morning poured into the valley, infusing color and warmth. Traffic grew heavier as the minutes passed. We parked at the post—a little hole-in-the-wall that Aprisa Ambulance leased with a couple couches and a TV. Bones strolled over to the convenience store. I unlocked the door, set my radio on the floor, and stretched out on a sofa. It smelled like dusty aged fabric. Bones walked in, laptop case strung over his shoulder, no plastic top for his coffee.

"Why don't you ever get a top for those? Aren't you afraid it'll spill if we get a call?"

"That's just it. If I get a top, then we're sure to get a call."

"That's the goofiest logic I've ever heard."

He lay down on the other couch and picked up the television remote. An episode of the seventies show *Emergency* emerged on the tube. "Hey, look," he said. "There we are."

"Roy and Johnny?"

"No. No. There. The guys with the white coats and the converted hearse." He sipped his coffee. "Burt and Ernie with the gurney."

I brought out Simon Letell's notepaper and unfolded it. The

markings still looked nonsensical. I set it on my stomach and looked up. "You ever heard of Arepo the Sower?"

"Does he live on Fourth Street?"

"No. Well, at least I don't think so." I straightened a corner of the paper. "You know our last patient from yesterday?"

"Yeah?"

"He AMA'd himself out of CCU."

Bones turned on his side. "Really?"

"Yeah."

He stared at my hands. "You healed him. You are a miracle worker."

"He died outside his motel room last night."

"Oh." He sat back. "You should have given him a piece of your garment."

"A piece of my garment?"

"'Surely then he would not have died.'"

"Would you shut up?" I folded up the note. "Forget it. I shouldn't have mentioned it."

He sipped his coffee. Roy Desoto cranked up the black phone to talk to Rampart. The show went to commercial.

Bones glanced at me. "So, how'd you find all that out?"

"Oh, now you want to hear about it."

"You have two minutes before *Emergency* comes back on."

I held up the paper. "I went back to Saint Mary's to return this."

"What does it say?"

"Nothing intelligible."

"Arepo the Sower? Is that what he said on scene?"

"Yeah."

"Wasn't there more to it?"

"'Arepo the Sower holds the wheels at work.'"

Bones stared at the floor. "I can't think of anything related. Have you Googled it?"

"The thought hadn't occurred to me."

"Let's do it." He sat up, unzipped his bag, and pulled out a silver and black Dell.

"Can you get Internet here?"

"I've got a mobile card." He powered up the computer. Roy and Johnny returned. I muted it. The Google search field popped up on the laptop screen.

Bones typed in the Arepo phrase. "Yahtzee."

"What?"

"Everyone says Bingo."

"What do you see?"

"Okay, one sec." He clicked a link and scrolled downward. "It is a rough translation of the Latin words *sator, arepo, tenet, opera,* and *rotas.*"

"Latin?"

His eyes narrowed. "Check this out. They can be formed into a palindrome square."

He turned the screen.

R O T A S

O P E R A

T E N E T

A R E P O

S A T O R

"Why would Simon say that to us?"

"He said it to you, not me."

"Does it tell where the square comes from?"

He clicked to another page. His eyes tracked left to right. "Looks like there's varying theories. The earliest finding is from a wall in Pompeii in 79 AD." He scrolled down. "Wow. If you take each of the letters in the square and use them once, you form the Latin words 'Our Father' in the shape of a cross with two A's and O's left over."

"Alpha and Omega?"

"I guess so."

We studied the cross formation.

```
                    A
                    P
                    A
                    T
                    E
                    R
A P A T E R N O S T E R Ω
                    O
                    S
                    T
                    E
                    R
                    Ω
```

I shook my head. "That's a trip."

"It looks like there's a lot of debate, but this page is suggesting that the inscription is early Christian. Like a pass code."

"To avoid persecution. Secretly meeting in catacombs."

Bones sat up and sighed. "Catacombs . . . catechism . . ."

I rubbed an eyebrow.

The radio beeped. Dispatch followed. "Medic Two, respond priority one for an unconscious subject, possible diabetic problem."

I clicked the radio. "Medic Two copy."

Bones packed up his laptop. A minute later we wailed down Prater Boulevard into an older section of the City of Sparks.

Bones drove aggressively but safe, for the most part. He only made me nearly soil my pants on one occasion—when he swerved late to get off the freeway and hit a curb going about fifty when the car beside us failed to yield.

"So left or right off Prater?" Bones said.

I glanced at the map book in my lap. "Left."

We pulled up to the curb of a fifty-year-old single-story house. A plywood ramp had been constructed over the porch steps. We rolled the gurney to the front door, where an elderly woman holding a thick, avocado-colored cordless phone pointed with a trembling finger down the inner hall.

Bones unlatched the gurney seat belt that secured the airway bag and defibrillator. I did the same with the larger first-out bag.

A small black terrier appeared from behind a recliner, demonstrating its disapproval with snarling incisors. We made our way to the back room. A man in his eighties lay on the bed with foam at the corners of his mouth and slow, snoring respirations.

Bones rubbed the patient's sternum with his knuckles. "Sir? Sir?"

No change. His skin was dusky.

"Jonathan, you got airway?"

"Sure thing." I pulled a pinky-sized, trumpet-shaped green tube from the airway bag. I lubed it up and slid it in the patient's nostril to make sure his tongue didn't block air from getting into his lungs. "NPA's in. You want me to bag him up a little?"

"Yeah, let's get his color better." Bones prepped the man's arm for an IV.

I pulled out the bag mask to supplement his breathing. The fire department crew walked in, and the room grew smaller with the six of us, not counting the patient or his wife. Bones asked them to get a set of vitals and to assist ventilations. I handed the bag mask to a fireman.

Bones pulled the needle from the patient's arm and handed it to me. I plunged a drop of blood from it onto the glucometer to check his blood sugar. The number 34 appeared on the digital display. Hence the reason he was unconscious.

I pulled the Dextrose 50% from the first-out bag and handed it to Bones. It was like clear syrup in a syringe.

He held up the medication cylinder and the needle attachment in separate fists. "Check it out—just like Roy and Johnny." He popped the caps off with his thumbs and posed.

I shook my head. "I thought you said we were Burt and—"

"One hundred over sixty." A firefighter unstrapped the blood-pressure cuff.

Bones noted it on his glove.

He connected the dextrose syringe to the IV line and spoke as he pushed it in. "Okay, Jonathan, I want you to stand with the light at your back so your shadow casts over our patient here."

I ignored him, as was often the best strategy, and gathered up plastic trash from the floor.

A bright light shone from behind me, throwing my silhouette over the patient's legs.

The fire captain held his flashlight and winked. "How's that, McCoy?"

Bones snickered. "Perfect. I have no doubt this man will be healed."

The patient drew a sudden deep breath and lifted his head. His eyes darted around the room in confusion.

Bones put a hand on his shoulder. "Hello, sir. I'm Paramedic McCoy with Aprisa Ambulance. We're here because your wife called us. Your blood sugar was very low."

The man scratched at the IV in his arm.

"Ooh," Bones said. "Don't pull that just yet. Let's get your head cleared up first."

I pulled the rubber nasal trumpet out of his nose and placed a clear, two-pronged cannula in his nostrils, hooking the tubing around his ears and cinching it under his chin. "There you go. Take some slow, deep breaths through your nose and let that oxygen work for you."

His skin color improved.

Bones nodded at the fire captain. "I think we're good from here. Thanks, guys."

The captain waved and his crew filed out.

We hung out with our patient for another fifteen minutes. He progressively became more alert and oriented and, after conversing with his wife, opted to refuse transport.

Non-transports didn't make any money for the company. But Bones didn't care about that. He cared about taking care of people and doing what was best for them.

That's part of why I liked him. It's why I knew I could trust him.

CHAPTER 06

North Post smelled like Orville Redenbacher popcorn. Stray unpopped kernels littered the corners of the microwave. Sitting there only provided more time to ruminate about Letell and everything that didn't make sense. Maybe I was just letting myself get too wrapped up in it. Things were looking up in my life. I was going from making a meager hourly wage to a full-ride scholarship to med school. I was going to be a doctor.

Emergency was on the TV again. "Are they having a marathon?"

Bones plopped on the couch. "Can you ever really get enough of it?"

The L.A. County electronic tones went off for Squad Fifty-One. The boys hopped in the truck to respond to a car over an embankment. Music accompanied their red pickup as it pulled out of the firehouse at twice normal film speed.

My radio beeped. "Medic Two, traffic. Priority one, 395 northbound for a multiple-vehicle accident. Subjects trapped."

Bones chuckled. "Say, 'Squad Fifty-One en route.' Say it."

I shook my head. "Medic Two copies, en route."

I hopped behind the wheel this time. Bones didn't bother with the map book. We knew where we were going. We screamed down Parr Boulevard and swung north on the freeway. Early afternoon traffic wasn't too bad. I shut down the lights and siren until I merged us into the fast lane, then lit it back up.

About half a mile beyond the Stead exit a fire engine's lights flashed. Traffic seemed at a standstill at the base of Anderson Hill leading into Cold Springs, cars stopped at odd angles on the freeway. I pulled up on scene next to the fire engine. Highway patrol wasn't too far behind us.

I fought the urge to jump out of the cab. I forced myself to see the scene, to look at the broad picture of it.

One car lay on its roof in the center median, white smoke trailing from its underbelly. A person dangled from a seat belt inside.

Again the urge to go right to the patient. Get them out of the car. Care for their injuries.

I resisted the tightening tunnel on my vision and forced myself to look at the rest of it. Two other vehicles with major damage angled next to each other over two lanes. Looked like a driver in each. No visible passengers. A fourth car, with no damage and no occupants, sat parked on the shoulder.

Bones reported a size-up to dispatch and requested the medical helicopter, AprisEvac.

I stepped out of the ambulance and snatched the first-out bag from the gurney. "I'll take these two. You got the rollover?"

"Yeah." Bones strode off, holding a handheld radio by his ear.

Debris littered the scene. I reminded myself to walk.

Tires screeched. A horn blared. I whipped around to see a highway patrol officer yelling at a driver who'd nearly crashed into his patrol car.

I turned back toward the accident scene, and from a short distance away the first car looked like some kind of convertible sedan. The driver's seat was reclined back, and a man lay in it motionless. I threw a glance at the second car—a black sedan with heavy front-end damage, a busted windshield, and an awake driver who looked like he might be trapped by a collapsed dashboard. One firefighter leaned in a window, talking to the man inside, another pulled a hose line between the three damaged vehicles. I came upon the driver's door of the first car, and my heart sank into my stomach.

This hadn't been a convertible.

The driver lay with the top of his skull missing, along with his brain—his life shanked in one transecting moment. He was someone's son, someone's friend.

But I couldn't see victims. I had to see patients. Problems to fix.

And this one made rapid triage easy.

Gone.

On to the next.

A fire department ladder truck and a light rescue unit arrived. I came to the driver's side window of the black sedan.

A fireman was in the back seat holding the man's head in line with his neck. "This is Jeff. He's forty years old, complaining of pain in his neck, his side, and his legs."

Jeff's face looked pallid.

"I'm going to ask you a few questions, Jeff. Try not to move your neck, okay?"

He winced. "Okay."

"Can you feel your hands and feet?"

"Yes."

"Were you knocked out?"

"No."

The door had folded over a foot against him. I reached for his wrist. Strong radial pulse, rapid. Skin felt cool and clammy. His body was compensating against shock, but time was short. We needed to get him out quick.

"Hang in there. We're going to remove the car from you instead of the other way around."

I heard the helicopter approaching.

Fire crews stretched hydraulic lines from the bumper of the ladder truck with steel spreaders and cutters in hand. The Jaws of Life. A tall truck captain walked toward me, his red helmet at an angle.

I put a hand on his shoulder. "Code fifty in the first car. This one in the black sedan needs rapid extrication. I'll tie in with my partner at the rollover and let you know what we've got there."

He nodded. "Sounds good." He turned his head toward his shoulder mic and spoke something into it.

The ladder truck roared into high idle. Firefighters went to work, prying and cutting.

Heavy helicopter blades whipped overhead from the AprisEvac MD 900. A flight medic stood with the door open and one foot on a landing skid, torso bent to get a clear view of the cylindrical tail boom. The pilot made his descent. Pebbles scattered and shot through the air.

I shielded my eyes and caught up with Bones in the dirt median. He knelt by the driver's window, talking to a man trapped upside down in the rolled-over vehicle. Firefighters with struts and wood cribbing worked to stabilize it.

"What you got?"

"One male patient. Stable. E-T-O-H."

The abbreviation for ethyl alcohol. It was a useful way to say that a patient was drunk without the patient realizing it.

"Got ya. Injuries?"

"Minor, actually."

"Need anything?"

He shook his head. "No. Once they get this thing stabilized, we'll get a bunch of hands to lower him onto a backboard. I've got enough guys here to do it. What do you got?"

"One code fifty. One trapped. Critical, though conscious."

"All right."

I walked back to the truck captain and shouted to be heard. "The rollover patient is stable but intoxicated."

He pointed at the black sedan. "So this patient on the bird first?"

I nodded. "Yeah, I think we can take the rollover patient by ground."

Back at the black sedan I noticed Jeff's color had deteriorated from pale to ashen. The firefighters worked to pry the driver's door open.

I really didn't want a second death on this accident. First one wasn't my fault. This one . . .

We needed to get moving.

At the passenger side I pulled out a bag of normal saline and spiked it with IV tubing.

The flight medic and flight nurse hopped out of the helicopter. Wearing white helmets, they carried bags and hunched beneath the rotors. It wasn't until the nurse drew closer and pulled off her helmet that I recognized her.

Naomi Foster.

The AprisEvac engines idled down, and the fire captain gave Naomi a quick rundown on the patients. Naomi caught my eye and turned to her partner.

I leaned in the passenger window and wrapped a tourniquet around Jeff's right arm. He looked to be in decent shape. He'd normally sport ropes for veins. But with his blood pressure tanking, nothing was visible. His body was trying to protect his core organs by shutting down peripheral circulation. I felt around for a vein in the antecubital space at the crook of his elbow. My fingertip found a faint rounded shape.

A familiar female voice spoke behind me. "Can you get a fourteen in that?"

I craned my neck, seeing only Naomi's torso through the window, her flight suit following her curves, name and title stitched into the fabric. She bent down and smiled, sandy chin-length hair dangling, eyes still the same striking blue.

I kept my finger on the vein. "I've got it by feel only. Better give me an eighteen gauge."

She raised and lowered her eyebrows, went to the roof, and returned with the smaller needle. She handed it inside with a wry curve to her lips.

She was going to shame me into a larger-bore catheter. The bigger the IV needle, the faster we could flow fluid into Jeff's body and improve his blood pressure. But also the more difficult of a stick.

"All right," I said. "Fine. Give me a sixteen."

A smile tugged at the corner of her mouth. She opened her other hand to reveal the larger sixteen-gauge.

I prepped the IV site on Jeff's arm with an alcohol swab, pulled his skin taut with my thumb, and inserted the needle. A flash of blood confirmed my placement. I popped off the tourniquet and held pressure above the catheter.

"Sharp out."

Naomi held a red needle container for me.

"Thanks."

I hooked up the IV line.

Naomi lifted the saline bag and spun the white wheel on the tubing. "Good flow. Running wide open."

The car rocked with a loud metallic pop. The driver's door creaked open. Another firefighter moved in to cut the hinges.

The truck captain walked up. "We're going to take the roof."

"Got it." I took the IV bag from Naomi and squeezed it under the passenger-side headrest. "Hang in there, Jeff. This fluid'll get your blood pressure up. They're going to cut off the roof and get that dash off your legs. All right?"

He kept his eyes closed. "Okay."

I picked up the first-out bag and backed out of the way. Firefighters went to work on the roof posts.

Naomi zipped up her medical bag on the roof and slung it over her shoulder. She took her helmet in hand and stood back beside me. "It's been a while, Trestle."

How long had it been? I didn't think we'd spoken for more than five minutes at a time over the past four years. "Where have you been flying out of these days?"

"Mostly Truckee."

"Ah." I glanced over at Bones. It looked as if he and the firemen almost had their patient out. "You like it up there?"

"It's pretty. But slow. I'm actually back here at County now." She tucked strands of hair behind her ears. No ring on her finger. "I like it. The days fly by. Literally. How about you?"

"You know, still working the streets. Four twelves. Did have a strange code the other day."

"What was it?"

"An older guy in full arrest on the sidewalk. We got him back. He said some bizarre things. I went to drop something off for him in CCU and found out he'd left the hospital already. I followed up and found him dead outside his motel room."

"Wow. That is weird."

"Yeah. Name was Simon Letell. Ever run on him downtown?"

"Sounds vaguely familiar."

I watched the firefighters lift the roof off the black sedan and carry it out of the way. "How're your parents?"

"My mother . . . She's had some health issues. But they're getting through it."

A hydraulic ram pushed against the dash. Plastic creaked and cracked.

The captain pointed. "Now get a new purchase point here."

In the median Bones and the other fire crew strapped their patient to a backboard.

I wanted to tell Naomi about the scholarship. I wanted to know if she was still living in Truckee and what was really going on with her parents, to hear about her life since we—since our friendship had reached its limit. But all I ended up saying was, "You must like flying."

To a disinterested nod.

The waning momentum reminded me of the other "conversations" we'd had in the past years. I didn't want it to end. "You been doing much on your days off?"

She eyed me. "Reading."

I scratched my jaw. "That's it? You just stay at home and read?"

Naomi folded her arms and creased her eyebrows. A strand of hair came loose from her ear and fluttered in front of her face. "Who said I just stay at home? I happen to get out quite a bit."

Dagger to the spleen. *Why did I even ask?*

The firemen reclined the driver's seat and slid a backboard behind Jeff.

Her statement shouldn't have bothered me. Of course she'd get out and be social, be seeing other people. . . . Other guys.

I cleared my throat. "So you get out quite a bit?"

"Yep."

"And like what, have a book club at the coffeehouse?"

Naomi pushed her lips together. "Jane Austen is a fine companion. Tea at three and a good read is all a girl needs." She flashed a quick look at me.

"That's all a girl needs, huh?"

She drew a breath—"Absolutely"—and pulled on her helmet. "You said your patient's name was Letell?"

"Yeah."

She kept her eyes on the car. "Deux Gros Nez happens to be a great café to read in."

I laughed and then did a double take. She'd just dropped where she hung out.

Her cheeks reddened. Maybe not noticeable to anyone else. But I could tell. My chest swelled.

Victory.

What did she know about Letell? I swung the first-out bag on like a backpack. "It's been a while since I've been to the Deux. Maybe I'll check it out again."

The AprisEvac engines throttled up.

Naomi smiled. "Maybe you should, Trestle."

Firefighters lifted Jeff out on the backboard and set him on the pavement. We walked to the board and helped secure him to it with Velcro Spider-Straps. I knelt low by his head so he could hear me. "Jeff, this is Flight Nurse Naomi from AprisEvac. She'll take good care of you on the ride to County. All right?"

He grabbed my elbow. "Thank you."

We lifted the backboard and walked to the bird. Naomi climbed in, and we loaded Jeff onto the helicopter cot. She slid the door closed and positioned the helmet mic by her mouth.

I backed away, watching her as the helicopter lifted, staring as she grew tinier against the blue backdrop, my heart pounding like the pulse of spinning rotor blades.

CHAPTER 07

Trent Matley squinted into the sun, pulling a cigarette from his lips, blowing smoke with purpose. His lanky arms dangled at his sides, short black hair spiked with a firm gel hold. He shook his head and cursed to himself for no apparent reason.

I sat on the bench outside the ER doors, the wood rough but warm, usually a pleasant place to finish up a chart. Trent's EMT partner redressed the gurney behind their ambulance parked next to ours.

Trent nodded. "'Sup, dude."

"Hey. Busy day, huh?"

"Tell me about it. All bull too."

I pulled out a pen for the chart's narrative section.

Medic Two arrived on scene to find a forty-year-old male awake, alert, and oriented, three-point restrained and suspended in the driver's seat of . . .

A horn blared. Light traffic halted by a crosswalk on Mill Street. I glanced at Trent. "So what'd you guys bring in?"

He stared across the street. "Seizure."

"And you don't consider that a bona fide call?"

He turned to me with a condescending look. "Dude. Really? How many seizures do we go on every day? It's not even an emergency." He took a pointed drag and shook his head.

Even from the far side of the bench his ego was edging me

out. But I expected that attitude from him. I shrugged it off and quipped, "That's why they pay us the big bucks."

The glass doors slid open and Bones walked through, Styrofoam coffee cup in hand. I still had half of my charting left.

Rolled-over sedan with moderate damage to the roof and passenger side.

The acrid stench of cigarette smoke wafted past the bench.

Trent watched his partner clean the back of their rig. "And they wonder why they can't keep medics around here. Pay them scrap to do what? Haul around drunks that aren't going to pay for the ride anyway."

I'd given up on coherent reasoning with Trent. A breeze flipped my chart. I flattened it out.

Positive ETOH, complaining of minor cervical and thoracic spinal pain.

The radio beeped. "Medic Two or Medic Nine, can you clear County for a call downtown?"

Nine had arrived a solid ten minutes before us. I waited for Trent to answer. He blew smoke and cracked his neck.

"Medic Two or Medic Nine, Aprisa."

I shook my head. *Forget it. We'll take it.* I tossed the chart in the metal clipboard and stood.

Trent flicked the cigarette on the concrete and depressed the transmit button. "Aprisa, Medic Nine's available." He ran his tongue under his lip. "See you, Jonathan." He pounded the side of the ambulance and shouted at his partner, "Dude, come on. Let's go."

The Washoe County Morgue was not one of Bones's favorite establishments.

But several rigs came available after Medic Nine took the

downtown call, so I managed to talk dispatch into allowing us an extended stay on the hospital grounds to follow up on Simon Letell and visit an old friend.

The morgue was its own separate but small building, set out on a far corner of the hospital's parking area. We greeted the receptionist in the lobby and descended the stairs into the basement. A glass wall, interspersed with steel support members, separated a small vestibule from the large exam room. Through the glass at the far end of the room I saw Dr. Eliezer Petrov's stocky frame operating the crematory oven.

His curly white hair stuck out from under the surgical cap he wore. He noticed us standing there, waved, and walked over. Pulling off a pair of latex gloves, he opened the door.

"Jonathan, great to see you again."

I shook his hand and patted his shoulder. "It's good to see you too, Doc."

Fog bordered his spectacles. He turned to Bones. "Hello, Thaddeus."

Bones couldn't stand that Eli used his proper Christian name. "Hello there, Dr. Petrov."

Eli wiped beads of sweat from the sides of his nose. "Takes a bit to fire that thing up, but once it gets going . . . You know we're one of the last morgues to still operate a crematory?" He leaned on the door and exhaled. "What brings you two down to the dungeon?"

My radio squawked. I turned down the volume. "There's a couple things, actually."

"Do tell."

"Well, for one, I've been awarded that full-ride scholarship to UNR Med School."

His face lightened with pride. "Jonathan, that is wonderful news. I am so happy for you." He pulled me in for a hug.

"Thanks, Doc. I couldn't wait to tell you. They want me to start with summer school in a month."

"A month?"

"Yeah."

"Will you still . . ." He motioned toward my uniform.

"I don't know. It's such a commitment. I don't think I could keep even per diem hours."

Dr. Eli folded his arms and took a deep breath. "Indeed. Well done."

"You've taught me so much down here."

"It might've helped on those MCATs, huh? What were you? Ninety-fifth percentile?"

"Ninety-eighth."

"Outstanding."

"It'll be a big challenge." I pocketed my hands. "But, hey, the other reason we're here is to check up on a patient."

"Oh, of course. Here." He motioned with his hand. "Please, come in."

The air smelled of bleach, not quite masking the permeating odor of decay. Bones's pale complexion turned a shade lighter. As many times as I'd been down there, I still felt blood drain from my head and had to focus on steadying myself. But once we dove into the science, the light-headedness mostly passed.

"One moment." Dr. Eli walked back to the crematory oven and shut down the burners. "So, this patient you had . . . ?"

"His name is Simon Letell."

"Ah yes. You're just in time. He's next up on the list for autopsies I'd ordered." Dr. Eli walked to a wall lined with oversized refrigeration drawers. He traced his finger down and tapped on a label. "Here we are." He opened the drawer and unzipped the black body bag that lay in it. "This look like your guy?"

Letell had the same vacant stare he'd had when I'd seen him lying outside his motel room. His skin was waxen and pale, with a clear line demarking pooled lividity.

"Yeah. That's him. I'm curious about cause of death."

"Well, all right." He clapped his hands together. "This will be fun." He walked to a small office cubicle, squared off by additional glass walls, and picked up a phone receiver. "Tech assistance for autopsy."

The tech transferred Letell's body onto a flat exam table. Bones and I donned surgical masks and stood off to the side. Dr. Eli stood at the head of the table, spectacles on and secured under his surgical hat, gloved hands in the air like a surgeon. A microphone hung from the ceiling, and periodically he would use a foot pedal to activate it, verbally recording the exam process.

The tech took a large scalpel and, starting near Letell's clavicles and extending to his navel, incised a large Y-shaped cut through the layers of skin and adipose tissue. He exposed the sternum, brought out a small circular saw, and wound the cutting blade into high RPMs.

The tech brought it down on Letell's breastbone with a high-pitched grinding whine and a cloud of bone dust.

Dr. Eli made his own incision over the back of the man's scalp and peeled the skin forward over Letell's face, revealing the skull beneath. It was still a strange sight—to see a faceless man with a bare skull. The tech moved to the cranium to begin his next cuts.

Beside me, Bones was as white as a sterile four-by-four dressing.

Eli studied him. "Thaddeus, are you feeling all right?"

Bones stared at Letell, the hint of a gyrating wobble to his stance.

"Remember, son, the body is but a tent."

Bones pointed at the stairway and managed, "I'm going to—"

"Sure." I nodded and smiled.

He took off through the door. Nothing with living people fazed him. But there was something about the dissection of a human body that got to him. Go figure.

It was times like that when I realized I shared a special bond with Eli. And not just with him, but with Vesalius and Da Vinci and Hippocrates. It was in my makeup to be a physician.

Eli pulled off the top of Letell's skull, set it aside on a stainless steel tray, and waved me over. Sliding his hands into the cranium, he made a few careful cuts with a scalpel and then cradled Letell's brain up into the light to examine it.

He depressed the foot pedal. "Cerebral surface tissue appears intact and undamaged."

He set the curled gray mass on a tray and used a blade to cut it into one-centimeter-thick slices. He stopped every minute or so to record an observation.

The areas of the brain echoed in my head as I watched every transection and incision. MCAT flash cards flipping through my mind—coronal, midsagittal . . . Colored-pencil images from my anatomy drawing book.

He progressed down to the neck and removed the entire windpipe. He handed me the trachea, all dangly and fleshy with ribbed cartilage up around the voice box.

Holding it up like a telescope, I stared past Letell's epiglottis and through his vocal cords. "It looks like there was some trauma around the larynx." I thought of how Bobbi the nurse said he'd yanked out his endotracheal tube.

Eli smiled. "Atta boy. Knowing your anatomy will save you."

He moved on to the heart, the lungs, each major organ—excising them one by one and verbally documenting his findings. Letell's coronary arteries were coated with a fine layer of plaque, yellow like a hamburger bun. There was a bit of blackened alveoli in the lung tissue, likely from a prior history of smoking. Letell's gall bladder sac spilled out a host of white BB-shaped stones when lacerated.

Dr. Eli finished up, bagging a few specimens for pathological testing. "Nothing obvious yet, I'm afraid. Definitely no other blatant trauma. I expect we'll learn more from this man's liver and kidneys than anything else." He peeled off his gloves and nodded to the tech. "Let me know when our next one is ready, if you would, Steve."

My radio chirped traffic again.

Eli raised his eyebrows. "Do you need to go?"

"No. It's for another unit."

"Care to join me in the office?"

We washed up and sat down in the glass-walled office adjacent to the exam area. Outside, Steve the tech sewed up the Y cut in Letell's torso with a pen-sized needle and thick thread. Eli set the bagged samples in a specimen refrigerator beneath a microscope on the far wall of the office.

"You still do most of your work down here?" I said.

"Hmm?" Eli looked up. "Oh, instead of in that closet-sized office in the old hospital wing?" He smiled and sat on the edge of a desk chair. "You know, my father always thought I'd be a family physician." He pulled a chain out from his scrub shirt. Two flat round pendants dangled at the end of it. He unclasped the necklace and held the brass circles out to examine them. "This was a gift from him when I made it into medical school." He pulled one off of the chain and handed it to me. "The Hippocratic Oath is inscribed on it."

I ran my thumb over the etchings.

"*Do no harm.*"

He rested his forearms on his knees. "Even though I work with the dead, I still endeavor to fulfill that oath."

I handed it back. "It's a special gift."

He put up a palm. "I would like for you to have that one."

"Doc, I can't take this."

"Jonathan, you are the closest thing to a son that I have. I am so proud of your accomplishment. I want you to have it."

"Eli," I looked at the pendant. "I am honored. This means a lot. Are you—"

"I insist. He gave me two for just this reason."

I clenched it in my fist. "Thank you."

He sat back in the chair and propped up his glasses. "So tell me—what was it about this patient?"

I took a seat and told him the story of getting Letell back from cardiac arrest, the strange things he had said, his last request to give a note to someone named Martin, and how I'd finally found him dead outside of his motel room.

Eli rested his chin on his thumb, his forefinger stretched across his lips, his eyes searching in thought. "What do you know about his Arepo comment?"

I shared what Bones and I had found on the Internet that morning.

He straightened. "Well, for one thing, he sure was determined to tell you that. So much so that he fought off the grave to say it."

I hadn't thought of it that way. "It's just so out of left field. I'm probably making too much out of nothing."

He nodded. "Perhaps." He took his glasses from his head and examined them. "When searching for the unknown, it is best to start with what we know."

"But where do you go from there?"

He sat back in his chair. "I've often found that when answers elude me, I need to cut deeper to see the story. Simon Letell related to you a message that coincides with an ancient Latin palindrome square."

"Right."

"How ancient?"

"Oldest depiction found is in Pompeii, from 79 AD."

"And many scholars believe it is early Christian in origin?"

"There's debate, but yes."

"And if I take all the letters from that square and use them once, I can form a cross that says, 'Our Father' in Latin with two Greek A's and two O's left over."

"Right."

"And you think that it's some kind of code persecuted Christians used?"

"Yes. Back when they had to meet in secret."

"Because they were persecuted." He looked as if he'd reached a conclusion.

"Right . . ."

"So, if we attribute what we know about these early Christians to Simon Letell, then we may have just learned something about him."

"You think Simon was being persecuted?"

"Assuming he was not simply insane or just disoriented, then it is a possibility."

I stared at the tile floor. "He was speaking in code?"

"Because he was forced underground, perhaps?"

I shook my head. "This seems really farfetched."

He fingered strands of his bushy white eyebrow and grinned. "Only one way to find out for sure."

"What's that?"

"Find Martin."

CHAPTER 08

Bones couldn't stop laughing.

We sat in the parking lot outside the morgue. "I'm glad you're amused by all this." I put my foot on the dash. "Mind if I use your laptop?"

He put on a cockney accent. "Right. Whatever you need, Inspector."

I felt like saying, "What does that make you? Dr. Watson?" But it was a lame comeback, so I just kept quiet. I got out, opened the outside cabinet where Bones kept his laptop bag and brought it back in. I opened the Web browser, and his home page popped up. In the Search field I entered the names Simon Letell and Martin.

Bones raised an eyebrow. "Yahtzee?"

"So now you're interested?"

"I have been equally interested and entertained."

I scanned the search results. One match. "Yeah. I found something."

"What?"

"Simon Letell and a Richard Martin are mentioned together on the UNR Web site." I followed the link and scrolled down the page. "Looks like Simon was a well-educated man . . . earned his master's degree in chemistry alongside Richard Martin some years back. Martin went on to earn his doctorate and is . . . presently professor at the chemistry school."

"At UNR?"

"At UNR."

Bones dropped the transmission in drive.

"What are you doing?"

"Taking you to the university."

"We already pulled strings just to be here."

"Don't worry. I've got it covered."

A sustained tone let out from the radio. I let my feet down off the dash and pulled out the map book.

"All units, this is an informational broadcast only. Please extend your congratulations to our own paramedic/soon to be UNR Med School lackey, Jonathan Trestle. Great job, Jonathan! Aprisa dispatch clear."

A scattering of radio mic clicks from other rigs gave the sound of static applause.

I smiled and looked at the floor. "Someone put you up to that?"

Bones extended his hand across the center console. "Congratulations, bud. It won't be the same out here without you. Just keep your head out of your you know what when you're an ER doc. All right?"

We shook.

"Now . . ." Bones pulled out his phone. "Leave this to me." He held it by his ear. "Hello. Hi, this is McCoy. Yeah. I know. He's blushing. Nice work. Hey, you mind if we swing by the university so he can check up on some scholarship paperwork? . . . It's not? Great. Thanks. We'll be listening." He hung up and pulled the ambulance onto Kirman Avenue. "Free and clear, Inspector."

We found the chemistry building off of Ninth Street, though only after Bones insisted on buying me coffee from the Record

Street Café. The mature trees and manicured lawns of the university were a nice alternative to the muddled concrete grays of parking lots and city streets. Spring burst forth at every turn, buds on cherry trees that would soon send tear-shaped petals twirling through the courtyards like snow flurries. I took a deep breath with the realization that I was walking on the campus that would soon be my new home.

The sixties-style three-story Chem building sported narrow elongated windows bordered by white walls that were interspersed with wide columns of red brick veneer. In the foyer we found a directory with white lettering affixed to a black background. Martin's name was listed under the heading *Faculty,* with 307 adjacent to it.

I tapped on the glass. "Third floor."

Bones motioned with his hand. "After you."

Time for some answers. I started up the stairwell, wondering what, if anything, Dr. Martin would reveal. I pulled Simon's note from my side pocket. Each step echoed, as though the building were vacant. Bones trailed behind, holding his espresso cup.

We crossed the second-floor landing and started in on the third flight. It occurred to me that we'd walked quite a ways from the ambulance.

I stopped. "If we get a call, we're going to have to hoof it back."

Our radios beeped.

Bones made a hands-in-the-cookie-jar face.

"Medic Two, respond priority one for a possible cardiac arrest."

Our boots drummed as we flew down the steps. I swung off the handrails around the corners.

We hit the ground floor. I pulled out my pager. "Did you get that address?"

Bones dropped his coffee in the trash. "No." He lifted his

radio. "Aprisa dispatch, Medic Two. Could we have that address again?"

"Ten-four, Medic Two. It's at UNR—room three-zero-seven of the chemistry school."

I froze. Bones looked at me.

The air snapped like a cable breaking.

He shot out the door. "I'll get the stuff."

I ran up the steps, two and three at a time.

Second floor. Blood rushing through my chest.

Third-floor landing. I threw open the door. The smell of sawdust and drywall came from the long hallway. Artificial light reflected off of Visqueen taped over the walls. White dust coated the tile floor, and there were sounds of power tools at the far end.

This can't be right. I sprinted down the hall. A Hispanic construction worker emerged from behind one of the clear plastic curtains.

"Excuse me," I said. "Did you call 9-1-1?"

"No, no."

I put my hands on my head and looked around. "Can you tell me where 307 is?"

"Tree-seben?"

"Yes. Yes. Three hundred and seven."

"Oh, oh. *Trescientos siete?*"

"Yes."

"*Sí.*"

"Where?"

"*No está aquí. Ahora está en el otro edificio. Temporalmente.*"

"*No esta?* What do you mean?"

"*Esta en el otro edificio. Para la física.*"

"*Otro edificio?* Other building?"

"*Sí, sí. Para la física.*"

"For . . . for physics?"

"*Sí. Con la construccion.*"

"Got it. Thank you so much." I took off back down the hall, hearing a faint and quizzical "*De nada*" from behind.

I sailed down the stairs and busted out the front doors. Bones wheeled up the gurney with all our bags.

I grabbed the foot of the cot. "Not here."

Dispatch came over the air. "Medic Two, I have an update on that location."

I pulled my radio from my belt. "Go ahead."

"Apparently room three-zero-seven has been moved to the first floor of the Physics building during construction."

"Medic Two, copy."

We bumped and rattled down the sidewalk, following a lawn sign over to the Physics building. A sandwich board in the foyer read *Adjunct Chemistry Offices* with an arrow pointing to a side hall. An office door hung open at the far end. We jogged down the hall, parked the gurney by the wall, and grabbed the bags.

A young Asian woman in a lab coat met us inside, her eyes swollen and red, her cheeks wet. Beyond her, a man with thinning silver hair slumped over a stout oak desk, his arms spread out on a scattering of papers. A plaque on the desk read *Richard Martin, PhD.*

I came beside him and lifted his head and chest. His arms remained extended, but now pointed toward the ceiling. Rigor mortis had already set in. Purple painted his face.

I set Martin down and looked up at Bones, his expression an amalgam of surprise and confusion.

Abaddon was staking his claims.

Two dead men and the wheels at work.

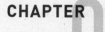

"Spitzer wants to see you in the office."

I looked up from the chart I was finishing to see Bones leaning in the doorway of the time-clock room at Aprisa headquarters.

"Why just me?"

"Oh, he tried with me, but I just changed the subject and deftly slipped out. Good luck."

"Wait. What is it for?"

Bones disappeared down the hallway.

Intolerable.

If Spitzer wanted to see me, then he could come see me. I turned my attention back to the chart I'd been trying to finish for the last twenty minutes. The clock clicked to ten past six. Late getting off shift, again.

"Hey, pal."

I looked up, this time to see the ingratiating smile of Dale Spitzer, the words *Paramedic Supervisor* engraved into the glinting rectangular name badge on his shirt.

Spitzer nodded at my chart. "Didn't get your paperwork done in time again, huh?"

"I guess I didn't effectively use the time between the ten calls we had in the past twelve hours."

I meant it to be facetious. He took it as a confession. "Well, hey, that's all right, pal. You'll get better. Just keep trying."

I'd been on the streets for four years—which like dog years, is more than it seems—but Spitzer still spoke to me as if I'd just made it out of paramedic school. I'd gotten past taking it personally, so now I just tried to have fun with his daily condescension.

"I can only hope I will get better, someday."

He patted my shoulder. "Come on, now. You'll get there." It was like listening to Barney in a paramedic uniform. "Hey, when you're done with your chart, why don't you come on down to the supervisor's office, and we'll have a chat."

I nodded. "Isn't that what we're doing right now?"

He breathed in through his teeth. "Yeah, there's just a little something we need to go over." He made a clicking sound and winked. "All right?"

I didn't say anything. In fact, I just stared at him.

He turned and greeted someone passing in the hall-way. "Hey, pal."

Spitzer spun around in his office chair, his elbows on the rests, fingers tented. I stood in the doorway.

"Go ahead and come on in. Close the door behind you, if you would, pal."

Okay, I'll admit, the whole "pal" thing still got to me. I honestly wanted to punch him in the gut, but I couldn't help imagining my blow being absorbed by a purple dinosaur belly. I sat on the edge of a chair.

"How's everything?" he said.

"Good."

Spitzer took a deep breath. "So, I'm sure you're aware this has been an issue before."

I pushed my lips together, looked to the side and then back at him.

"Response times," he cued.

I shook my head. "And . . . ?"

He rubbed the back of his neck and blew out. "Well, that's why we're here, Jonathan. This can't keep happening."

I scratched my chin. "I'm not sure I'm following you. I thought we were pretty dialed on our responses today."

"Five minutes and fifty-nine seconds. You know what those numbers mean?"

I'd placate him. "Of course. It's what the county contract stipulates."

"Right. And as long as we make those response times, you and I have jobs." He spoke as if he were talking to a preschooler.

I couldn't resist. "And what happens if we don't make those response times?"

He sat back, looking for an instant as if he doubted my credulity. "Jonathan, if we don't make our response times, we could lose our contract for service. Another company could replace us in this area."

I mimicked his breathing in through the teeth. "And that would be bad."

"Yeah, pal. That's why we've got to call 'on scene' every time, on time. If you don't do that, dispatch can't record when you actually got there. It's very important that you call 'on scene' before five minutes and fifty-nine seconds."

Something in the way he put that didn't sit right. "And . . . what if we're not actually able to be on scene in that time frame?"

"Come on now, Jonathan. You have a great job. You know how many people are lined up out there who'd take your place in a heartbeat?"

How many wet-behind-the-ears, fresh-out-of-paramedic-

71

school job applicants out there willing to be paid pennies to slog it out on the streets for a couple years? Yeah, I did. And the number was, unfortunately, limitless.

He stood and pushed in his chair.

I instinctually rose. Was this the part where we wrestled?

He stepped close, then patted my shoulder and inserted his right hand into mine, forcing a shake. "That's why we need to always be sure to get there in time." He looked me in the eyes, and all fabricated friendliness fell away. A moment later Medic Barney snapped back. "All right, pal?"

I wanted to tell him to shine on. To invite the line of folks wanting my job. They could pay them even less than the burger-flipping wage they paid me. And maybe that new employee would figure out sooner than I did that this job had a tendency to be a stepping-stone to somewhere else.

But I couldn't risk doing anything to jeopardize my "provisional" scholarship. So I just swallowed my ornery inclinations and nodded.

"All right." He forced a laugh and opened the office door, speaking for the benefit of everyone. "Keep up the good work out there, Jonathan. Stay safe."

CHAPTER 10

I woke late the next morning on my day off, paid bills and straightened things up. My dad napped in his room after lunchtime, a rerun of *MASH* playing on the TV atop his dresser. I walked out to the garage, into the dank smell of seventy-year-old cedar and cobwebs mixed with oil, strapped my kayak onto the trailer attached to my mountain bike, and suited up for the Truckee River.

The ride downtown was pleasant, cottonwood fairies floating in the air, dodging through the spokes of my bike wheels. High-rise condos flanked the river island, Wingfield Park. The theatre and pubs and coffee shops and food stops moved with scattered foot traffic. A couple families relaxed on the grass while children hopped from rock to rock with pant legs rolled up. A man wearing about seven jackets lay on his side by the bushes with a backpack for a pillow. A few boats paddled in the water, spinning and riding on the standing waves. Nobody I knew.

The spring snowmelt had swelled the riverbanks. I pushed off upstream from the kayak park, and the sudden buoyancy lifted my spirits and I felt the river. Its ebbs and swirls and choppy ripples moved in motion with my mind.

I dropped into one of the standing waves and carved and buffeted off the rolling pillow. I relaxed and let the river channel me downstream, and then with a light paddle I rested in an eddy. For the better part of the hour I cycled through this pattern. Paddle, carve, rinse, repeat.

It felt so different from work. So restoring. It reminded me of a psalm about trees planted by streams of water. It made sense that life in this town flourished by the river.

I played until my arms felt like rubber and then stalled by the north bank, staring at the sunlight shining through tree limbs. The days were growing longer.

I glanced at my watch—3:05.

I had a distant dim-light inkling that I was missing something. Somewhere I wanted to be. Someone . . .

Tea at three.

Naomi would already be at Deux Gros Nez.

I looked at the clear water dripping off my dry suit. A few hard paddles put me back in the current, thrusting forth through the next water feature with a rush of wave motion and rolling foam. I lifted my boat out on the south bank downstream and trotted past the Park Tower to my bike.

The slight incline pedaling Arlington toward California Avenue burned the cores of my quadriceps. I pedaled hard for speed. Halfway home I glanced at my watch—3:22.

Muffled sirens wailed in the distance.

I ducked my head and pumped onward, bouncing over uneven pavement to my garage.

I lifted the garage door to the groaning sound of rusted springs, left the boat and my bike as they were, and stripped out of my wet gear.

In my room I ran my fingers along the shirts hanging in the closet and picked out my favorite, a faded brown North Face short sleeve. I buttoned on a pair of blue jeans, threw on some socks, and skated down the hallway like a hockey player, grappling the frame of the bathroom doorway en route.

Comb your hair, brush your teeth.

I squirted a bullet of toothpaste in my mouth and shuffled a towel through my hair. Turning water full blast into the sink I rinsed my mouth, spat, and took one glance in the mirror.

A beanie would have to do.

Cinching one over my ears, I fetched my shoes, hopped out into the garage, slid into the Passat, and checked the clock on the dashboard—3:46. *She'll so be gone.*

Ignition. I shot glances in the mirrors, backed into the street, and fifty feet later halted at a stop sign.

An elderly woman with a walker inched through the crosswalk.

Lift. Shuffle.

Lift. Shuffle.

Lift . . . Shuffle . . .

She'd only made it to my passenger-side headlight.

I set the e-brake and opened my door. "Hi, ma'am. May I help you? Here." I reached for her walker and her arm.

She screamed.

I spun around. "No, no. Don't do that. No, see—"

She whacked my forearm with her handbag. I stepped back in disbelief. She hit me again, spoke something in Basque, and spat on my shoes.

I looked to the sky.

She faced forward and scooted on.

Lift. Shuffle.

Lift. Shuffle.

Back in my car the time glowed on the dash—3:51.

I set my forehead on the steering wheel and took a deep breath.

CHAPTER 11

Five minutes after four I ascended the exterior purple staircase of the brick building housing Deux Gros Nez café. Through the glass door I could see all the tables and the French-paned windows in the back.

No Naomi.

I exhaled and turned the doorknob. Dangling wind chimes clanked.

A girl with braided brown ponytails and a stained apron greeted me from behind the counter. "Howzit?"

"Good, thanks." I eyed the tables near the back wall.

Two middle-aged women chatted at one. A guy in his twenties clacked at a laptop keyboard on another. A girl scribbled on paper between two behemoth textbooks. A young couple cooed by a window at the north wall.

"Anything I can get for you?" Ponytails wiped her hands on a towel.

I took a stool by the bar counter. "Yeah, how about a cappuccino?"

"I can make an evergreen or a flower in the foam, if you'd like?"

"Sure. Anything but a heart."

She gave an intuitive nod and tamped an espresso brew handle clear. A minute later she frothed milk in a pitcher and spooned it into a small cup. She slid a saucer in front of me and leaned on her forearms. "One cappy."

I took a taste. "That hits the spot."

She grinned. "What's her name?"

I almost coughed cappuccino foam out of my nose. I set the cup down and ran the back of my hand along my mouth. "Just a friend."

She straightened. "Ah, I see. Just a friend?"

"Yes, actually. Always, in fact. I can't think of one I've known longer. Maybe you know her?"

"Oh yeah, I'm sure. Comes in here all the time. 'Justa Friend.'"

"Nothing gets by you."

"I'm that good." She wiped her hand on her apron and stretched it out. "I'm Sandra, by the way."

We shook. "Pleased to meet you, Sandra. I'm Jonathan."

"So, Jonathan, seeker of Justa Friend, what do you do for a living? Are you a student or—"

A wailing ambulance drove down California Avenue.

I pointed a thumb toward the door. "That." The sound faded. "I do that."

"Oh, you're a paramedic." She batted her eyes.

I laughed to myself and looked at the creamy liquid in my cup. I glanced toward the back windows.

Naomi appeared.

She sat at the middle table, right across from laptop guy.

I took another sip, then motioned with my head. "There she is."

Sandra feigned a gasp. "No. Where?"

"Right over there, by the window. She's sitting by that guy with the Dell."

"Her? With the dirty blond hair?"

"Yeah."

"That's Justa Friend?"

"That's her."

"That's Naomi."

"You know her?"

"Of course I do. She comes in here almost every day, same time. Why didn't you just tell me you were looking for Naomi? I could have told you I saw her go downstairs to the loo."

I scratched my chin. "Who's the guy?"

"Him, I'm not sure." She folded her arms. "This could get complicated. You better go over there and kick his—"

Door chimes clanked. New customers filed in. Sandra turned. "Howzit?"

I nursed my coffee for another minute and formulated a plan. I would stroll over and act as if seeing her there was a pleasant surprise. "And who might this be?" I would say, and she would go, "Oh, this is handsome and brainy laptop guy—he's a good friend of mine. Would you like to sit down and join us?" And I would say, "Oh no, thank you. I was just leaving but wanted to stop over and say a quick hello before I never talk to you again."

Or something like that.

I took a sip.

Let's do this.

I slid off the stool. Synapses double-fired, and my awareness of the room and the people in it heightened. Maybe it was fatigue from the river; maybe it was caffeine coursing through my bloodstream, or the band Pavement playing from the corner-mounted speakers. Whatever the cause, the moment was tangible, and time belonged to me as I took those first steps toward Naomi.

She turned and saw me. Her ocean-hewn eyes liquefied any animosity in my heart. Sunlight through the window met the gentle curves of her smile.

She was mine for another three steps.

Laptop guy looked up.

"Tanner," she said, "this is Jonathan—the guy I was telling you about."

He extended a hand. "Hey. I don't know how you guys do what you do. Quite the wreck you worked out there, I hear."

"Thank you." I shook his hand and glanced at Naomi.

"Tanner is my brother-in-law," she hastened.

Didn't see that one coming. Air filled my lungs like a trade wind.

"Well," Tanner said. "Soon to be in-law at least."

"Only one month left." She nudged him.

"Which reminds me"—he folded his laptop—"I need to meet up with Natalie before church tonight." He stood. "It was a pleasure to meet you, Jonathan."

I shook his hand with vigor. "You as well."

He picked up his things. "Bye, Naomi."

"See ya, Tanner. Tell Natalie I'll burn that CD for her, okay?"

"Sure will."

He walked out.

I stood there and studied her. I had no idea what to do next. I hadn't thought past the I-was-just-leaving part.

She looked around. "So . . . would you like to sit down?"

"Yeah, sure." I sat and ran my hand across the smooth table.

Naomi put her fingers by her mouth. "Did you think that he and I—"

"Was I that obvious?"

She sat back and bit the corner of her lip. "Just a little. But maybe only to me."

I rubbed an eyebrow.

"Well, if it's any comfort," she said, "I could never like a guy named Tanner."

"Is that right?"

"Oh yeah. I don't know what it is. My sister thinks it's the greatest name ever given to a man. Me . . . It just makes me think of cowhide."

I grinned. She ran a finger along the rim of her mug.

"What kind of tea do you have there?"

She looked in her mug and then took a long whiff. "Jasmine."

"Your favorite now?"

"Maybe. Have you ever had jasmine tea?"

"I don't think I have."

"Here." She held out her mug. "Smell this."

I leaned forward and let its fragrance waft into me, feeling its humid warmth, smelling earth and blossoms and honey.

Naomi sat back. "Good stuff, huh?"

I nodded.

"Wait until you taste it." She raised and lowered her eyebrows.

"Didn't you used to like chamomile?"

She waved a hand. "I finally admitted to myself that it just makes your tongue go numb." She nodded at my cup. "What're you drinking?"

"A cappuccino. Ever had one?"

She pursed her lips and made a sound like an air hose.

I raised my espresso in a toast. "To tea at three."

She clinked her mug against my cup. "Or four."

U2 played in the background. *The Joshua Tree*. Naomi cocked her head, listening. "You ever feel like that?"

I recognized the song. "Like I'm 'Running to Stand Still'?"

"Yeah."

I thought of my dad, of living in a rental house for four years, of striving for the best I could be at my job only to have it threatened because I didn't call on scene in five minutes and fifty-nine seconds. "All the time. How about you?"

"I used to."

"But not anymore?"

She breathed in, glanced out the window, then shook her head and smiled. "No. Not anymore."

"What changed?"

Something sparked in her eye. She sipped her tea. "I followed up on our patient Jeff last night."

"Oh yeah?"

"Contused liver. Doing well in ICU."

"Ah. That's good to know."

She nodded. "I heard about your scholarship. Congratulations."

"Thank you."

"You should be proud. You've attained everything you wanted."

Something like a vacuum opened inside me, a sucking black hole in the center of my gut. "Right. Yeah." I swirled the espresso dregs in my cup. "How about you? Anything big on the horizon?"

She shook her head. "No. Which is just great. I love flying. Since some of the older nurses retired, I have a better pick of shifts. One weekend day off now. I read and garden. And take care of my mom."

"You mentioned she had some health issues."

"Leukemia."

"I'm so sorry. How long have you known?"

"We found out this past year. She's getting good treatment but she's weak. We won't know if it will be effective for a while yet." She sat back. "I trade off with Natalie cooking for them a couple times a week. How's your dad?"

I laughed. "Honestly, I'm not sure what he'd do on his own. But his sickness is far from acute. It's more of the addictive, kill-yourself-slowly variety."

She nodded and cupped her hands around her mug.

It reminded me of my mother sitting at the breakfast table, a peace permeating her person.

"So," I said, "would I be wrong in thinking that you might know something about my patient, Simon Letell?"

She folded her arms. The relaxed Naomi I'd been watching shifted into Flight Nurse Foster. She looked toward the door. "I did hear his name mentioned at Aprisa a while back."

"How long ago?"

"About six months, I think." She stared at the floor, searching her memory. "I was in the billing office clearing up a misunder-standing on a chart. I think I'd filled out the wrong Medicare code or something. Spitzer and Shintao were in the next office having a heated discussion with the newest PR girl. Something about a guy and his multiple complaints. Shintao must have had a stack of them because it sounded like he was reading them off one by one, saying, 'Letell. Letell. Jones. Letell.' At first I didn't realize that he was actually saying a name. I thought, with his accent, that he was saying 'Let tell'—like 'Let's find out the story.' That's why the name rang a bell after you mentioned it."

"What were the complaints about?"

"That I couldn't tell. I only overheard a few snippets of

conversation before I didn't have a reason to be there anymore. It wasn't my business, and that kind of conversation was pretty much par for the course with those two. I don't know. Maybe it's not even the same guy as yours."

"Not too many Letells out there."

"Good point."

I would have to investigate more into it. But I didn't want to give the impression that I'd come just to pump her for information. "So, your sister is getting married soon?"

She bit her bottom lip and looked at the table. "Yes. I am really, really excited for her." She leaned her head to the side and brought her eyes up. "Can I ask you a question?"

"Of course."

"How do you feel about . . ."

"About what?"

"Ah, never mind. It was just a random thought. Whew, where did that come from? Look, see, there it goes. It's out the window." Her cheeks flushed.

Now I had to know. "Well, if it flies back in here, it's always welcome."

She shrugged her shoulders. "Thanks." Her fingers caressed the mug, eyes searching me. "You believe in a leading—right, Jonathan?"

"A what?"

"Like when you have a leading to do something?"

"I'm not sure I follow you."

"Is there anyone you trust so implicitly that you would follow them, even if you didn't know exactly where they were leading you?"

The last ounce of coffee in my cup had equalized with room temperature. "I don't think I know anyone like that. Maybe my

TOMORROW WE DIE

mother, when I was little. Well, my mother and God. When I think of her, I think of Him."

She studied me, looking into me.

"Don't get me wrong," I added. "Not that I equate my mom with God. Just little things—like her old Bible and the scent of its thin gilded pages. The feel of the silky bookmark ribbon. It makes me think of her and Sunday school and fists pounding on each other singing 'The wise man built his house upon the rock.'" I breathed in. "I don't know. When you mentioned trust, that's what came to mind."

She held my gaze, tranquility in her face. A cell phone chimed from her purse. "Sorry." She pulled it out. "Oh, wow. I forgot it's my night to make dinner for my parents."

"Oh, of course. I won't keep you." I turned in my chair.

"Come with me."

I stopped. "I'm sorry?"

"Come have dinner with us."

"You want me to see your parents?"

She grinned. "Yeah."

"But it's . . ." It'd been really long. "They probably won't want to see me."

She tucked a strand of hair behind her ear. "Maybe." She stowed her cell phone. "But let's just say, I feel a leading."

CHAPTER 12

Tunes broadcasted from an iPod tucked in the center console of Naomi's classic Volkswagen hatchback.

Switchfoot, "Beautiful Letdown."

The thirty-five-year-old German auto rattled as we exited the freeway for Victorian Avenue in Sparks. A bulging fabric grocery sack sat on the floor of the rear, a bag of tortillas flopped over the edge.

I rested my elbow on the door. "I can't believe you still have this thing."

"It's not a *Thing*." She hit her turn blinker. "You should know the difference."

I smirked and ran my hand along the seat material. "New vinyl?"

"Yeah. That and my dad rebuilt the motor a few years back."

Something old. Something new. I studied her. "Same, but different."

She looked in the rearview mirror. "You talking about the car now, or me?"

"Hard to pinpoint. But something's definitely different."

She glanced over. "Things have to grow. They can't always stay the same."

"So I've learned."

She stopped at a light. "Have you?"

Good question.

I had run full sprint from the prospect of our friendship progressing into a serious relationship. It still gave me a sinking, drowning feeling that conjured the memory of an event I fought daily to ignore—a day that pulsed and beat beneath the floorboards of my mind.

Love . . . marriage. I equated it to death. And regardless of the fact that not having Naomi in my life made it seem like a part of me was lost . . . I couldn't see how things could be otherwise.

So no, I guess I hadn't learned.

"Here we are." She pulled to the curb by the same single-story stucco home I remembered, with its small, well-trimmed lawn hedged by boxwood. A newly painted white picket gate opened to a brick path that led to their crimson front door.

Naomi's dad walked out onto the porch, his enormous smile accentuating his slender face. "Hey, hey. There you are." He bear-hugged her.

"Hi, Dad! Guess who I ran into?"

"I see." He placed a hand on my shoulder and looked me in the eye. "Welcome back, Jonathan."

Back . . . "Thank you, sir."

"Oh, please. You two aren't in high school anymore. Call me Gary." He turned to Naomi and rubbed his hands together. "What's the dinner plan for tonight?"

She lifted the grocery sack. "I was thinking I'd make tacos with the chicken I brought the other day."

"You are such a blessing. You know that?" He put his arm around her and kissed her on the cheek.

She elbowed him in the ribs. "All right, all right. I love you too."

We walked inside and unpacked the bag on a honey-stained

wooden island. Matching hickory cabinets filled out the kitchen, older in style but well cared for.

A female voice, just louder than a whisper, came from the end of a hallway. "Hello, sweetie."

A woman I hardly recognized leaned on a cane, a burgundy scarf wrapped around her head, her gray-blue eyes hovering over gaunt cheekbones.

Naomi's countenance wilted. "Mom."

They embraced.

I stared at the island, at the can of refried beans and the bag of rice, at the onion and peppers.

"Caroline," Gary said, "you need to conserve your strength."

She smiled at him. "Thank you, dear, but I'm fine. Besides, we have a special guest."

Naomi wiped her eyes. "Mom, you remember—"

"Of course I do. A pleasure to see you again, Jonathan."

"You as well, Mrs. Foster."

She walked over to me and then paused to catch her breath, leaning on her cane. Her hands were thin but elegant, her nails polished and manicured, a simple wedding band and diamond adorning her ring finger.

She placed her palm on my cheek. It smelled like aloe. "You look all grown up." She looked over the vegetables on the island. "Now, what can I help with?"

"Nonsense, Caroline," Gary said. "Please, come sit down."

Naomi picked up a knife. "We've got it, Mom."

Caroline grimaced. "But Jonathan's our guest."

I picked up the cilantro and took it to the sink to rinse. "It's my pleasure, Mrs. Foster."

She relented with a coy smile and sat at the kitchen table. "So, Jonathan, I heard a rumor about you."

I shook the cilantro out and patted it with a paper towel. "Uh-oh. Pure speculation, I'm sure."

"I heard you did a fine job on your MCATs. And that you've been awarded a scholarship."

"Yes, ma'am, that is in fact true. UNR Med School."

"Congratulations."

"Thank you."

Gary set a glass of ice water in front of Caroline. There was a deep, sincere love in the way he looked at her—a lifetime of affection and trust expressed in a glance.

I realized halfway into dinner that I'd been hunching over the table with food in one hand, drink in the other—rapidly chewing our Mexican meal. The fact that I'd been eating like a paramedic dawned on me when Gary Foster presented a question just as I'd stuffed another mouthful.

"Jonathan, do tell us about what made you want to become a doctor. Weren't you interested in being a professional kayaker or something along those lines back in school?" He smiled and waited.

I was a minute out, minimum, from finishing chewing. I raised my eyebrows and smiled back, brought up a finger and smiled again, dabbed my lips with a napkin and chewed faster. I scratched the side of my head, pointed to a painting of Sand Harbor at Tahoe on the wall, and grunted admiration. They grinned and bobbed their heads. As soon as I could take a drink of water, I did and exhaled.

"That's a really good question. You know, you get to help people, provide a valuable service. It can be exciting." I took another sip.

Who was I kidding?

It was for her. My mother.

It always had been.

I stared at the wood grain in the tabletop and stuck with a simple answer that still resonated truth. "And . . . it's nothing at all like what my dad has ever done."

The room fell silent.

Gary cleared his throat. He glanced at Caroline, then at me and raised his glass. "To what our fathers have never done."

I stood next to Naomi as we worked on the dishes. The Fosters' vintage dishwasher, though in great working order, was small, so we did most of the stuff by hand. I washed and she rinsed, her hip brushing mine. She took the soapy dishes from me with both hands, all the while humming.

The tune sounded vaguely familiar. Like the melody of a music box brought out only at Christmastime.

My cell phone rang. I held my hands out of the bubbles and searched for something to dry with.

Naomi pulled a towel from the stove front. "Here."

"Thanks." The number was local, but I didn't recognize it. "This is Jonathan."

"Jonathan Trestle?"

"Yeah."

"Jonathan, this is Steve from O'Brien's pub."

My heart bungeed to my stomach. "On Wells Avenue?"

"No, South Virginia."

"Right."

"Your father—"

"Don't explain. I'll be right over."

I pocketed the phone and clenched my teeth.

Naomi enshrouded a plate with a yellow cotton towel. "Everything okay?"

"I've got to go."

"What is it?"

"It's my dad. He—" I pressed my lips together. "His car broke down and he needs a ride home."

"Oh."

"Thanks for a great dinner. But I'd better go." I walked to the front door.

"Jonathan?"

"Yeah?"

She dangled her keys in the air. "You're going to need a ride too."

Her VW puttered up the on-ramp to the interstate. "If you want, you can just tell me where your dad is and we can give him a ride. Save you time."

"No. I mean . . . thanks. But it might be something that I can fix, so I want to stop by home to pick up my tools."

"Sure you won't need a hand?"

I stared out the passenger-door window. "I'm sure."

At the café she parked next to my car and turned off the ignition. "You sure everything is okay?"

I got out and leaned on the door. "I had a great time. It wouldn't be right for me to keep you."

"I don't mind. Really."

"I'll see you later." I patted the doorframe.

"Jonathan."

"Yeah."

She tilted her head. Her eyes pierced me. "Will you?"

I gave a slow nod.

"Then give me your hand." She held hers over the passenger seat.

I hesitated, and then stretched out mine. She turned it palm side up and wrote her number on it. She rolled my fingers into a fist.

"Don't lose that." A subtle smile turned her chin.

I breathed deep and quick. My eyes flashed hot and full of liquid. I tapped the top of the car, took two steps back, and walked away.

The only thing that made O'Brien's Irish was a kitschy brass four-leaf clover that twirled on a string behind the bar. Scribbled on one side was the dubious autograph: *Best Wishes, Bono*.

The pub was windowless and cavern-like, the air weighted with cigarette smoke. An Italian man in his fifties leaned behind the counter watching a soccer match on ESPN2.

"Are you Steve?" I said.

He didn't look at me. "In the back corner."

My dad sat by the jukebox, propped up against the wall with his head turned toward a wastebasket.

Jim Morrison crooned from a pair of tired speakers.

"The clock says it's time to close now . . ."

A silhouetted figure appeared in a booth with the quick flame of a lighter, followed by the red glow of a cigarette.

"Learn to forget . . . Learn to forget . . ."

I rubbed my dad's sternum hard with my knuckles. "C'mon, Dad. Wake up. You can't sleep here."

He inhaled and cracked open his eyelids.

"Wake up, Dad. Come on. You gotta get up."

He mumbled. His breath hung heavy and putrid, pungent like cognac and moldy bread.

I took his arm around my shoulder and squatted next to him. "Dad, you gotta get up."

I moved to stand, but his body slid away from me. I stood and leaned on the jukebox. "Fine."

I put my arms around his torso and heaved him up, bracing his body against the wall. I took a breath and, in one motion, moved my shoulder under his midsection and straightened up, spreading my legs for balance.

With my father in a fireman's carry, I turned to face the door, his ankles hitting the jukebox. I passed the bar and fished out a twenty from my wallet one-handed. I threw it down on the counter by Steve.

The weighted tavern door swung shut behind us.

Trash rustled in the gutter. Night encroached. I grabbed a plastic grocery bag swirling by the wall and hooked it around my father's ears.

He vomited once on the way home. At the house I tied the bag shut, threw it in the trash, and pulled him inside. His shoes dragged along the hardwood hallway. I laid him against the wall in his room with his head turned to the floor.

Across the hall in the bathroom I washed my hands, and as I did, blue ink ran onto the porcelain and down the drain. By the time I processed what was happening, it was too late.

Naomi's number was gone.

A box of pent-up rage busted open. I slammed the bathroom door against the wall. The knob broke the plaster. The entire door vibrated.

I looked for the closest thing I could throw and snatched a

dove-shaped glass candleholder from the top of the toilet. I hurled it down the hallway.

It shattered.

My father didn't stir.

Shards flinted in the darkness.

A memory came to me of my mother lighting a candle in that holder one Thanksgiving. She struck matches and wore a flower-print dress, her eyes accented by dark eyeliner that curved up at the corners. My father sat at the head of the table in a white T-shirt, his face unshaven, his cheeks rounding his jawline. He was grinning. The room smelled like stuffing and turkey. It was before . . .

I rubbed a finger over the small scar on my forehead. I clenched my fist. My eyes felt like cast-iron boilers.

My father hadn't stirred.

"See what you did." I wanted to grab him by the shirt and yell at him until he woke up and understood.

I thought about kicking him. Like someone would kick a dog.

But he wouldn't wake up.

And he wouldn't understand.

And even if he heard me and saw the anguish in my face, he would only cower back with an empty slew of resigned apologies.

I slid against the wall. My eyes blurred the only light from the bathroom. I wiped my nose with my shirt.

"Look what you did," I repeated, covering my head with my hands.

Sobs shrieked forth, shaking me like a prison break.

CHAPTER 13

The tires hit the road. I bounced in my seat.

Bones whooped the *Dukes of Hazzard* theme song from behind the wheel, siren wailing. "'Makin' their way, the only way they know how!'"

We rounded a corner. The tires squealed. I fished the map book off the floor.

Our call was for a seventy-year-old female with heart palpitations. We were understaffed again and pushing nine minutes in response.

I straightened the map pages. She lived in a gated subdivision in the hills off McCarran Boulevard. The street names on the page diminished into branching swirls. I leaned close to the book, my eyes tracing a descending orbit of streets with all too similar names.

Babbling Brook Circle. Babbling Brook Court. Brookside Drive branched off of Brookview Way, not Brookview Road. I checked my pager to confirm the address. Bones banked around another turn. My head spun. I put a hand on the dash.

Bones flipped off the siren and slowed by the keypad for the community gate. He punched in the numbers given to us by dispatch and watched it swing slowly inward. We passed through and swerved through a series of downhill streets until stopping in front of a two-story house that overlooked the city.

An older woman wearing a tennis outfit and visor met us in front. "She's inside. It's her heart again."

We carried the bags up a wide staircase. Ivory-colored spindles supported an oak banister. A white-haired woman lay in the master bedroom on top of a perfectly made bed, her face pale and diaphoretic. She breathed in rapid, shallow respirations.

It took only two seconds for me to know she was in bad shape. Bones knew it too and went to work. He placed her on an oxygen mask while I hooked up the cardiac monitor. He was already pulling out the IV kit by the time I took my first look at her heart rhythm.

Rapid, narrow. Really rapid. A hundred and ninety beats per minute. I felt her wrist. No radials. I felt her neck. She had a weak carotid tapping at that sewing-machine pace.

That heart rhythm wouldn't sustain life for long.

I tried not to think about our extended response time. It wasn't our fault.

I spiked an IV bag with tubing.

We'd left as soon as we were toned out and hauled across the valley to even get there in the time we did.

I pushed it out of my mind and went to my line of questioning.

Her name was Marie Straversky. She was allergic to penicillin. She'd felt this way a couple times before, but only briefly and not as bad. She'd felt nauseated and weak since she woke up an hour ago.

Bones deflated the blood pressure cuff. "Seventy by palpation."

Too low.

That gave us two definitive options. Administer a medication to try to reboot her heart or go straight to an electrical countershock.

I was weighing the second option when Bones said, "Edison medicine?"

I looked at her, still conscious, eyes implicitly trusting whatever we chose to do.

"Do what you need to, boys. I just want to feel better."

I shook my head. "No. Let's go with adenosine IV."

Bones taped down the IV he'd started. "One custom-crafted fourteen gauge at the AC."

"Thank you." I turned to our patient. "Mrs. Straversky, I want you to try something for me." I handed her a syringe and asked her to try to blow the plunger out of it for ten seconds. The act of bearing down could stimulate a nerve that slows the heart. She pursed her lips and dropped her heart rate from one-ninety to one-eighty-five.

Nowhere near good enough.

Bones handed me two syringes. "Six milligrams adenosine and ten CCs normal saline."

"Thanks." I hooked them both up to ports on the IV line. The adenosine lasted only seconds in the bloodstream, so it needed to be pushed rapidly.

The monitor continued its accelerated beeping. I glanced at Bones. "Ready?"

He nodded and pushed the printout button. The paper recording reeled out of the machine.

I made eye contact with Mrs. Straversky. "You may feel a sudden pressure in your chest." I drove the plungers into the syringes.

One. And two.

The beeping persisted.

No change.

"Did you feel anything with that?"

Her eyebrows tented. "No."

Bones handed me two more syringes, this time with double the dose.

I leaned aside. "If this isn't effective, we'll do the synchronized countershock."

He nodded.

The monitor beeped in time, drawing a long bed of needles.

I drove in the medicine.

One. And two.

No change. Mrs. Straversky stared at me.

The beeping hiccupped.

She groaned and clutched her chest.

The heart rhythm went flatline. Her eyes rolled and her head tilted back on the pillow.

Respirations stopped. As did her heartbeat.

The reel of monitor paper curled on the floor. Still flatline.

Come on now. . . .

A thin green horizon on a black background.

Come on. . . .

Bones's fingers twitched over the intubation kit.

Still pulseless.

"That's it. I'm tubin' her." Bones pulled out the laryngoscope handle.

"Wait."

The elongated tone continued.

Still flatline.

He clicked the blade in place. "Let's start CPR."

It beeped.

And again. In growing succession, like soldiers cresting a hilltop, they flicked on the screen.

Mrs. Straversky drew a deep breath.

Bones reached for her wrist. "I've got radials with that."

I checked the monitor. Eighty beats a minute. Then ninety. One-ten. *Slow down, slow down.* One-forty. One-seventy. Back to one-ninety.

The fire crew walked in soot streaked and smelling like smoke. The captain said they'd just cleared from a house fire. I asked them for another blood pressure while Bones explained to Mrs. Straversky that he needed to stick the two large defibrillation patches to her chest.

Her eyebrows knitted, her face morbidly pale.

A firefighter reported back on the blood pressure. "Fifty-four over thirty."

Her eyelids drooped and her jaw went slack. I shook her shoulder. "Mrs. Straversky? Mrs. Straversky?"

I switched the monitor settings for a shock that would synchronize with her rapid rhythm. "Charging to one hundred joules. I'm clear. Everyone clear?"

The firemen backed away with hands in the air. I put my thumb over the shock button, the red light passing through the nail bed. "Shocking at one hundred."

Her body jerked and relaxed on the bed.

I listened to the long somber tone of asystole.

I would breathe when she did.

It beeped.

And again.

In regular, marched-out succession, leveling at a beautiful rate of eighty beats per minute.

Color returned to her cheeks. She opened her eyes. "What happened? I have got a horrible headache."

Bones smiled. "We'll take a headache any day, ma'am."

On the ride to County Hospital she was talkative though tired. Her tennis friend rode in the front seat with Bones. I sat on the bench seat beside her, jostling with the motion of the rig, jotting down info on her chart.

She brought a hand to my forearm. "Thank you for coming to my house so quickly."

Quickly? "Did it . . . seem fast to you?"

"Oh yes. Compared to the other times."

"Other times were longer?"

"This isn't the first time I've had to call you handsome young men. Aprisa has been to my house before. Though I do live a ways up in the hills."

"But the ambulances, they didn't arrive faster the other times?"

She shook her head. "Oh no. I was fortunate that you boys were closer this time."

I patted her hand, got up, and sat in the captain's chair behind the gurney. "Mrs. Straversky, I'm going to call the hospital and let them know we're coming in."

"Thank you, dear."

I lifted the black phone from the wall and requested a patch to County's ER.

Mrs. Straversky would be all right. Our training, our tools— they did what they were designed to do. But had it taken us any longer to get there . . .

There was a reason the first ambulances looked like hearses.

CHAPTER 14

Bones swooned. "Has there ever been a sweeter voice to grace the VHF band?"

It was no secret that he was infatuated with the sultry-voiced new swing-shift dispatcher. She melted his butter like nothing else. If he were a Warner Brothers cartoon, his heart would be beating out of his chest, eyes star-crossed, with songbirds flitting about his head.

"Here she is, here she is." He pointed at the radio console as if it held her very essence.

"Ten-four, Medic Two. Post Rock and Victorian."

"Did you hear that?"

I looked at him sideways and dropped the transmission in gear. "Yeah. She said go to your post."

"It's not *what* she said." Bones tilted his head back against the seat rest. "It's *how* she said it."

The radio chirped. "Medic Two, did you copy?"

Bones took a deep breath.

I turned east onto Mill Street. "You going to answer that?"

He stared at the radio.

"Medic Two. Do you copy?"

Bones picked up the mic and cleared his throat. He spoke in an unnaturally deep tone. "Affirmative, dispatch. Medic Two copies. Thank you."

He held the mic over its dash clip. There was no response. His eyebrows angled and he said to me, "Maybe the thank-you was too over-the-top?"

The radio chirped. "Ten-four, Medic Two. My pleasure."

Bones exhaled and smiled. "Did you hear that?"

I stopped at a light and scratched my head.

He hooked the mic on the center console. "Wow . . . 'My pleasure.' Man." He pulled a foil-covered sandwich from the cooler at his feet.

"You are so gone for her." My cell phone vibrated. "Hello?"

"Hi, Jonathan." Dr. Eli's voice.

"Hey, Doc."

"I've been doing some background on our two deaths."

"Yeah?"

"Simon Letell has no surviving relatives. And as far as I can tell, no friends either. It's as though Dr. Martin was the last connection he had on the planet."

"How convenient."

"Exactly. It would seem, on the surface, that whatever secret Letell held has been effectively cast into the grave."

Bones pointed, mouth full. "Light's green."

"Thanks."

"What's that?" Dr. Eli said.

"Oh, nothing. I'm in the ambulance right now."

"Ah. Tell Thaddeus I said hello."

"I'll make sure to. Hey, Thaddeus."

Bones glowered at me.

"Dr. Eli says hello." I smiled and switched the phone to my other ear. "What about Martin? Was he married?"

"Yes. I was just about to get to that. His wife may be the best connection we have. She's in old Sparks, off of Stanford Way."

"Perfect. We're headed that way right now. Can you text me the house number?"

"Ooh . . . umm. Okay. Yeah, I think I can do that. Let me know if it doesn't come over."

"Thanks, Doc."

"No problem. And I have that autopsy on Martin coming up too. Perhaps that will shed some light on the situation. Take care, Jonathan."

Bones radioed dispatch to put us in the area of Rock and Victorian. Dr. Eli's text came through. The address was a bit outside of the one-mile radius of our post area.

I winced and looked at Bones. "Think you can ask dispatch for another favor?"

He shook his head. "I don't know."

"Come on now. Just because Jessica Rabbit is at the console—"

"We don't really have a good excuse this time. Besides, it would look like I'm just making up a reason to talk to her."

I sat back. It was too much for me to accept Martin's death as a coincidence. Something was going on, and I couldn't shake the sense that time was of the utmost.

"We need to get over there."

"No way. Our GPS signal will rat us out."

"This can't wait." I glanced out the window. "So what, then? How're we going to do it?"

Bones stared at the foil wrap around his sandwich. "There is one thing." He stripped off the aluminum and grinned. "I've always wanted to do this."

I stood guard by the back of the ambulance. We sat parked on Prater Boulevard. Two cars zipped by. "Okay, you're clear."

I gave Bones a boost and he clambered atop the box, aluminum foil in hand.

"How do you know which antenna to cover?"

He crawled forward. "I think the GPS is the big one in the middle."

"You think?" The light changed at the intersection two blocks away. "Hurry up. Here comes another round of cars."

"How long?"

"Ten seconds."

"That's not enough time."

"Hit the deck."

Bones dropped to his belly. I stood on the sidewalk with a hand on the ambulance, trying to look casual. The last car passed.

"You're clear."

"You think anyone saw me?"

"I think everyone saw you."

"Anyone of consequence?"

I thought about it. "Hopefully not. Hurry up."

"Okay. That should do it." He dangled his legs off the back of the ambulance.

I threaded my fingers and placed them under his boot. "I can't believe I'm touching the soles of your shoes with my bare hands."

"If you only knew where these feet have trod."

"I do know. That's the worst part."

He dropped to the street, the entire front of his uniform covered in dust.

I nodded. "Guess the roofs don't get washed much."

He brushed off. "We've probably got fifteen or twenty minutes before dispatch realizes there isn't really a problem with the GPS system."

I opened the back door and pumped disinfectant gel on my hands. "All right, then. Let's do it."

I parked curbside in front of a single-story stucco home, a sprinkler moved streams in a slow arc over a small lawn. I clipped my radio on my belt and walked up the front path. Bones trailed behind, hands in pockets. Standing to the side of the door, I gave a couple raps with my knuckles. A long-haired gray cat appeared on the windowsill beside the door.

I tapped the window. "Hey, kitty."

It hissed and let loose a high-pitched growl.

A bolt shifted inside, and an older woman opened the door and slid off a chain. She wore a long black dress that matched the color of the dark streaks interspersed through her silver hair. "Can I help you?"

The purpose of the black and the realization that she had only recently learned of her husband's death hit me. I'd been so focused on finding answers that I hadn't even taken her circumstances and feelings into consideration.

"Is there an emergency, gentlemen?"

"So sorry to disturb you, ma'am. Are you Mrs. Martin?"

"Yes, I am."

"We . . ." How did I put a professional spin on the real reason we were there?

I knew it was a stretch, but I went with, "We're here to offer our sincerest regrets and to follow up with you about your recently departed husband. We were the paramedics who responded to the 9-1-1 call for him."

She glanced back at Bones. He gave an acknowledging smile. She lifted her chin. I was sure she would send us on our way.

"Come in, gentlemen, please."

Sunlight pouring through a large front window lit her living room. Brass lamps with dangling crystals sat on coffee tables bordered by fine-quality cream-colored couches. She sat in a chair perched on ornate wooden feet.

She waved at the couch. "Have a seat, please." The tabby trotted over and hopped on her lap. She stroked the fur between its ears as it glared at me.

Bones stood behind the couch. I unclipped the radio from my belt and leaned forward. "We're very sorry for your loss."

"So you said, young man."

I swallowed. "Mr. Martin, he was—"

"Dr. Martin."

"Yes. My bad. Dr. Martin."

"Your what?"

"My . . . mistake."

She nodded. "Go on."

"Dr. Martin . . . did he know a man named Simon Letell?"

Her face lightened. "Oh yes. Simon. We had him over for dinner a couple months ago."

"So he and Dr. Martin were friends."

"Oh yes. Old friends. I still need to contact him about Richard's passing. But I can't find his number. Is he . . . I hope everything is okay."

"I'm so sorry to tell you this, but Simon Letell is dead too. He died the day before your husband."

Mrs. Martin turned her head, touching fingers to her lips.

I unfolded Letell's note. "Before he died, he handed me this paper. He said, 'Give this to Martin.'" I stood and offered it to her. "Do these markings make any sense to you?"

A perplexed look came across her brow. "No. I ... Are you sure it was him? Did he still live in that house off of Apollyon Way?"

Fitting street name. "No. No, I don't believe so. He'd been living in a motel downtown. It was Simon Letell, though."

She stroked the tabby harder between the ears. It lowered its little pentagonal demon head in rhythm, squinting at me and flipping its tail. "They *were* working on something."

I caught Bones's glance. He raised his eyebrows.

"They had this game," she said. "It started when they were in graduate school together. Little math games. Puzzles. They'd look for patterns in chemical formulas and create ways of encoding them. One was always trying to outdo the other, see if he could make a code the other couldn't break. It stopped a little after Richard started his doctorate."

"Letell couldn't keep up anymore?"

"Yes, I suppose. Simon is, was, very bright, though. I thought they'd just grown out of it."

"Had they started working on something new?"

"Yes. It reminded me of their little puzzles. But they worked together on this."

A grandfather clock gonged in the hallway. Bones checked his watch.

"Do you know why Letell—why Simon didn't go on to get his doctorate?"

"Oh, that was his plan. But his poor mother. She became ill and suffered a stroke. It left her weak on her whole left side."

"Did he go to care for her?"

"Simon brought her to live with him. He worked nights in a lab and cared for her during the day. He tried for years to take doctoral classes, one at a time." Her eyes trailed off. "He became reclusive. Never married. We lost contact. Stopped seeing him for years. Then about a year ago he and Richard reconnected. His mother had suffered some sort of heart failure and passed away."

Bones cleared his throat.

I glanced at the clock. "What exactly were they working on?"

She looked at the floor and shook her head. "We'd have him over for dinner. I think he liked the companionship. They'd go down to the basement, play pool, and . . ."

"And?"

"And talk."

"About . . . ?"

"That's it. I didn't really pay attention. I thought it was just two old friends meeting up again."

"They had to have said something. What led you to believe they were working on something?"

"I don't know. . . ." She took a deep breath. "I do remember Richard being distressed and speaking with a cynical tone about some kind of corruption." She studied the carpet. "Something that they couldn't yet pinpoint, that needed to be ferreted out."

A male dispatcher's voice came over the radio. "Medic Two, Aprisa."

"Corruption where?"

She shook her head. "I don't know. They were very cryptic. Whatever they'd found, they were being very careful that no one knew they had come upon it. I should have paid closer attention. I just . . . Like I said, I just chalked it up—"

"That's okay. It's all right. You don't need to blame yourself for anything."

"Medic Two, do you copy?"

Bones walked out the front door. "Aprisa, this is Medic Two. Go ahead."

I stood. "Thank you so much. We can only imagine how difficult this time must be for you."

"Medic Two, are you currently in your rig?"

I heard Bones's voice over the radio. "That's negative, Aprisa."

Mrs. Martin released the cat and rose from her chair with effort.

I clipped the radio back on my belt.

"Copy, Medic Two. We're having trouble with your GPS signal. What's your location?"

I turned to leave.

Mrs. Martin caught my hand. "Thank you, boys, for trying to save my Richard."

Her fingers were cold but smooth. I looked into her hazel eyes. "Take care, Mrs. Martin."

"Let me walk you to the door."

"Of course."

My radio again. "Medic Two? Aprisa."

At the entryway she waved and smiled.

I waved and jogged down the walkway to meet up with Bones. He climbed in the passenger side of the ambulance, holding up his radio. "Aprisa, we're in the area of Rock and Victorian post."

"Copy," dispatch said. "I'm sending out a supervisor with a mechanic to take a look at your rig."

I jumped behind the wheel and turned the ignition.

"Medic Two copy." Bones glanced at me. " 'Bout what time would you say we should expect them?"

I swung the box around.

The sultry-voiced dispatcher came on. "Medic Two, stand by for a landline."

"Copy."

I plodded through the residential neighborhood, eager to turn onto Prater and speed up. The rig cell phone rang.

Bones flipped it open. "Medic Two." He listened. His eyebrows relaxed and his face took on the appearance of a little boy gazing at his favorite toy through a window display. "Okay. Okay. Yes . . . Yeah. Okay, thanks. You too." He hung up the phone and leaned back in his seat, staring at the ceiling.

"What's going on?" I said.

No response.

"Hey, Danny Zuko. What'd she say?"

"What? Oh. She said they left ten minutes ago."

Ten minutes.

"Bones, we've got to be there now."

CHAPTER 16

The supervisor would be at Rock and Victorian post any moment. We'd be fired for tampering with the GPS. Not to mention for traveling out of our post area.

I traced my finger over the emergency light-bar switch.

No, no, Jonathan.

I made the turn onto Prater and laid into the accelerator. Bones stared out the window in reverie.

I shook my head. "You are so of no use to me right now."

I hung a left at Rock and barreled toward Victorian. In the distance I could see our post building. Still no supervisor vehicle. I let out a relieved breath.

We stopped at the light at the intersection of Rock and Victorian. The Aprisa supervisor's SUV approached on Rock from the south. From the angle we were at, they likely wouldn't see us. But I didn't have time to park in front of the post. The light changed and I made a quick right into the gas station on the corner and parked along the curb by the air pumps.

"Quick, Bones. Go buy some Twinkies."

"What?" Bones blinked as if he'd just woken up.

"Spitzer's going to be here in seconds. We need an excuse for why we're not parked in front of the post."

Realization flashed in his eyes. "Right."

The supervisor's car passed on the opposite side of the street. Spitzer. Tom the mechanic rode in the passenger seat. I waved.

Spitzer didn't return the gesture. They'd make a U-turn at the intersection and pull in next to us. From the way I'd angled the ambulance, I was pretty sure they couldn't see Bones.

I clenched my teeth. "That's them. Go, man. Don't let them see you."

Bones glanced in the side-view mirror and slid out his door. He disappeared between two cars and the gas pumps. Even I couldn't see him after a couple seconds. I was impressed.

Spitzer pulled up next to the ambulance. I shut off the motor and rolled down my window.

He got out like he was the town sheriff, aviator glasses on, strutting with his thumbs in his belt. "Hey, pal."

I nodded. "Hey."

Spitzer looked at the passenger seat. "Where's your partner? Snoozing in back?"

"Nah. He's inside getting a Twinkie."

"A Twinkie, huh?"

I glanced through the store windows. No Bones in sight. "You know Thaddeus. Super health foodie."

Spitzer laughed and stopped abruptly, pushing his glasses up on the bridge of his nose.

Mechanic Tom walked up wearing grease-stained blue coveralls. He nodded. "Hey, Jonathan."

"Hey, Tom."

Spitzer ran his tongue along the inside of his lower lip. "Why're you guys parked over here, anyway? Too long of a walk from the post for you?"

I raised my eyebrows. "Here? Oh, right. Actually, you know, Bones has been in there a seriously long time. I don't know what's up with him."

"Probably letting out a growler," Tom said.

Thank you, Mechanic Tom. "Yes. You know, I mean, that's probably it."

Spitzer folded his arms and stared at the convenience store. "You know, you guys really should use the post bathrooms. This is horrible customer service. That's why we provide these posts. They're there so you'll use them."

I tapped the steering wheel. "You're absolutely right. I really don't know what Bones was thinking."

How's that for throwing my partner under the bus?

Spitzer leaned an elbow on the doorframe and took off his glasses. "You know, these posts are a privilege, not a right. That privilege can be taken away at any time."

Bones walked across the parking lot, unwrapping a Twinkie.

Spitzer straightened and raised his chin. I could tell he was about to lay into him too.

Bones opened his door, and I said, "Feel lighter, Bones?"

Bones hopped up in the passenger seat, giving an inquisitive look. I gave him the heat-vision stare.

His eyebrows tightened and he swallowed a bite of Twinkie. "Oh yeah. Man. I seriously couldn't hold it. I had this Thai soup last night that you would not believe, and—"

"Okay, okay." Spitzer put his hands in the air. "Spare us the nasty details. Sheesh. You guys. Let's keep a demeanor of professionalism around here, huh?"

I turned toward Bones and rubbed the back of my neck, glancing toward the ceiling in reference to the foil. I turned to the window. Only Spitzer stood there. My heart dropped. "Where's Tom?"

I felt the back of the ambulance dip. He was on the tailboard. The back door opened. I leaned to look through the doghouse and saw a pant leg and boot disappear up to the roof. I dropped back against my seat.

We are so hosed.

The whole ambulance shook. I heard scuffling and movement.

I scratched my head and stared out the windshield. The ambulance rocked again, followed by the sound of boots clacking on the tailboard and then dropping to the ground.

Spitzer looked toward the back. Tom stood somewhere in the blind spot of the side-view mirror.

"Oh my." Spitzer put his hands on his hips. "Now that is completely unacceptable. Is that all you found up there?"

I rubbed my brow and shut my eyes. *Well, I was planning on quitting soon anyway.*

"Can you believe this?" Tom said.

Spitzer shook his head. "This will definitely get back to the board. There is no way we can allow this to happen." He turned to me. "Did you know about this, Trestle?"

I had no idea how to respond. I looked at Bones. He was texting on his phone. Probably putting out resumés.

Time to face up to it. "It really is—"

"Unacceptable." Spitzer pointed at Tom, who walked up, his coveralls stained with bird droppings and dust. "This is absolutely unacceptable. I know you guys are tired at the end of shift and you expect the vehicle service technicians to do everything for the rig, but come on. These rigs need to be clean. This is what we were just talking about. Pride in your job, guys. Come on now."

I swallowed down the wrong pipe and coughed. "Right." I coughed again. "Absolutely. Our oversight. We really do need to help those guys get this thing back in service each night."

I looked over at Bones. He smirked as he texted.

Spitzer's phone rang. "Spitzer. Yeah? Good. Satellite glitch? All right. Good work." He hung up. "Well, your GPS is working fine now. Just a technical issue, but you guys don't have to worry about that." He tapped on the door. "Just keep in mind what I said. *Professionalism*. All right, pal?"

I nodded. "Sure thing."

"Stay safe out there."

Spitzer hooked on his aviators and swaggered back to the SUV, scanning the near horizon as if to make sure no trouble loomed. He nodded to Tom. "Hey, brush that off before you get back in, will you?"

I rolled up my window. "Bones, how did—"

He twirled a piece of aluminum foil between his fingers. "Never again doubt my mad ninja skills."

"When did you . . . Before I came out of the house?"

"A good ninja never reveals his secrets."

"That's for magicians."

"Every good ninja is also a magician."

I started up the engine and shook my head. "You're incorrigible. You know that? You could have at least told me sooner."

He chortled. "But it was so much more fun this way." He unwrapped the second yellow pastry from the package. "Want a Twinkie?"

CHAPTER 17

"There she is."

The only person I saw through the windows separating the hallway from dispatch was an overweight woman with a microphone headset on, a computer mouse in one hand, and a bag of frozen bonbons in the other. I glanced at Bones. He had the boy at the toy store look again.

"That's . . . ?" I leaned my head forward to insinuate the rest of the question.

"Her." He smiled.

I tried to picture Bones's sinewy frame next to hers. The word *eclipse* came to mind.

Bones sighed.

"You want me to drop off your radio in there for you?" I said.

"No way. That's my chance to talk to her."

I handed him mine. "This should buy you another five seconds."

He took it. "Thanks. Wish me luck."

"Godspeed, friend."

He straightened and punched in the door code to enter dispatch. The sultry-voiced bonbon-eating dispatcher's face brightened, and she twirled her headset cord around her fingers when she saw Bones. He spoke, fidgeting like an elementary schooler the whole time. I chuckled and adjusted the strap of my workbag slung across my shoulder. Turning to leave, I nearly collided with Aprisa Vice President of Accounting, Lawrence Shintao.

Shintao stood in the center of the hallway, his graying hair combed straight back with plenty of body, lending the appearance, along with his sour disposition, that he'd been forced to inspect a huge operating ventilation fan for some time before coming in to work that morning. It was nearly six in the evening now.

"Mr. Shintao. Excuse me."

He looked at the name sewn on my shirt. "Trestle. I needed to talk to you. It was mentioned to me that you've been having trouble remembering to call on scene."

Here we go. Another "Did you get your TPS reports in" lecture. Only a few more weeks and I wouldn't have to put up with this anymore. Forever. I swallowed my frustration and nodded. "I did overlook that on a call last shift."

He took a deep breath and let it out slowly, like Mr. Miyagi in *The Karate Kid*. "This is a serious *infraction*."

"No doubt." He was going to give himself an *infarction* if he didn't relax.

"Serious."

I raised and lowered my eyebrows.

"You," he said, "do not strike me as a young man who comprehends the gravity of such a mistake."

I cracked the knuckles of one hand with my thumb, one by one.

"Perhaps," he continued, "you need some remedial radio training. I will speak with the supervisors to set that up. It is only four hours. You should be able to come in on one of your days off to get it taken care of."

Since when did the accounting VP become involved in operations discipline? I stood in silence, quite sure that if I opened my mouth, the conversation would rapidly digress into the inappropriate.

"Okay, then." He fashioned something resembling a smile across his lips and turned toward the business office. "Have a nice night."

I stood there and stared at the closed business-office door, feeling as if Shintao had sucked any tailwind I'd had from my sails. I took a few more steps forward only to encounter another executive-board member.

Dr. Kurtz grabbed me by the shoulders. "Hey, Jonathan." He grinned, crow's-feet wrinkling beyond his black-rimmed glasses, a bit of gray accenting his otherwise dark straight hair pulled back in a ponytail. "How've you been? You excited for school?" Fluorescent light mirrored off his spectacles.

I put up a hand. "Hey, Doc." I lowered my voice. "Shintao just finished giving me the third degree."

"No doubt, no doubt. That guy." He shook his head, giving it a quick tap with his fingers. "All numbers for him." He stepped aside. "You walking out to your car?"

"Yeah, actually."

"You know, I just realized that the person I was going to talk to is already gone, so I'm about to leave too. Walk with you?"

"For sure." I tilted my head from side to side to relieve tension.

Trent Matley strode down the hall toward us. "Excuse me, gentlemen."

I nodded and stood to the side.

"Trent," Kurtz said.

He stopped with eyebrows raised. "Yeah?"

"Let's talk later on those patient-comment forms. Shouldn't be a big deal."

Trent shifted and put a hand in his back pocket. "Right. Sure, no problem."

"And get some sleep, buddy. You're putting in a lot of good hours out there."

"Right. Thanks, Doc."

We resumed our stroll down the hall. I rested a hand on my workbag strap. "I didn't think you made too many board meetings anymore."

"Got to justify being medical director somehow."

I smiled at the self-effacing response. Every single medic in the company operated under his license to practice medicine.

He patted me on the back. "At least I get to see guys like you who do the real work around here."

I pulled my time-clock card from my wallet. "So, how's the medical school?"

He huffed. "What part? You know, you try to get in there and run things right? You try to get good candidates recruited and train them up to be good doctors. That's what it's all about."

"I sense a *but* . . ."

"Yeah, but . . . Anyway. I told them, 'Hey, you guys picked me to be dean. Let me run this thing and quit calling audibles from the sidelines.'" He gave an exasperated laugh. "You know what I'm saying?"

I smiled and nodded.

"But anyway, I'm rambling. How about you? You've got to be jazzed about the scholarship."

"Oh, like you can't believe. Thanks so much for the call."

"Should only be a few weeks now until you won't have to deal with guys like you-know-who anymore."

"That'll be nice. The summer-school thing was a bit of a surprise."

We came to the time-clock room and I swiped my card. "But I understand that the board wants to see my commitment. I do take it that means my scholarship isn't set in stone?"

"No, no. You know, people think it's like a one-time done deal, like a free movie pass. But it's not. It's an ongoing thing—for everyone, not just you. But here's the deal. You're super smart. I've watched you grow in your career. You're capable. And you've already got hands-on skills that put first-year residents to shame."

We walked through the door to the ambulance bay. "Well, I appreciate that."

A vehicle technician sprayed down the side of an ambulance with a pressure wand. I walked through the mist behind him, the moisture feeling brisk on my skin as I exited to the evening air. With the setting sun, the parking lot glowed burnt sienna.

I pushed the key-ring button to unlock my car and opened the trunk, sliding the strap of my workbag over my head.

Kurtz patted my shoulder. "You don't have anything to worry about. Just stay the course and you'll be fine. Set your sights on the future. Focus on your studies. Forget about this place. It was a means to an end. Right?"

I nodded and took a deep breath. He represented the world I wanted to enter. He had a keen understanding of the world I was coming from. "Thanks again, Doc." I closed the trunk.

"Good seeing you, Jonathan. You ever have any questions just come by my office. Anytime. I mean that."

I settled in the driver's seat and dropped the Passat in gear, eager to get home and out of my uniform. Despite Joseph Kurtz's encouragement, visions of Shintao's scowl and Spitzer's plastic smile still hung in my mind. What was it with authority and me? Why was I getting raked over by management? *Maybe I should have been a fireman.* At least they had a union to check and balance things.

It was the nature of the beast—an inherent, irreconcilable conflict for any business seeking to provide emergency medical care within a capitalistic context. Everyone should have the right to it. Not everyone can afford it. Therein lies the rub.

Call volumes were increasing faster than billing rates. In order to make County-mandated run times, the company would have to put more ambulances on the street. That cost more money. I could smell the underlying stress seething from management's pores. Even more than usual. Something was going on. Probably why Kurtz had been called in for a board meeting.

Our new schedule took effect tomorrow. Just when we needed to shed light on things, Bones and I would take our turn at the night shift. But I had the feeling that whatever was lurking in the shadows just might be more apt to rear its head in the open field of midnight.

CHAPTER 18

A light haze hovered in the kitchen that smelled of burnt bacon. My dad swayed by the counter as if he stood in a ship's galley.

He held a short glass of amber liquid with an ice cube. "Hey, Jonner."

He was unshaven, wearing tan slacks and a stained white T-shirt under an unbuttoned chalk blue collared shirt.

"Hey, Dad." I turned the burner down from high and moved the pan. "Your bacon's done." An unfamiliar patio table stood outside with an ashtray on it. "You just buy that?"

"Oh, that. Guy gave me a great deal at a garage sale down the street. Come here, you." He gave me a hug.

The stubble from his face scratched my cheek.

"You want some dinner?" he said.

Only bacon was out.

"Sure, Dad."

He opened a cabinet and reached for two plates with one hand. He set them down hard on the counter. I grabbed two bagels from the pantry and sliced them.

He put the bacon on the plates and stared at it. "There should be some scrambled eggs in the fridge." He opened the refrigerator door and searched.

I closed the door. "It's cool, Dad. I'm only hungry for this anyway."

The bacon was hard—harder than beef jerky. I had to suck on it for a while before I could chew it. I wished we had a dog.

Since we were doing breakfast for dinner, I said, "You want some orange juice?"

"No, thanks. My stomach can't take that stuff."

I poured a glass for myself and sat. He ate the bacon as if it were a cheese stick. His eyes were bloodshot behind his bifocals.

I palmed my bacon and pocketed it as I took a sip of OJ. "So, did you go to the bridge club today?"

"I've been lousy at it these past few weeks. Anyway, I might be coming down with a head cold."

"Again?"

"Yeah. I've been living on antibiotics."

"That's why you're sick, Dad."

"I'll tell you, if I could make money off of selling snot—"

"Dad. Please. I get enough of that at work."

He swallowed. "How was work, anyway?"

I exhaled. "It was . . ."

He flipped open the newspaper—stale headlines stretched across it.

I lowered my eyes and took another sip of orange juice.

"There's a couple good matinees at the Riverside tomorrow," he said.

"Oh yeah? Like what?"

"There's that one Siskel and Ebert gave two thumbs-up for."

"Dad, Siskel's been dead for—"

"Here it is."

I took a bite of bagel.

He spread the paper flat. "Remember, when you were just a

little squirt, how you used to love the movie-review section in the *Chronicle* with—"

"That little guy who would bounce out of his chair clapping if he liked the movie or be asleep if he didn't like it. Yeah, Dad. I do remember that. I thought you were getting sick. You still feel like going out tomorrow?"

"Sure. When was the last time we saw a movie?"

"I'm starting night shift tomorrow. I'll probably sleep till around noon, and then I wanted to do some kayaking downtown. How about a rain check?"

He held the newspaper up close to his face.

I finished the orange juice. "Hey, I was thinking that we could find you a place next to the university. Maybe a small studio."

"Five-fifty for a matinee now. Good grief."

I carried my dishes to the sink. "Dad, no one outside of a Peanuts comic still says *good grief.*" I let the water run hot. "I'll leave a twenty on the counter if you need a loaner."

"Remember when you were a kid and we used to see matinees for a couple bucks?" He shook his head. "Inflation. For the love of God."

"God has nothing to do with it, Dad. It's economics."

He laughed. He had a habit of laughing when I never really intended a joke.

I started down the hall. "I'm gonna take a shower."

"Oh, Jonner?"

"Yeah?"

"A man from the ambulance company called right before you came home."

"Who was it?"

"Not sure."

"What did he say?"

"Something about a woman you helped bring in." He squinted at the newspaper. "Video conference iPhone, huh? What'll they think of next?"

My neck muscles tightened. "Dad?"

He didn't look up. "Yeah?"

"Dad, what did he say?"

"Hmm? The guy?"

"No, Dad, Steve Jobs."

"He said it's a revolution in cellular—"

"Dad, no. Okay." I ran my hand over my eyes. "What specifically did the man, the guy, say about the woman?"

"Oh. Right . . . It was something from *Star Trek* . . . Spock?" He looked to the side. "No, that can't be it. Scotty?"

"Bones, Dad?"

"Yes. That's it. He did mention the woman's name. I wrote it down on a Post-it." He shuffled papers on the counter by the table. "Here it is. 'Straversky.' He said, 'Got update from nurse at County. Turn for the worse. On a ventilator now.'"

If we'd been there sooner . . .

"Thanks, Dad."

"Sleep tight—don't let the bedbugs bite."

I walked to my room, floorboards creaking with each step. A smoky haze lingered in the hallway.

CHAPTER 19

Evening blanketed the valley. The ambulance bay felt deserted as I sat behind the wheel of Medic Seven, waiting for Bones to return with the drug keys and radios. The first shift of our night rotations. The door across the bay swung open. I started up the engine.

Bones hopped into the passenger seat. "Priority one, downtown."

"What?" We'd be at least seven minutes out from that.

"We've got a call."

"I haven't even put us in service yet." I picked up the mic. "Aprisa, Medic Seven in service. Trestle and McCoy, twenty-one hundred to oh-nine hundred."

The sultry voice came back. "Copy, Medic Seven. Stand by for traffic."

I looked at Bones. "You told her we'd take a call right out of the gate, didn't you? To get on her good side."

"I did no such thing. System's just busy, I guess."

"Right."

The radio toned. Dispatch gave an address for O'Farrell's Hotel-Casino, seventeenth floor—man down, unknown problem.

I clicked the red master emergency light switch and pulled out into the street, gunning down the road for O'Farrell's.

From the moment we started, we were late. I could just picture Spitzer calling me into his office, questioning why we couldn't make it downtown in a Friday-night-traffic-impossibility of five minutes fifty-nine seconds. "According to our studies," he'd say, "you should be able to make that in five minutes forty-four seconds." Yeah, sure. As the cursor flies on Google Earth.

I took oncoming traffic on Mill and wailed under the freeway overpass, blaring the air horn. We passed County Hospital and weaved across lanes into downtown, passing under *The Biggest Little City* arch and parking outside of O'Farrell's Casino in the neon glitz.

Seven minutes thirty seconds into our response.

A female security guard, who looked to be about eighty years old and four-and-a-half feet tall, met us on the sidewalk. Bones pulled the front of our yellow Stryker gurney with one hand. I pushed the opposite end. Our airway bag, monitor, and first-out bag were all seat-belted on top of it. The guard led us through the labyrinth of slot machines, over heinously designed carpet, and under gaudy ceiling tiles to the guest elevators in back, using her elevator key to recall the car.

"I don't think our gurney will fit in these elevators," Bones said to her. "We usually take the freight elevator."

She shook her head. "Out of service."

We unlocked the seat belts. I grabbed the first-out with both hands, and Bones lifted the airway bag and monitor.

The elevator car arrived, and the ubiquitous Barry Manilow accompanied us to the seventeenth floor. I wondered what kind of difference, if any, an extra two-and-a-half minutes would make in this case.

We exited into a long, narrow hallway, Bones whistling "Copacabana." A different security officer, this one sweaty and potbellied, waved and pointed to us from the end of the hall.

"Yes, hello." Bones nodded back. "We see you. Yesss, we see you."

"You think he wants us to hurry?"

"What was the nature of the call again?"

"Another unknown man down."

"That's right. Excellent memory, Jonny-boy."

"You save lives. I save you."

The guard kept waving at us.

"I think he wants you to run, Jonathan."

"How about no, Bones?"

A fire captain appeared in the doorway. "GSW to the left temple. Looks self-inflicted."

Gunshot wound to the head. *Time to drop it in gear.*

"He's agonal," the captain continued. "We're setting up to bag him right now and I'm having my engine operator bring up a board and c-spine stuff."

A mammoth revolver lay on the bathroom counter. A police officer questioned a sobbing woman sitting on the toilet. A few steps more and a queen bed came into view with a middle-aged man lying supine with snoring respirations, the right side of his head shaped like a volcano cone. One firefighter in turnout bottoms and boots squatted on the bed, suspenders strapped over a blue T-shirt. He wore clear trauma glasses and held a purple bag-valve mask with latex-gloved hands. Oxygen tubing trailed from the back of it to another fireman who was in the process of pulling out a green and silver oxygen bottle. He opened the valve, and pressurized oxygen shot out with a hissing sound that muffled when he connected the tubing. I went to the patient's head.

The firefighter looked up, eyes wide, hands full. "We found him like this on the bed."

The glow of streetlights disseminated through the room's thin white curtain. The television flickered a *Jeopardy* answer in white letters—*Robert Young is best known for the patriarchal role in this '50s TV program.*

"Will he take an oral airway?" I said.

"He looks pretty clenched down."

Bones unzipped the airway bag behind me. "They need an OPA?"

"No, he's trismussed." I turned back to the fireman bagging. "How's that compliance?"

"It's not." He wasn't getting any air into the lungs.

"Let's drop an NPA, Bones."

He flipped the green trumpet-shaped tube through the air. "Need some K-Y?"

"No, I'm good." I wiped the nasal tube through pooled blood on the man's upper lip and slid it flush with the opening of his nostril. Placing my stethoscope in my ears, I listened to breath sounds beneath his armpits.

"Sounds like he's aspirated a lot of blood." I whipped the stethoscope back over my neck.

The fire engine operator came through the door with a blue backboard, a pair of rectangular foam head blocks, and a set of Velcro Spider-Straps. He slid the board onto the bed. The fireman who was bagging stopped and placed his hands on the patient's head to stabilize the neck.

"On your count."

"One, two, three."

We logrolled the man onto his side, checked his back for any hidden trauma, and then laid him back on the board. I strapped a cervical collar on his neck. Bones and the others secured him to the board with the Velcro straps. We taped his head down last and picked him up.

Bones shuffled backward while carrying the board. "We'll have to tilt him diagonal to fit in the elevator."

We strode down the hall, a firefighter at the head still bagging. I wanted to intubate him, but with all the moving we were doing, the risk of dislodging a good tube was too high. Not to mention that, with his teeth clenched down, it'd be a blind intubation through his nose. The security lady stood next to two elevator doors, holding them open with an override key.

We lifted the board upright and angled the patient inside the first elevator, leaving only enough room for Bones and one fireman, one to support the patient and one to bag.

The doors closed, and Bones lilted, "'His name was Rico. He wore a diamond.'"

I stepped into the second elevator with the rest of the fire crew. The car descended. No more Manilow. Kenny G. this time. Could a saxophone be more grating? I curled a breathing tube around my fingers to form the best angle for a nasal intubation.

The car jerked, and the doors opened to the middle of the casino floor. Slot machines bleeped and dinged, shelling out change in resonant bins. People ambled about with quarter-filled plastic cups and beer bottles, some zoning out by slots with cigarettes smoldering in opaque ashtrays. The digital readout for the elevator next to us showed it descending from the third floor.

We'd beat them down.

I knelt in front of the doors and strapped on a surgical face mask with a clear eye shield. I had the tube in hand, lubed and ready to go.

The green number one glowed against the black background of the elevator readout. Two women stepped in front of me.

"Excuse me, ladies. You'll have to take the next one."

They stopped and frowned at me and my face mask, endotracheal tube in gloved hand, stethoscope dangling from my shoulders.

What an inconvenience for them.

The elevator doors opened.

Their eyes grew wide at the sight of an unconscious man strapped to a board, blood oozing from the side of his deformed head.

Bones and the fireman laid him on the casino floor. The ladies arced around to the other elevator, striking back looks of disgust. A man persisted in playing a slot machine behind me.

I pulled out the nasal trumpet and eased in the breathing tube.

Bones knelt beside me. "Careful now, Jon-boy. No room to miss."

I exhaled, steaming up the visor edges. Visions filled my mind of the famous X ray they show in paramedic school of a nasogastric tube curled up inside a patient's cranium. This man's gunshot may have created a pathway for a misplaced tube to end up right in his skull.

Okay, Jonathan, tube the lungs, not the brain.

I advanced with care, timing my movements with his underlying respiratory rate. Condensation filled the tube as I drew closer to the larynx.

"Almost there . . ."

I felt it nudge past the vocal cords and used a syringe to feed air down into a small balloon cuff that would secure the tube in his windpipe. I pulled the stethoscope from around my neck and placed it above his stomach and then his lungs.

"Tube's good. Let's go."

We lifted him on the gurney and wove through the casino floor, out into the city with its lights and activity and Friday night buzz. We loaded him in the box and took off code three, lights and sirens to County Hospital.

This guy didn't need a medic. If anything, if he even still had a chance, he needed a surgeon and more time.

Take away those and the wages of trauma were death.

CHAPTER 20

The bustling cyclone of nurses and techs silenced once Dr. Thomas Wheatland lifted his hands above the gunshot patient on the trauma table.

He reminded me of an Old Testament prophet.

"I believe Paramedic Trestle was still giving his report." He eased his dark-skinned hands into a pair of blue nitrile gloves. "Go ahead, Jonathan."

Eyes shifted to me.

Well, all right, then. "High-caliber handgun, looked like a three-fifty-seven, self-inflicted to the temple. Agonal and trismussed on our arrival. Nasally intubated with a size seven-and-a-half tube, good confirmation on lung sounds bilat and end-tidal capnometry. Head-to-toe otherwise atraumatic. He's got a fourteen gauge in the left AC."

Dr. Wheatland nodded. "Thank you, Jonathan."

Activity resumed.

I'd had many counter chats with Wheatland over the years— he called them curbsides—following up on patients, gaining his insight on treatment modalities. Ever since I'd caught a case of Wolff-Parkinson-White Syndrome in the ER that changed the way he treated a cardiac patient, he had given high regard to my "mere paramedic" assessments.

I peeled off my gloves and scrubbed my hands with surgical soap in the washbasin.

My role as paramedic was difficult to characterize—moving from "para-god" powers in the eyes of lesser-trained first responders to the disdainful attitudes of occasional disgruntled RNs. Though higher in the medical food chain, some couldn't get past the physician-level authority extended to us and not them by big daddy doctor. All that attention in the course of a call. Finish my paperwork, load up the gurney, and do it again.

No sooner had we rolled the cot away from the trauma table than Aprisa squawked from our hips that we had another run.

Bones tossed the gurney sheet in the bio bin. "Are we the only ambulance in this city?" He picked up his radio. "Go ahead with traffic for Medic Seven."

"Medic Seven, Aprisa. We're level zero. Can you come available?"

We rolled the gurney through the automatic doors. Bones's keychain jingled against his hip. "Affirmative, Aprisa. Go ahead."

"Medic Seven, priority one. Infant choking, Damonte Ranch High School at the baseball field."

I loaded the gurney in back. Bones slid behind the wheel. I hopped up in the cab. "It's a mess back there."

"Among other places." He flicked on the lights and switched on the siren. We bounced onto Mill Street and shot east.

I figured eleven minutes out on this one—at best—even with Bones driving at warp nine-point-eight. But there was a fire station not too far from there.

I picked up the radio mic. "Aprisa, Medic Seven."

"Go ahead."

"Do we have fire responding on this as well?"

"Stand by. Will attempt to contact their dispatch to confirm."

What if they weren't available?

We shot down the freeway like a bullet through a barrel, outrunning our siren, fighting time with speed—passing other cars, other people in their houses, shoppers in stores, folks living life and wrapped up in their own concerns. We were just another ambulance. An annoying sound interrupting a show or the first stages of sleep. A requisite part of the city din. And at the forefront of my mind lay an infant turning purple and flaccid and the distressed faces of family wondering where 9-1-1 was.

"Medic Seven, Aprisa."

I clicked the mic. "Go ahead."

"Reno Engine Fourteen just arrived on scene."

I exhaled. "Copy."

What if they hadn't been available? What if they'd been out on a fire like the downtown crew when we rolled up on Simon Letell?

Bones pulled us up on scene outside of the baseball field at the high school, towering white lights refracting in the cloud cover. The engine company stood around a teen mother holding a crying infant in her arms—noisy babies were always a welcome sign. Everyone's body language looked relaxed. One fireman held a small oxygen mask near the baby's face.

The mother's cheeks were red and tear streaked. "I just didn't know . . ."

"That's okay," the fire captain said. "That's why we're here. Sounds like she swallowed down the wrong pipe for a moment."

The mother sniffled. "I just didn't know what to think. I'd never seen her hack and cough like that."

The captain nodded to me. "Didn't sound like she wanted to go by ambulance, guys. Baby's doing good now."

He relayed the vital signs they'd taken. Bones had the mother sign a refusal of transport form, and we hopped back into the rig.

He offered to drive again so I could work on the chart for our gunshot patient. I balanced the clipboard on my thighs and began my incident narrative.

Bones caught the freeway north toward Rock and Victorian post at dispatch's request. It marked the center of the valley and subsequently was the highest-priority post. Being sent there meant we were still the only ambulance available. Busy Friday nights weren't atypical, but this had the stench of understaffing.

"Four hundred thousand people, Jonathan. And only one of them has to call 9-1-1." Bones smirked and clicked on the stereo. "I meant to tell you, I found out a little more about your guy Letell."

I looked up. "Really?"

He nodded, eyes scanning the traffic lanes. "I called a buddy of mine at NMHI."

The Nevada Mental Health Institute.

He changed lanes. "He used to be an ER nurse. Now he's in admitting over there. State retirement. Pretty sweet gig. I asked if he knew about a Simon Letell. He said even if he did he couldn't tell me."

"HIPAA violation?"

"Right. I told him that Letell's dead and didn't have any relatives—so he was all right with that."

"What'd he say?"

Bones gave a "Sorry to break this to you, but you're not getting a bike for your birthday" sort of smile. "Letell was bipolar and suffered paranoid delusions. Big conspiracy theorist. He wasn't violent. Just off his nut."

I leaned my elbow on the door and rested my head in hand. "Are you sure?"

"That's what he said." He merged onto Interstate 80 East. "Sorry.

142

I know you were aiming to be a super sleuth. Guess you'll just have to settle for being a plain old doctor."

I sat back. A jetliner descended toward the airport. I felt my shirt pocket and the stiff crinkle of Letell's note inside it.

Chicken scratch.

Dispatched toned. "Medic Seven, traffic."

CHAPTER 21

We screamed down Moana, Bones bobbing over the steering wheel, lip-syncing Bob Dylan—"From a Buick 6."

"I've got this graveyard woman . . ."

The asphalt, damp from a quick evening shower, sucked in our headlight beams. I flipped a page in the map book. Bones took oncoming traffic and rode the air horn.

He swung us through an intersection and back into the direction of travel. The transmission shifted and I jerked back in my seat. Streetlights fanned. I pointed to the next intersection and glanced at my watch. "Hang a right here."

Ten minutes and counting.

A pressing feeling told me that we were walking a tightrope that was ready to snap.

The call was for respiratory failure after a severe asthma attack. I dug nails into the ceiling as Bones whipped around the corner. The back end of the box fishtailed out. I'd have grabbed a fistful of ceiling fabric if I could have. Bones steered in the direction of the skid and straightened her out.

He pushed his lips together and, with a penitent look, lowered his head. "Whoops."

I let out a quick and forceful breath. "Okay, it's coming up. Another right. Creekbend Way is your warning street."

He straddled the white lane divider. "I'm looking for Willowbend, right?"

"Yeah."

We pulled into a residential court. A woman holding a phone by her ear flagged us from the driveway. She knelt next to a parked car with the passenger door open. A man lay supine and unconscious on the concrete.

I clicked the mic. "Medic Seven on scene. No fire." We grabbed the equipment and set it by the patient. "How'd he get here like this?"

The woman fit words between hyperventilating sobs. "I tried to get him into the car . . . for the hospital. He passed out."

I tilted his head and chin and listened. No breathing. I found a rapid and thready pulse at his neck. A fire engine pulled up next to the curb.

Bones pulled out the defib pads. "No pulse?"

"No, he's got one."

He tossed me the BVM. I set the mask over his face and squeezed the bag. His chest didn't rise.

Bones plugged the oxygen tubing onto the tank. "How's compliance?"

"I can't get any air in."

Bones cut off the patient's shirt and slapped the defib pads on his chest. A rapid heart rhythm spiked across the screen. "Sinus tach at one-thirty."

The fire captain bent beside me. "We just cleared that multiple-vehicle accident on 395. What do you need?"

"Try to bag some air into him."

Lightning flashed in the west. I clicked the laryngoscope blade on the handle, red and blue light bar reflections glinting in the curved metal. Fat raindrops pattered on the pavement.

And that day flashed in my mind.

No. Stay focused.

I hooked up a syringe to a breathing tube and tested the balloon cuff at the end of it.

The rain drilled harder. Thunder boomed overhead.

I saw the car.

No.

Her car.

Focus.

Wrapped around that tree. A water-curtain deluge. The body-sized hole in the driver's-side windshield . . .

I blinked and strapped on a mask with a plastic eye shield.

The firefighter bagging glanced at me. "You ready?"

I nodded and lay on my belly upon the concrete. Wetness soaked in through my cotton shirt. The firefighter pulled the bag mask away, and I tilted the man's head and inserted the curved blade, sweeping his tongue to the side, shining the small light down his throat.

Thunder again.

The police car in the pouring gray . . .

Focus, Trestle.

I stared down the dark red tunnel. Rain fell in sheets. The plastic fluid barrier on my mask streaked with water. I tore it off and squinted to see.

The esophagus was lower, and larger. The trachea more anterior—higher, smaller, and would be marked by those pearly gates, the vocal cords. The area where they should have been looked swollen like a tomato.

"What do you see?" the firefighter said.

I pulled out the blade and sat up. "Nothing good."

Bones handed an in-line albuterol treatment to the firefighter. "Try bagging him with this."

I looked at Bones. "I don't think I'm going to get a tube down that."

The firefighter squeezed the bag with difficulty. "Compliance is still poor."

He was bagging against a shut door. Any air that did get in was routing straight to the stomach.

Bones peeked at the monitor. "We still got pulses?"

I put two fingers on the carotid. "Thready. But there. Let's trach him."

If our patient couldn't breathe through the normal anatomy, we'd cut a new hole straight into his windpipe.

Water pelted plastic. Above us, two firefighters held a red tarp. The fire captain shone a flashlight beneath. I swabbed iodine in a circle over the man's throat, angled the scalpel in my hand, and froze.

Now sheltered from the rain, a crucial detail came into view— a cut in the man's throat, just above the sternum. I separated it with my fingers, revealing a gaping hole with a burgeoning pool of dark red blood. Across the top part of his chest I felt fluid beneath the skin, like water under the moisture barrier in a crawl space.

I pulled back the tarp. Cold rain met my cheeks. "Where'd this come from?"

The woman still stood on the driveway, phone in one hand, and in the other . . . a bloody razor tip.

I pointed to the patient's neck. "Did you do this?"

Water poured off her chin. "I had to . . . I had to get him air. You guys were taking too long. No one was here. I had to get air in him. I saw it done once."

"We've lost pulses," a fireman said.

"All right. Let's start compressions."

We needed an airway. The man's body articulated with the compressions, like a piston-driven machine.

I found the anatomical landmarks on the throat and made my scalpel incision. "All right, I'm in the trachea. Tube."

Bones handed me a short breathing tube. I twisted it into place. The firefighter connected the bag mask and squeezed.

The man's lungs lifted and relaxed for the first time since we'd been there.

"Okay, good. Let's logroll him toward me and bring the flat underneath." I kept one hand on the tube and the other on the man's shoulders.

Rookie move. We rolled him and a rush of blood spilled from the lower laceration in his neck.

The puddle extended on the concrete. I made my feet. "Okay, back down. Back down."

Bones came beside me to lift him. "She must have lacerated a big blood vessel."

As soon as we loaded the gurney in the back of the ambulance—why did it have to be in the ambulance?—all that air we'd bagged into his gut violently discharged his stomach contents.

On instinct I turned him away, and moving with the speed of experience, Bones avoided a solid shot of emesis. But more than the vomit, the blood pool in his neck also streamed out, cascading down the side of the gurney and coating the floor like a dark watery syrup.

I laid him back and stuck a suction catheter into his mouth. Bones tossed me a fat stack of four-by-four dressings for the throat.

He opened the side door. "Guess I'll be going now."

Up front I heard the driver's door open and shut. Bones spoke through the doghouse, "I'll give the report to Saint Mary's."

One firefighter kept bagging. The other resumed chest compressions. I spiked an IV bag and hung it on the gurney pole. I kept slipping on the bloody floor. I couldn't find a vein and poked him twice with no success.

It was Airway, Breathing, then Circulation. And I'd spent most of my time on A and B. He had no blood pressure, no pulse, but his heart still produced an electrical rhythm on the monitor. It wasn't anything that could be shocked, but even if it had been, with no fluid in his bloodstream it'd be like whipping a dead horse.

The back-up alarm sounded off, and the ER doors drew closer, several nurses already waiting beside them. I walked on the balls of my feet and opened the back of the ambulance. The nurses' eyes grew big at the mess we brought.

We rolled the patient inside, and in a breath all the whirlwind energy and focus I had was whisked from me and laid out beneath bright lights on a sterile table, activity all about him.

I faded into the corner with my rain-soaked uniform and blood-stained shoes. I shed my gloves. Bones wheeled the gurney out.

I wiped my brow with my shoulder. The double doors to the ER seemed to shift and warble. An EKG tech pushed through them, and the faint sound of music trailed from behind. I followed it to its source in the hallway.

It was the same song Bones had been singing in the ambulance.

Dylan railed, "I need a steam shovel momma to keep away the dead. I need a dump truck baby to unload my head."

The ambulance sat in the parking lot, rear doors open, with a slow trail of blood dripping down the back.

CHAPTER 22

Wingfield Park lay quiet at nine thirty Saturday morning.
I leaned on a guardrail overlooking the Truckee River. A couple
unshaven men slept on the grass. No kayaks were in the water.

The Passat led me here after shift. I'd changed uniforms halfway through the night shift, but the second one I was wearing still
smelled like ambulance and the host of odors that came with that.
My mind hung in a hazy state of sleep deprivation.

I unfolded Letell's note. Slashes and dashes and dots. The scrib-
blings of a disturbed man. Clear water rolled beneath, bubbling,
curving over and around rocks. I thought of tossing the note in—
and I never litter—thought of giving the paper back to the earth,
letting the river take it and letting my life move on. . . .

I folded it in half and eyed the water.

Martin was dead—swallowed, like Letell, by the ground.

Tossing the note would be giving it to him, washed back to the
dirt, finally to rest.

I creased the paper into an airplane, pinching it between my
forefinger and thumb. I angled my hand to throw it and flicked
my wrist forward.

The moment I let go, I saw something—a freeze frame. The
plane glided up to a pitch and then paused in the air. The dashes
and the lines and the dots, once broken, but now folded at new
angles, came together.

And formed numbers.

Numbers!

It hit me too late. The paper plane circled down toward the water. I considered jumping after it, but the river was a good twenty feet below and not super deep. There was a short bridge across to Wingfield Island and the water's edge. I sidestepped to it, shuffling my hands across the railing, keeping my eyes glued to the plane. It spiraled and came to a graceful landing in a pool near the opposite bank, listing to one side.

Stay there, baby. Stay there.

I ran across the bridge, nearly colliding with a woman pushing a cart full of cans. I made it over and clambered between trees and down the rocks to the shore.

No plane.

I searched the water, squinting to see if the paper had sunk. Beyond the relatively still pool, the river flowed at a good clip, and there a darkened paper caught my eye just as it entered the stream.

I pulled my phone from my pocket, chucked it on the shore, and jumped feetfirst into the river. The current swept me along, and I lost sight of the note. The sharp cold bit through to my skin, and the weight of the water dragged down on my clothes. I navigated through a standing wave, stroked with both arms to get out of the white water, and then brought my legs forward again, shooting downstream.

And there I saw it.

Floating just beneath the surface, in an eddy by the river-walk wall, just beyond another wave.

The ink would be running.

There could be nothing left.

I slid through the next wave and paddled to it. My feet met muddy ground, stirring up clouds beneath. I brought my hands beneath the paper plane and lifted it to the air. Barely visible across the folded and waterlogged wings lay Letell's streaked markings and the numbers they formed.

9. 53.

I drew a deep breath and glanced at the riverbank I'd jumped from. A woman with her back to me leaned over to pick up a palm-sized black object off the ground.

"Hey." I waded toward the middle of the river. The water strength caught me off guard and forced me to find balance. "Hey. Wait. That's my phone. That's—" I cut myself off in surprise recognition.

Naomi straightened and held my cell in the air. A smile turned her cheek. "Is this why you never called?"

Freshly clean from a hot shower, I changed into jeans and a T-shirt. I shuffled a towel through my damp hair and heard Naomi say something from the living room.

I called down the hallway. "What was that?"

"I said, I never knew that Matisse and Picasso were such good friends."

She'd been reading the Louvre coffee-table book. I hung the towel and walked down the hall. "Personally, I'm more of a fan of old Hank."

Naomi found me in the river on her walk home from Java Jungle. Come to find out she owned an apartment less than a mile from there. She offered to buy me tea after I went home and dried off. Fortunately, my dad wasn't there passed out on the floor.

She turned a page. "Good ol' Henri. Look at this one from 1894. *Woman Reading*."

I looked over her shoulder. "Much darker tones than his later stuff."

"All you see is her back and the fact that she's reading a book.

But it's so interesting. *She* seems interesting. What is she reading? Who is she?"

I clicked on the stereo. Something ambient and lounge streamed on. The paper airplane lay intact, drying on a small towel spread over a corner of the table.

Naomi closed the book. She wore jeans and a thin forest-green hoodie with a flowery pattern stitched across the shoulder.

"So," I said, "do I get my phone back now?"

She pulled it from her pocket. "This thing's pretty neat. I downloaded a couple apps for you."

"Oh, you did?"

"Oh yeah. Check this one out—you can take a photo of a pill, and it will identify what medication it is."

"Get out."

"Serious."

"That's amazing."

"Mm-hm."

I nodded. "Can I have it back now?"

She stood and laughed. "You think I'm not going to give it to you, huh?"

I made a swipe for it.

She dodged. "Ha. Nice try. I was going to give it to you. Now I don't think so."

She stood between the couch and the coffee table, the wooden edge at just the right height behind her leg . . .

I hurdled the sofa in one move. She shouted and laughed, but I caught her off-balance. I wrapped my hand around the phone. She stumbled backward and I with her. We crashed on the area rug.

She shot me a defiant look.

I pinned her arms down. "You going to make me pry it from your fingers?"

"You don't have to."

"I don't?"

"You just have to ask nicely."

"Isn't that what I've been doing?"

"I never heard you say please."

I looked up at the ceiling and exhaled. "Please may I have my phone back?"

"You didn't look me in the eyes and say it."

I held her liquid-blue Tahoe gaze. "Naomi, would you please give me back my phone?"

She forced back a smile. I relaxed my grip. Her fingers curled around my hands.

The phone vibrated. We held it up, Eli's photo flashing on the screen. Naomi glanced at me.

Acoustic strumming filled the room.

She searched my eyes and propped herself up. Strands of hair fell to her face. She didn't tuck them back.

"What happened with us, Jonathan?"

I swallowed and looked away. Images flashed through my mind.

Broken glass.

The wedding ring dropped into my father's palm.

I looked at her lips, alive and full, her eyes penetrating.

My voice came out hoarse. "I don't know."

"Don't give me that." She sat straight. "You know."

I couldn't look her in the eyes.

In his palm.

Empty fingertips.

She stood and folded her arms. "What was it?"

I balanced on my hands.

She brought up her shoulders. "What?"

Shattered glass.

A curtain of rain.

I got up. My phone vibrated with a voice-mail notification. I pocketed it.

She drew close. "Don't hide from me. You were my best friend. If anyone has known you, I have." She found my eyes. "Are you going out with someone? Are you? Does she know you like I have? Since fourth grade and through youth group and high school and senior prom. Does she know you like that, Jonathan?"

I whispered, "There's no one else."

"What?"

"I said there's no one else."

"Then, what is it? What *was* it?"

I looked at the ceiling and blinked. "I remember the first time I saw you. The only girl with braids and five different colors in your outfit."

She bit her lower lip. "Green tights?"

I nodded and smiled. "All through high school I'd be in class or in baseball practice or . . . It didn't matter—I knew that after whatever I was doing I would be with you."

She touched my fingers.

I drew them back. "But . . . we . . . It was changing."

Her eyebrows knit. "And why was that bad?"

"It was becoming more."

"You didn't answer my question."

"It wasn't bad. It isn't. I just . . ."

The diamond falling.

"You just what, Jonathan? This is what I don't understand. This is what I have never understood."

I shook my head.

She stepped back. "I deserve to know. Give me that at least."

My phone vibrated again.

Eli.

I looked her in the eye and answered. "Hello?"

"Jonathan. Where are you right now?"

"I'm at home. What's up?"

"Can you come by?"

"The—"

"Yes."

He had to mean the morgue. "Yeah. Sure. What did you find?"

"Just come by." He hung up.

His voice didn't seem right. He sounded frightened. The phone vibrated again—this time for a text.

Use back door, code 8-4-2-8.

This wasn't like Eli. He'd found something. My mind ran through scenarios. He could have got back the lab results from his samples. Maybe that had provided a cause of death. Perhaps something turned up on the Martin autopsy. I glanced at the paper airplane.

Naomi crossed her arms. "What did he say?"

"I don't know. But he wants me at the morgue right now."

She cradled the airplane note in the towel. "Don't forget this."

I grabbed my car keys. "Will you come with me?"

"It's starting to dry." Naomi examined the paper airplane in the front seat. "There are more numbers on here."

"Where?"

"Underneath, when you fold the wings down. They're all over."

I parked half a block away from the morgue building. The parking lot around it was empty. We left the paper out of sight in the car to dry further and walked to the back of the building. I looked around before descending several concrete steps to the rear door. A steel keypad hung to the right of it. I punched in the code, and we entered a short hallway lit only by the light coming through the glass walls of the autopsy room. Our footsteps echoed. I stopped at the locked glass door and knocked. Eli walked over, wrinkles etched deep in his brow.

He opened the door. "Anyone see you two come in?"

"Doc, what's this all about? What's got you so—"

"Just come in. Come in." He closed the door behind us and glanced both ways between the stairs and the basement corridor. "Come, take a seat in the office." He nodded to Naomi. "Hello, dear. Missed you last Sunday at church."

She smiled. "Hi, Eli. Missed you too. I had to work an extra shift."

We followed him in. He moved from one desk to the next, stopping midway as though he'd forgot something. "Take a seat. Take a seat."

We sat in two office-style swivel chairs. I leaned on the armrest. "So where does the 8-4-2-8 come from?"

"What's that?"

"The door code. Are those just random numbers or . . ."

"Oh, right. No. Eighty-four inches by twenty-eight inches. Standard casket dimensions."

Morgue humor.

Naomi laughed to herself.

Dr. Eli pulled a stapled packet of papers out from under a thick book and stood straight, as if preparing himself for a speech.

"Doc," I said, "would you sit down?"

He exhaled. "Right. Okay." He pulled up the chair and perched on the edge of it. He held the papers up. "Letell's lab results."

"What'd you find?"

"Poisoning."

I caught Naomi's eye. "With what?"

"That will take some narrowing. I don't know if it was unintentional or . . ." He glanced out the office windows. "Or intentional."

"What do you mean?" Naomi leaned forward. "Like suicide?"

"Possibly. . . . Or murder."

I sat back. "Murder?"

He nodded.

"Where'd you find the evidence?"

"In the liver."

"So that makes you a key—"

"Witness. Yes."

I ran my hand over my cheeks and down to my chin. "What about Martin? What have you found with him?"

"Your report said his body was stiff on your arrival, correct?"

"Yes."

"The onset of rigor mortis begins anywhere from minutes to several hours after death, depending on the environment." He stood, the papers trembling finely in his hand. "I'd hoped a careful study of Martin's liver would turn up more answers. Perhaps a similar cause of death."

"And . . ."

"Not *and*. But."

"But . . . ?"

"But I never had the opportunity to study his liver."

"Why not?"

He looked at Naomi, then back at me. "Because Martin's body has gone missing."

CHAPTER 23

The simple fact that Eli, one of the kindest, most levelheaded men I'd ever met, had been thrown into a state of fear gnawed at me to no end. I needed time to piece things together. I asked Naomi, since we were already on hospital property anyway, if she minded following up on Mrs. Straversky, who Bones said had taken a turn for the worse.

At the work area outside Mrs. Straversky's intensive care room Naomi thumbed through the chart.

A nurse wearing teddy bear scrubs and a Littmann stethoscope walked up. "Hey, girl."

"Hi, Sharon." Naomi embraced her. "Is this your patient?"

"One of them. We've got half as many nurses up here now as we did this time last year."

Naomi nodded. "There've been big cuts."

"Deep." She gave me a once-over and smiled. "Who's your friend?"

"Oh. We work together at Aprisa. This is Jonathan."

Just, "We work together"? I shook Sharon's hand. "Pleasure to meet you."

Naomi tucked a strand of hair behind her ear and ran her finger down Mrs. Straversky's chart. "What's the story with her? Jonathan said when he brought her in, she was doing good."

I crossed my arms. "Rapid a-fib conversion. Strong vitals."

Sharon fingered a roll of clear tape that hung on her stethoscope. "Prolonged a-fib?"

I thought of the time it took Bones and me to haul across the city. "Yeah. Could have been going for a while."

Sharon looked down. "That's probably what prompted the CVA."

"She had a stroke?" Naomi said.

"Yeah. That's why she's on the vent."

I leaned around the doorway to Mrs. Straversky's room. She lay unconscious with a tube protruding from her mouth. A ventilator humming beside her bed. Two poles with IV pumps and tubing stood beneath a flat-screen monitor that displayed vital signs.

Her rapid pulse rate could have caused her heart to pump ineffectively. Stagnant blood may have coagulated and eventually traveled through her bloodstream until it lodged in a tiny vessel in her brain.

I turned back to Sharon. "You think she threw a clot?"

"Yeah. Head CT scan shows embolic stroke."

That was it then. If we could have fixed her heart rate before that clot formed . . .

Sharon shrugged. "But what can you do, right?" A woman behind the nurses' station called for her. She waved. "Be right there." Then to us she said, "Got to show our new intern how to place a Foley."

Naomi smiled. "Oh, joy."

"Let me know if you two need anything."

"Bye, Sharon."

Naomi sighed and glanced at her watch. "I forgot you worked last night. You must be tired."

"Coffee would help."

She bit her lip. "I've got the perfect place to enjoy a cup."

The rooftop breeze made Naomi's hair dance. "Bet you never had a cappuccino on a landing pad before."

I shrugged. "Ah, I'm sure I have at some point."

Naomi elbowed me. "You're full of it."

I grinned and sipped from the cup's plastic top.

Sky hues warped and reflected around the helicopter's blue exterior. I ran my hand along the curved body.

She led me around the front and pointed at a short metal protrusion on the nose. "Watch out—this gets really hot."

I pulled my hand from the helicopter's body, feeling like a child in a glassware aisle.

She smiled. "Come check this out."

I followed her to the far landing skid, and we sat on the rough step tread. Downtown rose from the valley in a small patch of staggered gray blocks with a white sphere nestled between them. Beyond, the Sierras stretched out in clear view beneath patchy gray-and-white clouds, the winter snowpack retreating to the highest elevations.

I raised my coffee in a toast. "To the best seats in the house."

She tapped her lid to mine and took a sip. "The city seems so small compared to the mountains. Look. You can see all the way to Job's Peak." She balanced the drink on her knees, cupping her hands around it. "Eli really is a special man."

The espresso hit my throat, warming my chest. I felt my mind wakening, fatigue retreating. "Remember our youth group trip to Mexico?"

"The one where our bus driver got arrested—"

"For a bag of Yerba Mate tea. Yeah, that one."

"Poor Mitch. They thought he was a drug mule."

I laughed. "Eli was my group leader on that trip. You know he drew up the plans for that medical clinic?"

"No, I didn't. I'm not surprised. He's amazing."

"When I told my dad that I wanted to pursue medical school, he treated it like I'd told him I was going to a Giants game. But Eli was ecstatic when I told him. He gave me books and invited me to autopsies and introduced me to instructors up at the med school. He was the one who suggested I become a paramedic first."

"In some ways he's been like a father to you."

"Yeah. How's your father and mother?"

"My dad is doing everything he can. But Mom's weak. The prognosis is tepid at best. But we're prayerful." She cleared her throat and stood. "Best view seats but not the most comfortable. You hungry?"

"Famished."

"There's that great little sandwich place down in the cafeteria."

"Let's do it."

We sat at a small table next to the windowed wall of the dining area. A delivery truck rolled through the alley below. Steam billowed from the rooftop of a lower building. A din of lunchtime conversation permeated the room. Tables of doctors and nurses and respiratory therapists, some tables with patient visitors. I took a bite of sandwich—turkey with cranberries, cream cheese, and sprouts on wheat bread.

Naomi stared out the window. "I didn't get the chance to tell you."

I swallowed. "Tell me what?"

She rested her forearms on the table and picked at the edges of her sandwich. "I spoke with a couple of the other flight nurses about Letell. I think I have a decent picture now of why he and Aprisa didn't get along so well."

"What'd they say?"

"I didn't know this, 'cause I don't read the paper, but I guess Letell had been a rather vocal dissident against the company. He'd written numerous editorial articles and blog posts on how Aprisa had taken upwards of twenty minutes to get to his house to care for his ailing mother." She pulled a single sprout from her sandwich and nibbled it. "In past cases the fire department had been able to respond and stabilize her until the ambulance's arrival. But the last straw for him was when he called 9-1-1 for his mother and the local engine company was already committed on a fire."

"Is that when she died?"

Naomi nodded. "I guess by the time the ambulance crew got there, his mother was already too far gone for them to even work on her."

I clenched my teeth and breathed in. "That's not good."

She looked at her sandwich and shook her head. "I'd be mad too."

"So, what then?"

"He goes on this negative PR rampage—phoning and writing all the major media outlets. He even hired a lawyer to sue Aprisa for wrongful death."

"Wow."

"Yeah. But you know Aprisa. They put their PR machine in full motion." She took a bite of sandwich.

"Launched a defensive campaign."

"Exactly. And they were effective."

"How?"

"Someone dug up records of a past psychiatric history—a

period in the seventies that he'd suffered from post-traumatic stress after serving overseas. They used that as a springboard to paint him as a raving delusional."

I nodded. "Bones has a buddy that works over at the mental health institute. He said Letell had a paranoid schizophrenic background."

She took a deep breath. "The defense worked. Reporters dismissed Letell's rantings as unsubstantiated. With the expenses of legal action, Letell lost his house and moved into a motel downtown."

"Probably the one I found him at." The sky looked like a faded blue canopy. In the distance a jet streaked a long white line across it. "So he was going to sue for wrongful death."

She chewed. "Mm-hmm."

"And he'd already been upset about delayed response times."

She nodded.

I rubbed the back of my neck. Maybe it wasn't just the night shift and weekends. Maybe we were becoming chronically understaffed. "Don't get me wrong—I'm just going to play devil's advocate for a minute—but as unfortunate as his mother's death is, those things happen. We can't always be there in time, right? What's the county contract for Aprisa say, anyway? Ninety percent in under five minutes and fifty-nine seconds?"

It was a rhetorical question. I knew full well.

But she shrugged her shoulders. "That's for you ground medics. We just fly everywhere."

"Well, it is. Ninety percent. And that means every month ten percent of patients may not get an ambulance in that time frame, and as far as the county is concerned, that's just fine."

She raised and lowered her eyebrows. "All business."

"Right. Despite how wrong it may seem for Letell and his mother, the county has said this is what's acceptable."

"Tort law."

"Exactly. The king can do no wrong."

"So there's no recompense."

"Yep. No wrongful death. Just an ugly PR situation that was quickly brought to a close."

She squinted her eyes at me. "You're too good of a devil's advocate."

I sat back and put my hands up. "Hey, I want to be a doctor, not a lawyer. You know what Shakespeare says."

"First thing, let's kill all the—"

"Right." I looked at the crumbs in my sandwich carton. Only a few eaters remained in the cafeteria. The empty stainless food tray conveyor disappeared into the kitchen through dangling rubber tentacles. "But . . ."

"But . . ."

"But Simon had already been complaining about ambulances taking too long to get to his house. His mother died. He complained again. Then he loses his house."

"And his life." Naomi glanced around the room and leaned forward. "What have you seen on the streets? Is it taking longer than usual to get to calls?"

I nodded.

"More than ten percent of the time?"

"Much more. It's got to be an issue with the county by now."

She ran her hand behind her ear as if to tuck a strand of hair, though none were loose. "You'd think we'd have heard something if it was."

I rubbed my chin. "The run charts should reflect response times."

Naomi studied my face. "What are you considering?"

Good question. This was unfolding fast.

She sat back. "Are you suggesting . . ."

"We verify. That's all. We simply verify the numbers I've been getting on the ground with what's in the files."

Her mouth dropped open.

I looked behind me. Nobody there. "What? What is it?"

"You said numbers. Times." She brought a hand up. "Letell's numbers . . . What if they were times and dates?"

I brought my hands behind my head. *Of course.* "For his mother's calls?"

She picked up her purse. "There's only one way to tell."

I called in sick for the evening shift and dropped off Naomi with the plan to pick her up again after dark. She had keys to access the business office. We would slip inside through the ambulance bay and gain access to the billing office when no one but the dispatchers were likely to be around. We discussed surveillance cameras but didn't think there were any inside, just one by the east side of the building. If we went in through the helicopter-pad entrance we'd bypass that. Then we would just have to cross the ambulance bay. There might be a vehicle service technician restocking ambulances as we walked through. We'd have to see what the layout looked like when we got there and avoid being spotted. Just to be on the safe side. It wasn't like we were breaking any laws. Just stretching the rules. Just . . . verifying.

I slept hard through the afternoon, woken only by the grumbling hunger in my gut around seven thirty. I grilled up a couple chicken breasts and made Caesar salad, leaving half of it in the fridge for my dad, whenever he got home.

Romaine and red onion joined a slice of chicken on my fork. I took a bite and studied Letell's note.

9. 53. Nine minutes fifty-three seconds? But when? I decided to follow my instinct and read from left to right. I turned the paper on its side and folded it. 1. 22.

January twenty-second?

I grabbed a pen and jotted down the set of numbers on a sticky note. Above it, in succession from left to right, ran a second set. 17. 55. And 2. 25.

I wrote on the sticky note: *Seventeen minutes, fifty-five seconds; February twenty-fifth.*

There were three more sets of numbers that appeared with different fold configurations—none of them reflecting a response time within the standard. All of them revealing dates that coincided with the last winter.

I sat back and thought through the feasibility of it all. Why wouldn't someone within the company have spoken up by now? The fear of being fired could have silenced any tumult. Guys were driving faster to get to calls and avoid being reprimanded or let go. We were isolated and divided. Grief over long response times probably never made its way outside of the ambulance doors or the supervisor's office. With dispatch being its own keeper, the alteration of a response time or two, or twenty, could be as simple as the stroke of a computer key.

So that's what we'd *verify*—that the stats weren't being manipulated to look better than they were. It was a simple plan with a plain reason.

I never imagined the avalanche of consequences that were to follow.

Moonlight hung pale over the valley.

Way too bright for my first covert mission. I wore a baseball cap, as if that'd obscure my identity, and followed Naomi through the field that backed up to the helicopter pad. The reserve helicopter sat with rotors tied down, a small fluorescent light mounted on the building corner the only illumination. We skirted past the landing skids to the door leading to the flight-crew room. Naomi used the master key she'd been given when she worked a temporary desk job as continuing education coordinator. She turned the knob and cracked the door just enough to peek inside.

I glanced around. "What do you see?"

She raised a finger, then opened the door enough for me to slide past her into the small flight room. Light flowed in from the opposite door to the ambulance bay. Lockers lined the walls, interrupted only by an angled drawing board that held a large map of northern Nevada and California. Outside a car's engine started up. I glanced at Naomi.

She took baby steps inside the room, letting the door against her back slide shut. "The swing-shift vehicle tech is going home."

That meant that Joey, the night-shift tech, should be committed for at least thirty minutes doing the stockroom inventory. I poked my head through the ambulance-bay door. At least a dozen ambulances sat in the four garage bays, some parked three deep. More in that garage than out in the city. To our far right was the mechanic bay, with an ambulance perched on a hydraulic lift. The stockroom stood opposite, adjacent to the access door for the hallway that led to the business offices and, beyond that, dispatch.

I reminded myself that we weren't doing anything illegal—at least not yet. I raised my eyebrows and Naomi nodded. I stepped through the door and felt instantly naked in the bright bay light, trying my best to be relaxed and stealthy at the same time.

We'd made it halfway across, amid sounds of plastic shuffling in the stockroom, when a metal pipe clanked on the floor in the mechanic bay. I caught Naomi's eye, and she tugged on my arm, retreating us between two ambulances.

Someone cursed. Naomi stood behind me, her breath warm and constant on my neck. The voice carried out again, something unintelligible and unhappy. I recognized it. *Mechanic Tom.*

I tilted my head back and brought my mouth by Naomi's ear. "He must be working late."

She lifted my wrist to look at my watch—*11:17.* "That's really late."

She was right. He got off at five. Six thirty on a late night. I whispered, "What do you think we should—"

"Jonathan," she said, full volume.

I creased my eyebrows, angry and confused that she spoke so loud.

"Jonathan, I think—" she forced a laugh—"we've been caught."

I turned my head to see Mechanic Tom staring at us from behind the ambulances. He held a chrome exhaust pipe streaked with welding scores. His Adam's apple shifted.

172

He ran a thumb across his brow and cleared his throat. "Look, I don't know what you two lovebirds are up to, and I don't really care. As long as you don't care to mention that we saw each other here. Deal?"

I breathed out. Tom had been working on a custom motorcycle, and the company would come down on him hard if they found out he was using Aprisa supplies for personal use. I forced a smile. "Your secret's safe with us, Tom."

He glanced around the bay, then nodded. "Good. I know Joey in the stockroom has my back. Wouldn't take six-packs—just free use of my boat when he needs it." He shook his head and looked at the floor. "Shrewd little businessman. But I can get you two something if—"

"Don't worry about it," Naomi said, draping her arms around my shoulders. "We never even saw you." She kissed me on the cheek and placed my arm around her waist. "Right, honey?"

I cleared my throat. "Right. Exactly. Sweetie. See who?"

Tom huffed. "All right, then." He walked off, staring at the muffler and cursing something under his breath.

Naomi leaned back against an ambulance and exhaled. She smiled and pocketed her hands, glancing out at the bay and then back at me. "Now what?"

I brought my hands to the bridge of my nose in a tent. Tom wasn't a snitch. He was a simple guy. If anything did go down, I don't think we'd have to worry about him.

The fact remained that two men were dead. One body missing. Bones and I'd been screaming across town to barely make it in twice the time we should have been. Patients like Mrs. Straversky had suffered. Letell had given us clues—dates with times that were way out of the requirements. Someone didn't want that to be common knowledge. Someone who had a stake in Aprisa's business success.

I ran my fingers along my eyebrows to my temples. "We press on. We get in there and we find out if someone has been changing these response times."

Naomi put a hand on my wrist. "Hold on. I know we talked about this. But what if Letell's numbers are wrong? How do we know that the numbers Aprisa has for these dates aren't the correct ones, if, in fact, they are any different in the computer?"

"We see who the medics were on those calls. We find out from them directly."

"But who's to say if they'd even remember?"

"Letell's mother. The full arrest. That one should stand out for the crew that responded to it. Especially if they had a long response delay."

She thought about it. "Okay. I'm with you."

I took her hand and led her across the ambulance bay. It seemed to fit with the front we'd portrayed. But it felt like more than that. Her hand fit in mine as if it had been fashioned to be there.

We approached the door. Joey made quiet rustling noises in the stockroom. I pushed through and let the door close behind us. The ceiling-mounted Exit sign lit the hallway. To one side sat the time-clock room and, midway down, the business offices. Beyond that was the entrance to dispatch. Naomi let go of my hand and took the lead to the billing-office door.

No need for a relationship ruse anymore.

She pulled the key from her pants pocket and took a last look both ways. This was it. No explaining this away. Even if we tried to play the lovebird shtick again, we couldn't justify sneaking into the billing office. No. I saw it in her face, and we both knew it.

I thought of med school, of the actual number of days I had left to work for Aprisa. Only sixteen shifts. We could still turn back. We didn't create the problem. We weren't the ones understaffing the city. It was well beyond our pay grade. I could keep quiet, do my duties to the best of my abilities, and have my scholarship with no fear of it being revoked. Let karma sort it all out.

I saw Letell's face, pale and stricken and determined. His hand on my shirt collar. "*Give this to Martin. . . .*"

I had to go forward.

Naomi inserted the key and turned the knob. She led us inside, past darkened cubicles to a small office with a windowed wall. The door to it was locked as well, but her key gained us access. Metal blinds covered a small window on the far wall. The desk held a couple small frames with photos of the current continuing-education coordinator holding a toddler. Naomi pulled up the swivel chair and powered on the computer. A longer set of plastic blinds hung on the windowed wall by the door to the office. I drew them shut. The familiar Windows start-up refrain played, and the blue log-in screen cast a pallid light on Naomi's face.

She tucked that same rebellious strand of hair back and let her fingers fly across the keyboard. The screen changed.

I folded my arms. "Won't she see that someone else has logged on?"

Naomi shook her head. "She gave me her password when she left for maternity leave. I never set up my own." She double clicked an icon. "What's the first date and time you have?"

I'd copied Letell's numbers onto a note on my phone. "January twenty-second, nineteen minutes and forty-three seconds."

She entered in the date, then whistled. "There's more than a hundred entries for this day. How are we to know which call he was referring to?"

I propped a hand on the desk and looked over her shoulder. "This first date has to be for his mother."

"Do you know that address?"

Mrs. Martin had mentioned it in passing. *How could I forget?* "Look for Apollyon Way."

She filtered the results. "Yeah. Here we go. The house number is 2720."

I watched her click through to the response times.

Dispatch: 09:51:01.

Enroute: 09:52:14.

On Scene: 09:56:55.

I did some quick subtraction. "This says it only took five minutes and fifty-four seconds to arrive from the time of dispatch."

Naomi sat back. "And Letell is claiming almost twenty. What's the next date?"

I read it off. And each one after that. Not one time corresponded with the computer's. Conveniently, each time listed in the database showed the ambulance being on scene in less than five minutes and fifty-nine seconds.

I pulled a flash drive from my pocket and plugged it into a USB port. "Let's get a copy of this."

A *thump* sounded outside the office.

"What was that?" Naomi whispered.

I shook my head. Everything stayed quiet. I tiptoed to the office door, coaxed the bolt free from the doorjamb, and slid it open to a fine sliver.

My heart trampolined into my throat.

"Oh, Shintao."

CHAPTER 25

Naomi raced to shut down the computer.

I waved at her. "Get under the desk."

"What?"

"No reason for both of us to get caught."

"Jonathan, I'm not going to leave you hanging."

"Just get down."

"We'll play off like we're lovebirds again."

"Won't work. I've already thought through it."

Shintao approached.

I furrowed my brow and waved her down. The computer monitor flicked off. She slinked under the desk.

The office door pushed open. Shintao stood in a black overcoat, the green exit sign giving him the appearance of a stage villain in limelight. I was ready for him to pull out a nunchuck-looking device that converted into a coat hanger.

I made like I just happened to be on my way out, delivering my best nonchalant air. "Mr. Shintao. Surprise to see you this time of night. Putting in some late hours?" I had every reason to be there. Of course. Completely natural.

His head twitched as if he just did a hard reboot. "I . . . I have ample reason to be here by virtue of an emergency board meeting I called."

They would have held that meeting in the supervisors' office adjacent to dispatch.

He straightened the lapels of his overcoat. "You, however, Paramedic Trestle, have no reason to be snooping around the business office near midnight."

I laughed. It sounded so hollow and fake. Daytime Emmy worthy. "No doubt, no doubt." I shook my head. Chuckled. Wiped an eye.

He let out a long, slow breath through his nostrils. "And so . . ."

I raised my eyebrows and nodded. "And so." My mind flipped through options. A: Keep playing it off. B: Push him over and run. C: Tell the truth. D: . . . I didn't have a D yet.

Shintao waited. With his shoulder-padded overcoat he looked like a helmetless Samurai.

"Look," I said, "I won't lie to you. I've been backed up on charts for a week now. We've been getting slammed out there. I know billing demands that we have them done by the end of shift, but I can't keep up. I've got a life outside of work, you know."

His head tilted up. He was listening. I just had to set the hook.

"I took what you said the other day to heart. I didn't want to risk getting put on your bad list again, so I figured I'd come in here and get them done before the next business day." My statement about his advice could go one of two ways—either he'd take it as me blaming him for my predicament, or his already inflated ego would be puffed up further by the thought that I feared his reprimand. I was banking on the latter.

His body language relaxed from guarded to a swagger. He motioned with his hand when he spoke. "So you thought, Mr. Trestle, that you would make your situation better by further breaking company policy. Is that it?"

I rolled with it, channeling my pumping adrenaline into a façade of penitence. "I know. I know. Looking at it now . . . it was such a foolish thing. I just keep making things worse. I don't—"

"No, no. Don't put yourself down. You've made a mistake. Now stand up to it."

I nodded my head. My eyes were actually watering. I couldn't believe I was getting away with it. "You're right. You're right."

"Of course I am."

"Yes. Of course you are."

He studied me, reassessing my credibility.

Don't lay it on too thick, Jonathan.

I had to recover—be a little defiant to dismiss suspicion. Out of nowhere I pounded the desk.

Shintao jumped. In my peripheral vision I saw Naomi wince and grab the top of her head.

"You guys just don't give us enough time to do what we need to do."

Shintao crossed his arms. "Ah, so it is management's fault?"

I looked away and clenched my teeth.

He cocked his head to catch my eye. "Then why is it that everyone but you is able to keep up, Mr. Trestle?"

Recovery. He was still on my line. Time to reel him up and get out of there. "I just need to get faster at my charting."

"Thorough is good. Speed will come in time. Don't be too hard on yourself. I will schedule a four-hour remedial charting class for you to attend. That should help."

I pocketed my hands and nodded.

"But keep in mind, Mr. Trestle, that violating company policy is not the way to get ahead. Am I understood?"

"Yes, sir."

"Very good. Now, go home. And stay after shift next time if you need to finish reports." He stepped aside and stretched his hand toward the hallway door.

I was hoping he'd follow me. "Thank you. Can I walk you out?"

"I'll be right behind you."

I had no choice but to walk on. I had the feeling he was watching me the entire way out, but I didn't dare look back. I opened the door to the hallway and threw a quick peek. He'd disappeared from sight, and the door to the continuing-education office was now closed.

I walked down the sidewalk in front of Aprisa. Once I made it half a block and was out of sight of the building, I doubled back between a couple businesses and hopped a fence into the field that Naomi and I initially approached the building from.

I sat on the front bumper of my car and waited. Twenty minutes passed before my phone vibrated with a text from Naomi.

I'm out.

I wrote back, *Meet you at my car.*

She hiked back through the field, her form silhouetted and slender in the moonlight.

It was difficult to make out her expression.

I stood. "You all right?"

She rubbed her head. "I do have a headache."

I bit the inside of my cheek. "Sorry about that. Did he see you?"

She shook her head.

I inhaled a deep breath. "I can't believe we made it. We actually made it."

She stared at the pavement.

"What?"

"He found the flash drive."

Shock at two hundred joules. I had difficulty finding words. "What?"

"He didn't see me. But I saw him take the drive. He put it in his jacket pocket."

I punched the hood of the car. My knuckles burned. "That's it. I'm screwed." I ran my hands through my hair. "That's it. He'll see exactly what I was doing in there."

"Maybe it won't mean anything to him. Maybe he's not involved."

"How could he not be? He's the numbers guy. He can't be in the position he's in and not know."

"We don't know that for sure."

"So . . . what? What do I do now?"

"Keep showing up for work."

"And act like nothing is wrong?"

"Exactly."

"And just wait for the hammer to come down? They're going to know."

"Maybe. Whoever 'they' are."

"Which leaves me as a target. They'll be lying in wait."

"Which may bring them out of hiding." She sat beside me on the car. "But we'll get the jump on them."

"What do you suggest?"

"I think it's time we take this to the police."

CHAPTER 26

Daytime made the previous night's events seem like the substance of a dream.

From my pillow I stared at the light edging around the drawn blinds.

All would continue to be as it had been. Right? The sun followed its predictable path. The days grew warmer. I could just forget about everything, quit Aprisa now and take a couple weeks' vacation before starting med school.

The plan sounded outright plausible. A very practical and reasonable course of action. Why let myself get further caught up in something I had nothing to do with? I needed to attend to my future, my aspiration.

That shattered windshield flashed in my mind.

Angled shards surrounded a torso-sized opening. They protruded into the rain like clear flanges of an explosion frozen in time.

That memory was the whole reason I was going to become an emergency physician. To redeem lives. To snatch back Death's spoils.

My duty lay to her. To that day.

But Simon had given the note to *me*. I bore the last message of a man condemned to death.

A stranger.

A lunatic?

Could I let him lay unnoticed in the grave?

I unclasped the pendant chain from around my neck and held it in my palm. The Hippocratic Oath, etched in tiny seriffed font, held all the joint and marrow separating conviction I needed.

Do no harm.

The clock flashed eight thirty. Naomi was working today.

It was my cross to bear. I rose and turned the blinds. Morning poured into the room.

Time had arrived to bring it all to light.

Reno's aging police headquarters sat on Second Street, about a block east of the central fire station. Its cream-colored walls rose from the pavement in Art Deco defiance, its distinct lines a contrast to the modern skyscrapers just to the west. It seemed fitting, and made it feel as though I were walking into a color episode of *Dragnet.* I imagined hard-boiled detectives and the clang of manual typewriters. The story I was about to see was all true. Only the names had been changed to protect the innocent.

A woman in a badge uniform with brunette ponytailed hair greeted me from behind a thick glass window at the reception area. She asked if I needed a work permit or a report filed.

I hesitated, then gave her my name and told her that I needed to speak with a detective about two possible murders. She sized me up in one long still look and lifted a phone receiver. Her thumb and forefinger dialed a three-digit extension.

"Detective Humbolt, please." She glanced at the desk and then to the side. "Yeah, Evan, there's a gentleman here to see you about a double homicide." She hung up and shifted a stack of papers. "There's seating on the far wall."

"Thank you." I tapped the counter once and retreated to a

slatted wood bench anchored to the far wall. A couple magazines lay in a steel-wire basket. *Good Housekeeping*, a copy of *Popular Mechanics* with a computer-generated image of Automobiles of the Future on the cover. I reached down to pick it up.

"Mr. Trestle?" A clean-cut man with a light brown Republican hairdo and a pressed black suit stood in an open doorway.

I rose, wondering how *he* knew my name.

He extended a hand. "I'm Detective Humbolt." We shook firm and quick. "Please come on back."

I followed him through a maze of narrow hallways. Cork bulletin boards held wanted posters and stolen-vehicle advisories. Two street cops sat talking around a small table in a break room. On the second floor a short hallway opened into a room filled with packed cubicles. Phones rang. Two men leaned on the gray fabric-lined wall at the mouth of one cube, stopping to nod at Humbolt, then tightening their expressions and evaluating my innocence in the five steps it took me to pass them.

We turned the corner at the end of the room, the smell of burnt coffee wafting down the path, and passed a water cooler with an empty cup holder alongside it. Humbolt had stretched the distance between us with my sightseeing, so I skip-jogged to catch up.

He stopped at the last cubicle. "Please, have a seat."

A chrome-framed fabric chair lodged between an L-shaped oak laminate desk and the cubicle wall.

I sat with enough room for my knees to face forward, my shoulders squared so that my hands rested on the tops of my thighs.

Humbolt started to sit but paused. "Can I get you some coffee?"

I waved a hand. "No, thanks."

He unbuttoned his coat and sat with a heavy breath, making quick examination of the fan of files spread across his desktop. The edge of the bottom one read *Crown Motel*. He shuffled them together and dropped the stack into a side drawer. The polished wood handle of a holstered sidearm flashed beneath his coat. It struck me as not unlike glimpsing a stagehand in the wings during a play. One knows that he's there but has the sense that he's not meant to be seen.

Humbolt folded his hands on the desk and tilted his head, staring at me. "Fourth Street, right?"

A vague memory formed in my mind of a suited detective mingling with the officers who'd taken my statement on the night I found Letell. "You were there."

He nodded and picked up a white coffee mug. Taking a swig of the dregs, he grimaced, like it was hard liquor. "Gets cold fast."

I swallowed, not sure how to break the ice.

He shifted in his chair. "So tell me what you got."

I hadn't noticed how tired his face looked. But now, under the fluorescent light and against a backdrop of muted cubicle drab, the spidery red showed at the corners of his eyes. Short silver strands emerged in his hair, tucked back in neatly combed rows.

"Another man has died. A friend of Simon Letell's." I expected him to say that he was already familiar with Martin's case.

But he kept silent, elbow on armrest.

"Dr. Richard Martin," I said. "The last thing I heard Letell say on the day he died was 'Give this to Martin.'"

Humbolt's eyebrows pinched. "Give what to Martin?"

I eased Letell's original note from my pocket, folded once over in its airplane shape. Letell's handwriting had dried in bled smears.

I handed it to Humbolt, who took it by the corner between thumb and forefinger. He examined it, appearing unimpressed.

This wasn't going to be easy. I realized how foolish it must look to him. Here I was claiming that two murders had taken place, and as my first piece of gripping evidence I produced a water-damaged and crinkled paper airplane.

Humbolt cleared his throat. "So Letell hands you this note and says, 'Give this to Martin'?"

"Yes."

"And was that at the motel?"

He should've known from my written police statement that I'd found Letell dead at the motel. He was testing me, probing. "No. It was after we'd shocked him out of v-fib."

"After what?"

"Defibrillated him. Downtown. That was the first time I saw him. He was in cardiac arrest on the sidewalk, and a bystander was doing CPR. We shocked his heart out of a lethal rhythm, and he regained consciousness."

Humbolt looked like he was reading a timeline that floated in the air above my head. "And that was all he said?"

"Yes."

"Nothing about being attacked or threatened?"

"No. No, that was it."

"And at the motel, later, did he say anything else then?"

"No, I . . ." What was his angle? "It's in my report. I found him dead at the motel. He didn't say anything. He was dead."

Humbolt leaned on an arm of the chair, thumb on his chin, forefinger across his lips. "And were you able to revive him that time?"

"There was no reviving him."

"Why's that?"

"Rigor mortis was already setting in. Dependent lividity. Signs of irreversible death."

"How long had he been like that?"

"Couldn't have been more than a few hours."

"Why's that?"

I folded my arms across my chest. He knew the answers to his questions. I was feeling less like a witness and more like a suspect by the second. But my body language was bad timing. It showed him that I felt uncomfortable.

I brought my hands back to my lap. "He had been at the hospital we took him to earlier."

"How'd you find Letell at the motel?"

"A nurse gave me his key to return to him. He left it at Saint Mary's. Look, I put all this in my report."

Humbolt put a hand in the air. "Of course, of course. Forgive me. It's been a while since I've looked at it."

Whatever. I was beginning to think I'd made a mistake coming in.

He read my unsettledness and quipped, "What is it they say? Only two things are certain, death and . . . memory loss?"

"Taxes," I said, unhumored.

He fished a legal pad from the thin drawer of his desk and wrote down the facts. "Okay. What else?"

"The coroner is an academic mentor of mine. I asked him about Letell's cause of death, and—"

"Poisoning."

"Right. You must—"

"Have a copy of the coroner's report. It comes to me with any suspicious death."

"So you suspect foul play?"

He blinked. I could tell for a second that he'd said more than he wanted. He wrote something random on the legal pad. "Just standard procedure. Cover the bases." A quick, dismissive smile said the conversation was now moving on.

I rubbed my ear, considered leaving, but couldn't think of where to go from there. I didn't know if I could trust Humbolt, but what other avenue did I have?

"What else?" he said.

"I searched out this guy Martin."

"To give him the note?"

"To give him the note."

"And let me guess. You found him—"

"Dead. Yes."

"At the university."

"Right."

"And where had you been the hours preceding Martin's death?"

I stood. My voice came out louder than I expected. "A man came back from the dead to tell me to give that"—I pointed at the note—"to Martin. That night I found him dead at a motel, and when I tracked down Martin, he was dead too. Letell was poisoned, and now Martin's body is missing from the morgue."

Humbolt studied me. Like a disinterested kid on a field trip watching a caged monkey rage at his onlookers.

He didn't acknowledge that I was standing, didn't regard my heaving breathing or that I'd raised my voice. He picked up Letell's note and pointed at a row of numbers with the back of his fingers. "So what are these?"

"Dates." I ran the back of my hand beneath my nose and looked away. "Run times."

"Run times for what?"

"Ambulances."

He sat back and motioned to the seat I'd been in. "Please."

I was tired of being led along. I leaned both hands on his desk and lowered my voice. "Every one of those times and dates coincides with ambulance runs to Letell's former residence. The times in Aprisa's database don't corroborate what is here. Letell's beef was that the ambulances had been taking too long to get to his house and that, ultimately, his mother died because of it. But according to Aprisa's stats, the ambulances arrived at his house every time within the six-minute time standard set forth in their contract with the county."

Humbolt intertwined his fingers and pushed his lips together. "How convenient for them."

"Exactly."

"But who's to say they're wrong and he isn't?"

I pointed to my chest. "I am. I've been out there. Especially on night shift I've seen it. Fewer ambulances. Longer response times."

"Significantly longer?"

"Yes."

He cocked his head. "Say you're right. If response times aren't being made, who records that?"

"Dispatch makes a computer entry when a call comes in, when they dispatch it, and when we radio on scene."

"So Aprisa is accountable only to itself."

"In a sense. Representatives from the County Board of Health do periodic audits."

He twirled a pen between his fingers. "And what standard is Aprisa held to? How often do they need to make this six-minute mark?"

"Ninety percent of the time."

"What happens if they don't?"

"Fines. Eventually revocation of their contract for service."

"Their exclusive contract?"

"Yes."

Humbolt leaned back in his chair. "Meaning another ambulance company could come in."

"Right, and corner a monopoly on the transport cash cow. The problem though for any private ambulance company would be offsetting the costs. There's the employees, equipment, dispatch, billing personnel. Collection is difficult. If they get payment from even half the people transported, that's doing pretty good."

"So it's not an easy buck."

"Not if you want to do it right." I straightened. "Therein lies the rub."

Humbolt nodded. "Sounds to me that if someone didn't care about doing it right, they could make a killing."

CHAPTER 27

Humbolt's phone rang, one square of five on the bottom row blinking white.

He stretched to answer it. I scanned the room over the cubicle walls. A few heads faced computer screens. A woman in business attire crossed the far side with files in hand.

"I see." Humbolt scribbled something on the yellow pad. "Uh-huh. All right." He hung up and stood. "Mr. Trestle."

I stretched out my hand. "I won't keep you any longer. Thanks for meeting with me, Detective."

He stepped around the desk and buttoned his coat. He shook my hand. "You should know your rights."

I nodded. "Definitely."

He didn't let go. A set of handcuffs jingled and glinted in his opposite hand. He clicked a bracelet on my wrist.

"You have the right to remain silent. Anything you say or do can and will be used against you in a court of law." He placed one hand on my shoulder and bent my right arm around behind my back.

I twisted. "What's going on?"

He shoved my shoulder into the cubicle wall.

"What is this?"

"Mr. Trestle, you are under arrest for narcotic theft." He patted my pockets. "Anything in here that will poke or cut me?"

"What? No. Narcotic theft?"

"You'll be escorted down to the detention area. A hearing will be scheduled for tomorrow afternoon."

"Are you kidding me? This— I came in here to provide information that might help solve a murder—two murders—and you're going to throw me in jail?"

"Hey." He turned me around and looked me in the eye. "Remember that part about remaining silent? Keep it in mind. Let's go."

Who could I trust? As much as I wanted to, I dared not contact Naomi with my one phone call for fear of implicating her. But I had already mentioned Eli, so I reasoned that it was safe to call him. I had to hope he had his cell phone with him and that it was turned on. But he only carried it for "emergencies," and as expected, I was sent to his voice mail.

In the basement I recognized the detention guard from the streets. A slow nod and laissez-faire expression fell across his brown features. His name tag read *Sonny Rysen*, but I remembered guys calling him Bad Moon. I wondered what had gotten him off the beat and assigned to dungeon duty.

I explained that there was no reason for me to be down there and that there'd been a huge misunderstanding, all the while thinking how cliché it must sound to him.

He raised a hand. "Hey now, I judge not, lest I be."

He paid me the professional courtesy of a private cell, which, though itself not much, was much appreciated. It was windowless with a single bed along a white-painted cinder-block wall and a stainless toilet in the opposite corner. They'd taken my street clothes and given me orange scrubs and shoes without laces. I laid my head on a pillow that had all the cushion of a folded blanket and stared at the ceiling.

How many movies had I seen, how many books had I read, where the main character ended up in a similar predicament? Even Paul the apostle praised God with Silas from behind bars. The earth shook and their cell doors swung open. Seemed very much like fiction now, with my present powerless circumstance every bit real.

Cold like metal bars. Empty like whitewashed walls.

I have a memory of picking up my dad from jail. As a kid, jail is the ultimate punishment. That's where they put the bad guys—pirates and thieves and scoundrels. Though sometimes Zorro or Jim West might end up in the predicament. But they always escaped with a knife hidden in a boot or a wagon tied to a barred window.

I shifted on the bed, mattress springs jabbing my flank.

To see my father, unshaven with his eyes half-glazed behind bifocals . . . It didn't evoke images of an incarcerated hero. My mother didn't say much. She didn't try to explain. He hugged me, the stench of alcohol on his breath. My mother stayed stoic, never letting go of my hand, perhaps for fear that I'd somehow end up in jail as well.

I'd been asleep for some time when a familiar voice echoed down the hall. I blinked and propped up on my elbow.

"Yes. No. That I assure you. Thank you."

"Right this way, then, Doctor."

Eli.

Bad Moon signaled the duty clerk to buzz my cell door. A loud metal clank followed, and it slid open.

Bad Moon smiled. "Done found the truth for you, Jonathan. At least according to this man, you're innocent. And so be it—free."

I exhaled. "Thank you."

"Ain't nothing. Thank the fella who dropped some coin to bail you out."

Eli walked up and grabbed me in a tight hug. He pulled away and gripped my shoulders. Fissures etched deep in his face, an angle of concern in his eyes. "I came as soon as I heard."

I patted his arm. "Thank you."

I changed back into my clothes, signed some paperwork, and followed Eli up to street level. The sky had shifted into shades of mauve.

Eli wiped his glasses with a corner of an untucked shirt. "Where did you park?"

I had to think about it. "I'm . . . right over here by the—" I found myself pointing at a tow truck hoisting a Passat by an expired meter.

I ran into the street. "Hey, wait! Wait!"

The driver climbed in the cab. "Tell it to the company." He grinded the truck into gear and drove forward.

I ran my hands through my hair.

A blaring horn and rushing air whipped past my hips. I looked both ways and walked back to Eli on the sidewalk, heart pounding and legs trembling.

"Come on." Eli motioned. "I'll give you a ride."

CHAPTER 28

We walked around the corner to High Street, and I pulled out my cell to dial Naomi. Eli fished keys from his pocket next to a burnished bronze, late-sixties International Scout II. A chrome roof rack perched atop the bone-white upper half of the two-door SUV.

"Where'd you get this ride?"

He grinned with a hint of Millennium Falcon pride. "Something I've been working on in the garage out back."

Naomi's line rang seven times before rolling over to voice mail. "Hi, this is Naomi. Sorry I couldn't take your call. I'll get back to you as soon as I can." A beep followed.

"Hey, it's me." I looked around, searching the city, not sure how much was safe to say on a recording.

Eli climbed in.

I opened the passenger door. "So, I . . ."

Eli reached under the driver's seat and produced an obsidian black revolver in a leather holster.

"Just give me a call." I pulled the phone from my ear. "Doc"—I checked both directions—"what're you doing? We're right next to the police station."

He flipped the bullet cylinder out, his index finger straight along the three-inch barrel. "Close the door."

This was a new side to Eli.

My door squeaked, falling hard and fast against the car with the camber of the road. I watched him insert six thirty-eight-caliber slugs into the chamber.

He clicked the cylinder in place one-handed, holstered the piece, and tucked it between the gearshift and the four-wheel-drive levers.

"I'm sorry I don't have another one for you." He started the engine.

Do I need one?

We pulled into the street.

I couldn't take my eyes off the revolver. "Where are we headed?"

"Out of here."

"Out of where? Reno?"

"More is at stake than your job." He threw me a glance. "We've stepped on a hornets' nest, Jonathan." Eli merged onto Interstate 80 West. "Open the glove box."

I turned the knob and lowered the long rectangular door. A FedEx envelope lay inside, addressed to me.

"That was on your doorstep."

"You stopped by my house?"

"Better me than you."

I scanned the side-view mirror. "Are we being followed?"

Eli checked his mirrors. "It is possible." He switched to the fast lane, increasing the hum of the Scout's tires over the road.

"What made you think to go to my house first?"

"Before I got your message about being in jail, someone from the police department called. They gave a name and inquired about your whereabouts last evening, if you'd been with me, and if so, had you been showing any signs of being under the influence. I responded that no, you hadn't been, and that I'd never once seen you in such a state from either alcohol or drugs."

We began the uphill toward the mountains. Semis slowed in the other lanes. Eli glanced in the rearview mirror. "When I asked him to repeat his name, he hung up. That's when I realized I had no way of knowing if that person was in fact from the police department. And I'd just told whomever it was that you didn't have an alibi with me for wherever you were last night."

"Or wherever somebody wanted to place me as being at."

"Right. Something felt off. So I called your cell phone from the morgue but got no answer. I left work early and stopped by your house. When you weren't there I turned on my phone and saw that you'd left a voice mail. That's when I saw the envelope on your doorstep."

"Had it just been delivered?"

"That's what I gathered. I took the liberty of opening it once I was back in the car. I hope you don't mind."

I examined the envelope. "Of course not." The first line on the return address read *AAMC: MCAT.* I pulled out a single sheet of paper on professional letterhead.

Dear Mr. Trestle,

It is with great regret that the MCAT review board must censure your recent exam results as required by our regulations. Recent video evidence has revealed that you did not adhere to the strict protocols set forth to ensure each candidate's answers are entirely self-derived. The censure includes a four-year ban from retaking the exam.

We hope that a character of utmost integrity will guide your future endeavors.

Sincerely,
Ronald Smith, CEO
Association of American
Medical Colleges

I knocked my head against the seat. This couldn't be happening. "Someone's trying to frame me."

"Not trying, son. In one fell swoop you've been marked as a thief, addict, and cheater."

"'Recent video evidence'?"

The car wandered into the corrugated median. The pistol vibrated on the center console until Eli corrected back into the lane. "I have received two death threats this week."

"What? How?"

"First by phone. I was the last one at the morgue, finishing up reports. The call lasted ten seconds."

"What'd they say?"

"It was a digitally modified voice. It said, 'Leave it or join them.'"

I checked my cell phone to see if Naomi had called back. No messages. "And what about the other?"

"A note."

"In the mail?"

"No." He took a deep breath. "In a stomach."

"In a—"

"Man . . . his fifties. Homeless. The paramedics found him in an alley. No witnesses."

"So an autopsy was ordered."

"Right. When I examined the stomach contents, I found a tiny laminated note rolled up like a scroll and tied with floss."

"What did it say?"

"Same message."

Evening darkened the mountain canyons, obscuring the Truckee River below.

I folded the MCAT letter. "Who doesn't want us to know about the times?"

"What times?"

"Letell's note contained dates and response times for Aprisa ambulances. When we compared them against Aprisa's database, the numbers didn't match."

"Let me guess—Aprisa's all fit neatly into their county mandate."

"Exactly."

He nodded. "Losing a lucrative contract—that could be motivation."

"But enough to drive someone to murder?"

"Who stands to gain the most from Aprisa's success?"

I leaned an elbow on the door and rubbed my chin. "Maybe we should be asking who stands to lose the most from its failure."

"Fear is a powerful motivator."

"Shintao caught me downloading run times last night."

"Shintao?"

"The Aprisa accounting VP."

Eli ran his thumb over the steering wheel. "So Shintao could be savvy to the fact that you know the times don't add up."

"Assuming he himself knows. Then yes."

"And today you are arrested on false charges, your MCAT scores are discredited under false pretenses, and your hopes for medical school and a scholarship are stripped away."

"Someone knew how to hit me where it hurts." The mountainside raced past the passenger window.

"Who else knows about the scholarship?"

"Pretty much everyone."

"How did you first get notice of it?"

"Dr. Kurtz."

Eli's cheeks tightened, as if he had tasted a tannin-laden wine.

Kurtz? "Why would he want me out of med school? He's been the main guy working to get me there."

"He *is* paid by Aprisa to serve as their medical director, correct?"

"Yes."

"What about profit sharing? Do employees have a buy-in with the company?"

I shook my head. "Aprisa is a Reno start-up. It's not publicly traded."

"Yet. Anyone not particularly fond of you?"

"You mean . . . do I have any enemies?"

"Put bluntly."

"I happen to be a very well-liked individual, Eli."

"At least you were." He gave a quick smile. "Sorry."

"I've found a new talent."

"What's that?"

"Turning public tide against me."

"Who knew?"

I ran my hands over my face and exhaled. "Where are you taking us, anyway?"

"I have a small cabin in Tahoe. Emerald Bay. We can regroup there for a bit."

"At some point I've got to talk to Kurtz. If anyone can clear this up, he can. He might be able to use his pull with Aprisa or maybe talk to someone about the MCATs. I'd like to see them produce that alleged video."

Eli nodded. "Itself doctored, I'm sure."

"Out of anyone, Kurtz's position would be one of the most influential with both Aprisa and the MCATs."

Eli rested a hand on top of the wheel. "But you said yourself, he's been nothing but an advocate. Why undo what he's done for you?"

I shook my head. "I'm calling him."

"You sure that's wise?"

"I need to ask him where the scholarship stands, if nothing else."

"Jonathan, I—"

"It's ringing." I leaned my elbow on the door with the phone in hand.

The line picked up. "This is Joseph."

"Doc, it's me."

"Jonathan? How are you?"

"Oh, just great. Super, really. Let's talk about baseball, or maybe the weather. Or, you know, why I am being framed for narcotic theft."

"Hold on, now, Jonathan. You know I had nothing to do with that. The news came to me after the fact."

"You had no idea?"

"You think I would just stand by and not come to you if I had?"

"I got thrown in jail, Doc."

He sighed. "Jonathan, I am so sorry."

"Sorry doesn't help. I got a letter from the MCATs. That news to you too?"

"Look, let's slow this down a bit."

"You knew about the MCATs?"

"I received a phone call with an inquiry related to an investigation."

"So you knew about it. Were you planning on telling me?"

"Believe it or not, I do get those from time to time. I figured it was a random audit. I know several of the members on the governing board, and I assure you they are all top-notch."

"Is that right? So you're saying you believe them?"

"Believe them about what?"

"They accused me of cheating."

"On what grounds?"

"Video evidence."

"Jonathan, this is not good."

"You want me to believe you knew nothing about this?"

"How could I possibly know? I understand you are upset and that this could have dire consequences for your scholarship. But I do not appreciate your calling me out with an accusatory tone."

I watched the yellow line of the road wind past the car.

Kurtz cleared his throat. "Look, why don't you meet with me tomorrow, and we will see what options we have. Get a game plan going."

I glanced at Eli. "All right. Where? At the med school?"

"No. I'm . . . I have a full schedule lined out. Let's meet up at the Old Country."

"That dive on Fourth Street?"

"I know. But it's only a bar in front. If you park around back you'll find some of the best German meals you've ever tasted. Tell you what, I'll buy."

"About what time?"

"See you at six thirty?"

I took a deep breath. "Okay, Doc. See you then."

CHAPTER 29

We wound along 89 and the west shore of Lake Tahoe, rising to about midslope over the lake. Eli shut off the headlights and pulled across the highway onto a dirt road. He drove ten yards in.

We waited.

Two cars passed.

He shifted the transmission into four-wheel drive low, turned on the running lights, and crawled forward.

The highway disappeared as we rounded a corner. I braced a hand on the doorframe. "You think we're in the clear?"

He adjusted his grip on the wheel. "Hard to know. If someone really wants to find us, they eventually will. Just might take them a day or two." The car rocked with the uneven road. "I do have supplies down at the cabin."

The dull amber lights didn't seem sufficient. "Can you see well enough?"

"I've been coming down this path since I was a child." He turned left before I could even tell the road went that way. He held a ten-and-two grip on the thin and wide steering wheel. It jerked left to right in short quick jabs. "You mentioned a 'we' before when you spoke about comparing the numbers to Aprisa's database. Were you referring to Naomi?"

"Yes. But I don't think anybody knows that she was involved."

"Shintao didn't see her?"

"No."

We kept quiet for the better part of the winding descent. Eli pulled the Scout to a stop by a woodshed behind a small log cabin. A waning half-moon cast a dull white fan over Emerald Bay, visible through a filtered tree view and not more than a couple hundred yards away. Eli grabbed a cloth grocery sack and a small flashlight from the rear, then led the way to the front door.

"How come I never knew you had this place?"

"I could've sworn I'd mentioned it. It's been in our family for a century. Always a place of solitude and healing for me."

We stepped up on a small wood porch. Eli crouched and felt the short planks that ran perpendicular to the front cabin wall, stopping at one to the right of the entry. He lifted it and picked up a green box from below. He blew off a coating of fine dust and set it on the porch top.

"Here." He handed me the flashlight.

It looked like a vintage ammo box. I kept the beam focused on a small combination lock attached to the side latch. Eli spun the wheel and released the bolt.

He opened the lid and produced a key ring from inside the box. "My father wanted this cabin to be available to anyone who needed it. Rather than copy a bunch of keys, he made up this system."

He replaced the box and board and unlocked the front door. Inside smelled of musty pine.

"Come on in. Over here in the kitchen."

I followed him with the light to a drawer where he pulled out a book of wooden matches. An oil lantern sat on a small dining table. Eli lifted the glass and lit the wick. A warm, bulbous glow filled the room. A cool breeze angled through the front door.

"I'll get that." I walked back and shut it.

The place looked to be about a thousand square feet, with two bedrooms off the back hallway, each big enough for a double bed and one chest of drawers. Eli lit lamps in each and one in the living room. He took logs from an iron holder by the stone hearth and went to work building a fire.

"Take whichever room you'd like, Jonathan. I'll try and get this going—see if we can warm things up."

It didn't take long before he had a ripping fire going. He propped the stoker in its holder.

My phone vibrated. Naomi's number. "Hey."

"Jonathan?"

"Yeah."

"I called as soon as I got your message. We were slammed with back-to-back flights. What's up?"

I gave her the rundown and invited her to meet at the cabin, pausing to ask Eli how to describe the exit for the dirt road.

He shook his head. "It's difficult to find in the daytime, let alone at night. She's likely to draw attention." He folded his hands and leaned his elbows on his knees. "Tell you what. Have her find a parking space in the Vikingsholm parking lot. Tourists occasionally park there to watch the moonrise over the lake. She'll be less likely to stand out that way."

"Sometimes the best place to hide is—"

"Right out in the open. Exactly. Tell her to take the long hike down to the beach by the Vikingsholm castle. I have a two-person kayak stored in a redwood container by the beach. In this moon, you should be able to see well enough to take it across and pick her up."

I nodded, relayed the information to Naomi, and hung up.

Eli brought a small water backpack from the front closet. "There'll be less of a chance this way of her leading someone directly to us. Take this when you go. There's a first-aid kit, flint and steel, and a thin fleece blanket should you need it. I'd do it myself, Jonathan. But these arms are about worn out for the night." He rubbed his shoulder and winked. "Besides, you know a thing or two about kayaking."

"No problem. I'd like to go get her myself anyway."

"I know you would, son."

I studied his face. "What's that supposed to mean?"

"You think that after watching you two grow up I'm that unobservant?"

"Observant of what?" I paced behind the couch. "I, for one, do not need to be shackled down."

"Shackled?"

"Eli, as far as I'm concerned, marriage equates to the old ball and chain."

"Who said anything about marriage?"

"You did."

He shook his head.

"Didn't you?"

He grinned. "I will say this—Naomi waits. But she won't forever."

I huffed. "How about you? It's been a long time since Maureen passed away. You haven't retied the knot."

"She was my one."

The fire popped. I looked at the floor. "Name me one happily married couple."

"There are plenty of them."

"Name one."

"How about Naomi's parents?"

I'd forgotten about them. "All right, fine. Name another."

"There's no need. Because not everyone loves their spouse the way God intends them to."

"There's what God intended and what actually happens."

He knitted his eyebrows. "Oh yes, yes. Of course." He warmed his hands by the fire. "You know, I've been meaning to tell you that I've felt a burden to pray for your father lately."

"Could take a lot of praying."

A strong gust eddied down the flue. The fire waved and shook.

Eli stretched. "Well, you'd best leave in about forty-five minutes. Should work out pretty close time-wise for you to cross the bay and meet up with her."

CHAPTER 30

It was the womb of Lake Tahoe.

Eagle Fall's twisting umbilical fed the pear-shaped basin below. A simple stone house perched on a tiny island in the center, ensconced by lunar-lit snowmelt.

There was a quiet to Emerald Bay. All the more on the water's surface. A rhythm to the drip-paddle-splash and the coursing glide of the kayak. No towering buildings at river's edge. No distant siren echoes. Just peace. And the Lake of the Sky.

The alpine air entered my lungs, crisp, light, brisk. I felt at home. In my element.

The moon's shimmer followed me on the water. Objects ashore melded into amorphous shapes and blobs of inky green.

I scanned the mountainsides, eyes trailing up snow-covered draws to the craggy outline of Jake's Peak and down to where I estimated the highway lay.

There was a saying about shooting ducks in a barrel....

I moved my arms faster, my smooth glide becoming a swift carve, the water unsettled and rolling in a broad V-shape from the boat.

I found myself praying for cloud cover.

Through my jacket pocket came warmth from a stainless-steel Thermos Eli had filled with hot tea. Already sweating from the paddle, I stripped off the wool beanie he'd provided from the cabin's front closet.

Near the beach I brought the oar into the boat and made ground at a slow coast, coarse pebbles rolling beneath the hull like poured coffee beans. I rolled up my pant legs and took off my shoes and socks, stepping into the biting cold water to pull the kayak ashore. I set it down and placed my hands on my hips, looking at the distance I'd just covered.

Her voice came from the tree line. "Jonathan?" She wore a dark fleece jacket and a beanie with tassels that hung like two braided hair locks.

Somehow, the expanse of the water and the vacuum of space—the silence and solitude of it all—freed my inhibitions. I ran and grabbed her around the waist, lifting her. Her arms fell around my shoulders, eyes piercing mine.

I let her body slide down.

Our cheeks caressed, warm breaths disseminating in the air.

She smiled. "Hi."

"Hey."

"Everything all right?"

I didn't think—I just spoke. "I've missed you."

Naomi brought her lips together and tilted her head.

I didn't want to let go of her.

"You . . ." she began. "How long have you missed me, Jonathan?"

A simple question. The answer like a thread entangled in a scab.

Water lapped.

It was the pool at Bethesda.

I swallowed. "All my life."

Our eyes locked, and for a moment I knew her. The sheer power and truth of it delivered a defibrillating jolt.

I let go of her waist.

My eyes clouded. I turned toward the boat and blinked it away.

I shuddered, the cold reaching my core. I felt vulnerable. Like a nine-year-old boy seat-belted in the back of a wrecked Plymouth.

Naomi walked down the beach and knelt by the fore of the kayak. She ran her hand over the rope handle. "I like your ride."

A shadow darkened her face. A gray barge—the lone cloud in the sky—sailed in front of the moon.

I smiled and took a deep breath. "Yes, ma'am. One midnight kayak ride, courtesy of Dr. Eli and a God-sent cloud cover."

She turned to the bay. "That's Fannette Island, right?"

"Yes."

"I've only ever seen it from far off."

It didn't make sense. It wasn't a prudent decision. But I heard myself say, "Then it deserves a closer look."

She bit her lower lip and cinched down her beanie. I shoved the boat halfway in the water. She climbed in and I set it afloat, quick-stepping through the shallows before hopping aboard.

We placed the oars and paddled. The small island jutted up like a jagged cone, and the teahouse, encompassing the size of a large kitchen at best, reigned in stone solitude with glassless windows and a missing roof.

I rowed and related to Naomi the story of the narcotic-theft accusation, being jailed downtown, about Eli bailing me out, and the letter from the MCATs.

She didn't reply, then suddenly sang, "'I've seen better days, been the star of many plays.'"

I swung my oars back in the water, grinning. "'And the bottom drops out.'"

The teahouse features amplified, growing prominent and higher in my field of vision until the island approached and shadowed it with trees and granite and the pale blur of the clouded moon.

We slowed. The water waved smooth and transparent. Boulders and sea serpent roots interspered the sandy bottom.

I shifted my oar. "Let's bring it around to the opposite side."

We skirted the west aspect and slid onto the island's one sandy shore, barely the length of the kayak.

I hopped off the nose of the boat and grasped the front strap. Naomi climbed forward, did the same, and we dragged it to the base of a towering mud wall.

We found a narrow, winding path and worked our way between boulders. Branches made handrails. Every stone got tested.

At the top the wind picked up, whipping like an angry cat, blowing in my ears and biting at my neck. I pulled on Eli's beanie. Moss and grass shoots filled cracks of the mortared teahouse walls. I got the feeling that the house stood watch. Had the sense it was looking toward the neck of the bay leading to the greater breadth of Lake Tahoe.

Naomi posed at the threshold, looking like a flapper from a 1920s film. "Right this way, darling."

A vision unearthed of my mother standing at the door of our new house. *"Right this way, darling."*

My gut corkscrewed.

I didn't want to go in.

CHAPTER 31

"Jonathan?"

I blinked.

"You all right?"

I pinched the bridge of my nose.

"You okay?"

"Yeah. It's nothing. Just a weird flashback. You and your Greta Garbo."

"Come on."

I heard my father's voice, "It's how much?"

The real estate agent spoke appeasing words, reassuring.

My father turned toward the door, refusing to look at my mother. "Let's go."

"Stuart."

"No."

"Stuart, I like this place. It's safe and it's cute."

"It's too small."

"Not for us three."

I squeezed my mother's hand. "Mom, I—"

"Jonathan." His voice struck like a sledgehammer. My body tensed. My eyes burned hot.

"Jonathan?" Naomi said.

I refocused.

She ran a hand along a glassless window frame. "We finally

make it to the teahouse, and we don't even have any tea." She made a pouty lip.

I walked to the middle of the house and stared at the canopy of stars above. I pulled out Eli's Thermos. The lid squeaked as I unscrewed it.

Naomi looked surprised.

I held up the lid cup. "Care for some tea?"

She walked up and put her hands around the Thermos. "It's nice and warm."

Steam waved as I poured. She lifted the cup to her chin and breathed in, eyes closed.

"Jasmine!" Her eyes flipped open. "You brought jasmine tea." She gave a coy smile.

Thank you, Doctor Eli. He was an observant fellow.

I pulled out the rolled fleece blanket from the backpack and spread it over the stone-tiled floor. I sat back on my hands. "Incredible view."

Naomi sat cross-legged, cradling her tea, shoulder touching mine. "It's not so breezy down low." She took a sip. "So is this where you take all the girls?"

I laughed.

She ran a finger along the rim of her beanie, fingers feeling for a strand of hair to tuck. "Is that how you work it? Lead them into thinking you're in some kind of mortal danger? Soften them up and get them all worried over you?"

"Are you worried about me?"

"Of course."

I nodded. "Me too."

She inched closer. "You're warm. Wait. You didn't answer my question. How'd you do that?"

"How'd I do what?"

"Get me to cozy up to you without even telling me if this is your secret wooing spot."

"I'm not trying to trick you."

"You still haven't answered me, Jonathan Trestle. Look me in the eyes and tell me you haven't taken any other girls here."

"I promise. You, Naomi Foster, are the only one."

She stared as though I'd said something once heard in a dream. She took a token sip of tea and looked up at the stars. "Hey look, there's Copernicus."

"That's not a constellation."

She handed me the cup. "Here, pour yourself some."

I did, held it to my lips, and blew on it.

The wind slid through the windows, whisking overhead. I traced my finger over the sand and mortar that separated the irregular floor tiles. The grains tumbled coarse under my fingertips.

Naomi folded her arms and leaned forward. "Still hot?"

I nodded and offered her the cup. She took it, fingers lingering a moment with mine.

"So," I said, "how're things looking for your mom?"

"She has good days and bad."

"More good than bad?"

She breathed deep. "No."

"What's the prognosis?"

"Mixed. The cancer isn't spreading right now. She's weak from all the chemo and radiation. It knocks her out. She stops treatments this month."

"Permanently?"

"For a few weeks. We'll see what happens." She looked away. "I can't imagine losing her."

I brought my knees up. "God willing, you won't have to."

There was silence, and then I felt her hand between my shoulders. "I'm so sorry. I know that you . . . that your mother . . . We were both so young." She set the cup down. "You've never really spoken about it. All I know is that there was a car accident."

I stared at the floor, running my finger along the sandy cracks. Up, down, right, left. My mind repeated the pattern, trying to order the chaotic emotions within me.

"It's okay. You don't have to tell me if you don't want."

I saw the memory take shape. "I was nine. In that new house we'd bought. Sitting on a rug in my room. It was oval shaped and multicolored. Brown-sugar yellow, plum, red. I was playing with a balloon, trying to keep it from hitting the floor. My parents were yelling at each other in the living room. It made it hard to concentrate. I was mad at them. They didn't want to watch me with the balloon.

"My mother cried out. The sound was like something sharp driven into my chest. 'What?' she kept saying. 'What? Who is she?' The balloon fell. I ran out of my room and yelled at her, saying why couldn't she be quiet, I was trying to play.

"And something like a light switched off in her. She looked older. There were curves to her face I didn't recognize. She twisted the diamond ring off of her finger, reached out her hand, and dropped it in my father's palm. Then she turned to me and said, 'Come here, darling.'

"I forgot why I was angry. I ran to her side and buried my face in her ribs. She told my dad in one quiet, resolute sentence that we were leaving.

"That was the end of it. The transecting of what I had known and what would become.

"I remember the rain whipping at the living-room window. I can see Death waiting in it now, his scythe sharp and clear like water."

A meteor streaked and vanished overhead.

"My dad protested, but my mom cut him off with a finger in the air, saying, 'No. No more. You've lost the right.'

"She walked me to my room and stuffed a bunch of clothes into a backpack. I kept asking her if she was all right, and she kept saying, 'Mommy's fine,' hiding her face from me. I protested. I wriggled free and grabbed my stuffed bear from my bed and my favorite shirt from a drawer. She walked me through the living room. My father was in the same place he stood when we'd left the room. He looked like a wax-museum statue. My mom pulled me through the front door and strapped me in the back of our Plymouth."

My heart raced. I'd never told the story like this before. I tried to slow my breathing.

Naomi tilted her head. "It's okay. I'm here. I'm listening."

I swallowed. "We drove out of the city, along a narrow and winding road. Rain dumped so thick. I couldn't see the lines on the street. That's when she lost control of the car. A tree as thick as the grill swung at us like a pendulum. The hood wrapped around it. She wasn't seat belted and was ejected through the windshield.

"I sat there in the car and called for her. Rain pelted the rooftop. Water poured in on the dash—a body-sized hole in the glass above the steering column. I sat for a long time and just called out for her.

"I finally climbed out and went searching through the downpour. A couple school-bus lengths away I found her, face up in the mud. She didn't look hurt. But she was pale, white, and staring up at the rain. Like she was looking to see where that pendulum had swung from. I nudged her shoulders. I shook them. I tapped her face. But she wouldn't blink. She wouldn't talk.

"The rain splashed on her eyes, and she wouldn't blink. I kept saying, 'Close your eyes, Mom. Close your eyes.' If they'd just been shut, like she was sleeping, or knocked out, I could have had hope. She was there but she wasn't. And there wasn't anything that I could do."

I wrapped my hands around my beanie. "I knelt by her until I was soaked through and shivering. I don't know how long. When the first policeman came I barely had any sound in my voice. 'Help' was all I could manage. 'Help.'"

Naomi put both hands on my face. Tears streamed down her cheeks.

I shook my head. "You don't have to cry for me." A well of pain swelled inside.

She cradled my head.

Her empathy unsettled me.

And then I felt them. Hot stinging tears. I wrapped my arms around her and let my sorrows escape.

I heard the sound of her heart, the rhythm of air entering her lungs. And I felt a peace in place of the pain, like a weight had been lifted.

We stood, fingers intertwined, her eyes at once unsettling and electrifying. We crossed the threshold of that old stone house.

By the kayak we lingered. Our clothed bodies couldn't have been any closer. Steam danced with our breaths.

Our lips hovered close.
And we kissed.
Her warmth became mine, and mine hers.
She smiled. I couldn't help but grin.
Tomorrow we may die, but right then we'd live forever.

CHAPTER 32

I awoke on the cabin couch, a blanket half covering my jeans, beanie all cockeyed over my forehead.

My neck was stiff from the position I'd slept in against the armrest. Naomi's feet tucked beneath mine, the lion's share of the blanket up to her shoulders. She slept on her side, head resting on a tasseled pillow.

I had woken to many things over the years—the sound of dispatch tones and musty posts, often to an empty bedroom with vacant light streaking through the blinds. But I'd never woken in her company. I saw a glimpse of what life could be. The peace in her face, the trust in her slumber—a foreshadowing of what could be mine, completely.

Trails of smoke filtered up the flue, the firebox floor now filled with soot, ash, and the charred remnants of hardwood. A vague memory returned of coming in the cabin door late, the only light from the smoldering fireplace, and the stark difference in temperature between the small back bedrooms and the heart of the cabin.

I remembered sitting back on the couch with Naomi, my arms around her, her head back on my shoulder.

We spoke about my dad. That none of the choices he'd made in this life were my fault. That regardless of his inability to forgive himself, I needed to forgive him and love him, as much for my own sake as for his.

"Everyone has a different path to redemption," she said.

I leaned my head on hers, smelled her fragrant hair, closed my eyes, and then it was morning.

A teapot whistled. I propped myself up to see Eli lifting a black kettle with a rag in hand. He was dressed for the day in jeans and a flannel shirt. The impressive beginnings of a white whiskered beard grew on his face. A few days' growth would give him the look of an older version of Grizzly Adams. He smiled and held the teapot in the air with an inquisitive look. I nodded my head and mouthed, "Please."

He poured three cups and placed two with saucers on the coffee table. I slid my legs out from the blanket and went to work building a new fire, rolling newspaper and placing it between wood cribbing. Naomi stirred. I struck a wood match and lit the papers in several places, adding thin wood strips Eli had set beside the stash of logs. A healthy fire soon popped and waved. The heat felt wonderful.

Naomi sat up and covered her mouth with a closed-eye yawn. She ran fingers through her hair and gave her head a shake.

I crouched and warmed my hands. "Good morning."

She bit her bottom lip. "Good morning, Mr. Trestle." She noticed the tea on the table and glanced at me.

I nodded toward the kitchen. "Compliments of our gracious host."

Naomi turned. "Eli." She leaned her arms on the back of the couch. "How are you?"

Eli set four pieces of bread on a wire-frame tent over a gas burner. "Welcome, Naomi. Did you sleep all right?"

"Just perfect."

He pulled red jam from a pantry. "I grabbed bread and a dozen eggs before leaving yesterday. I'm afraid I don't have any other perishables."

"That's fine. Thank you."

He pulled out a skillet and lit another burner.

The scent of pine mixed with hot tea, toast, and eggs in cast iron. I didn't want to leave.

But I knew this was only a buffered reality. An alcove set apart from a raging sea. Outside the walls of this cabin my life lay in shambles.

I needed someone with power to stand up for me. I didn't really care about not working at Aprisa anymore. I was a short-timer anyway. But I needed to at least get into the School of Medicine. If the accusation against me for cheating was retracted, then perhaps I could keep my scholarship. Dr. Kurtz was my best hope for a defense, both with Aprisa and the MCATs.

We ate breakfast around the coffee table. I couldn't remember when eggs and toast had tasted so good.

Naomi warmed her hands around her teacup. "I'm scheduled to pick up the second half of a shift today for another flight nurse."

I nodded. "You start around two?"

"Yeah. I'd like to be there by one thirty at the latest."

Eli set his spectacles on the table. "There is information I'd like to secure at the morgue. I'm approaching a conclusion. But there's some data I need to check to be sure." He stared at his plate. "Whoever is out for you, Jonathan, obviously does not want me interfering."

"Which means they'll be looking for you."

"Yes. But if they are, then they'll be looking for me in the car I normally drive. Not the Scout parked out back."

Dr. Kurtz didn't want to meet until that evening. But he'd

never been too busy to meet me at his office before. I wasn't willing to wait for the Old Country. If he had anything to offer, he could give it at the university. "I could drop off Naomi at her car and you down in Reno at the morgue and then head to the university to meet with Kurtz."

Eli cleaned his glasses with a shirttail. "Yes. Yes, I think that's wise. See what headway you can make with him, then come get me." He hooked the wiry frames around his ears. "As far as we know, no one is aware that Naomi is involved. You two haven't been seeing each other regularly before this, so there's not much reason for her to be suspected."

He scratched his beard stubble and turned to Naomi. "Still, I'm concerned. Whoever is covering up Aprisa's actions is also willing to kill for it. I'd feel best if you spent the night here again after your shift. Do the same thing as last night. If you can, drive a different car up and park in the same lot. The moon will be thinner this evening. We should be good for at least one more night."

The cabin didn't have electricity, but it did have hot water. It felt good to start anew and be clean after a shower, even if I had to pull on the same clothes I'd been wearing. Before long we were jostling uphill in the Scout.

Across the bay, the Vikingsholm parking lot was already filling up with people of various nationalities carrying cameras and speaking in different languages. We said a quick good-bye to Naomi, who didn't waste any time getting into her car. The plan was for her to let us go first and then leave a few minutes later.

I didn't like separating from her. Ten minutes into it, I called to make sure she'd left the lot without problem. No answer. After passing Tahoe City on the north end of the lake, I still hadn't heard back.

Eli adjusted his seat belt. "She probably just doesn't want to talk while driving."

I took a deep breath. "Right."

"It'll be okay."

We merged onto Interstate 80 toward Reno, and I wished I could believe him.

CHAPTER 33

My knee vibrated while I sat in the lobby outside Dr. Kurtz's office. Framed photos of past med-school deans lined the walls. Like a timeline of presidents, each was labeled with a small brass plaque stating the individual's name and dates of service. All WASPs. Only the last four photos were in color, with Joseph Kurtz, M.D. engraved beneath the last, a blank space following his starting date. School of Medicine Dean was not a position prone to turnover.

The thick cherrywood door to his office opened. Kurtz appeared in a predictable black button up, ponytailed hair, and circular glasses. Very John Lennon-esque.

Imagine there's no MCATs . . .

"Jonathan." He motioned toward his office.

No smile for me this time.

I followed him in, glancing at the receptionist busy penning something at the welcome desk.

Kurtz sat in a high-backed leather chair, the kind with rows of big buttons that cinched the fabric. Windows behind him looked out from the second story onto a grassy courtyard surrounded by university buildings.

"Have a seat." He flashed a courteous smile.

I ignored the offer and examined the glossy walnut hutch that lined one wall. *Taber's Cyclopedic Medical Dictionary.* The *Physicians' Desk Reference* for pharmaceuticals. A few framed photos of Kurtz shaking hands with prominent figures.

He clicked a pen. "Or not."

I studied my dim reflection in the cabinet varnish. "I'm not a thief."

A crystal trophy engraved with the heading, *Lifetime Achievement in Medicine* cast a swath of rainbow.

"And I didn't cheat."

He crossed his fingers, elbows resting on the table. He stared at a black writing mat, nodding.

"I need you to believe me, Doc. Aprisa might fire me, but I need that scholarship."

"Jonathan. There is no more scholarship."

"But there can be. I've been . . . They've got it wrong. They're saying they have video evidence that I cheated, which is impossible. Because I didn't. I need time to clear my name."

"Time that the university isn't willing to take."

"But you . . . This isn't right."

"Right or wrong has little to do with it. This isn't like back in my day, Jonathan. Drug abuse can't be excused by social revolution."

"Right or wrong has everything to do with it. Don't you get it? I'm being framed."

"Hey, now." He put his hands up. "I understand emotions are high. But we don't need to jump to rash conclusions."

"There's nothing rash about it."

"I understand you're under a lot of stress right now—"

"Stress? I'm being set up."

"Okay. Okay."

"They're trying to shut me up."

"Jonathan. Shh. Come on now. Why would Aprisa even want to do that?"

I froze.

Who said anything about Aprisa?

I pocketed my hands and nodded, pacing behind two leather chairs positioned in front of his desk. "Right. Right." I scratched my neck. "Why *would* they? You're on the board. You tell me."

He searched for things to straighten on the desktop. "Look. You can be frank with me. If you've got a substance-abuse problem, I know people. There's a great program I can get you hooked up with. It's best, at this point, to just come clean. That's going to be your only shot of getting back into med school. Eventually."

I stared at the frames hanging on the opposite wall. His undergraduate diploma abutted his med school diploma and his license to practice medicine.

My heart dropped in my chest.

My eyes fell upon a plaster imprint, measuring maybe eight inches square, hanging next to the frames. Jutting between deep grooves stood a series of Latin letters markedly familiar.

R   O   T   A   S

O   P   E   R   A

T   E   N   E   T

A   R   E   P   O

S   A   T   O   R

My heart beat like mad. I kept my back to Kurtz.

His chair squeaked. "Friend of mine brought back that casting from Italy."

My eyes moved back and forth. Letell had led me to this square.

Martin had worked at the university. He worried about corruption. He would have known exactly who Letell was cryptically pointing to.

Kurtz cleared his throat. "It's a magic square, reputedly. Imparts success and good fortune."

I steadied my breathing.

"Which I'm sure you feel in want of now. Forgive me. Perhaps I can get you a copy. If you'd like."

I turned and walked to the edge of the desk. "I didn't steal any narcotics. I am not an addict, a cheater, or a liar."

"Hey, it's not for me to judge."

"You know it! What's in it for you, Joseph?"

He stood. "How dare you? Come in here like this . . . Yell at me. Disrespect me in my own office?"

"Disrespect you? Are you listening to yourself?"

"Video evidence doesn't lie, Jonathan."

"You think I don't know how easy it is to doctor a video?"

"Not with the MCATs."

"Look me in the face and tell me that you don't believe me."

He turned aside.

I set my chin. "All right, then. I get it. I get it. Your believing makes no difference. Why would it?"

"I think I've heard en—"

"Why are you altering Aprisa's run times?"

His lips fell apart. He looked down and let out a cynical laugh. He dropped into the chair and ran his hand over his mouth. "Fools rush in, Jonathan." His face hardened. "So why are you running into places the very host of heaven avoid?"

"The company paying you dividends on profits, Doc? Is that it? How petty is that?"

"You had such a bright future. Now here you go. Chucking it to the side of the road—and for what? To what end, Jonathan? What benefit? You've earned your reward." He slid open a desk drawer and produced a matte black pistol with a rubber-lined grip.

My heart skipped.

He locked his eyes with mine. He pointed the gun at the floor and pushed a button on the desk phone. The receptionist answered, and he said, "Judy, did you hear yelling from inside my office just now?"

"Yes, Dr. Kurtz. Is everything all right?"

"There is a bit of a situation. Have the university police come right away."

"Yes, sir."

"You are aware, Jonathan, that assault alone is a crime. The simple act of making someone think you're going to commit battery."

"I don't even know you anymore."

"You've betrayed my trust."

I betrayed him? "You think I have no defense? There are others at Aprisa who can clear my name."

"You have no friends at Aprisa. You've already been fired by unanimous board vote this morning." He stood up and ran his free hand along the top of the chair. "This is bigger than you, Jonathan. And I am sure, now that you have a record, certain detectives downtown will be curious about the fact that you showed up, off duty, at a prospective murder scene. You've brought this on yourself."

"You knew I found Letell dead at that motel.... Is it because you killed him? Is that why you called me right after with news about a scholarship? You've been trying to distract me. Telling me to put

Aprisa behind and look to my future." I shook my head. "This will spiral out of your control. You—"

"Have a seat."

"I'll stand."

"Sit." He straight-armed the pistol.

If it were the movies, my line would be "What're you gonna do? Shoot me?" To which I'd seen varied results. Depending on the writer, not all of them favorable.

I pushed my lips together and sat on the edge of a chair.

Kurtz stripped off his glasses and slid them on the desk. He pulled his ponytail out and shook his salt-and-pepper hair free. It hung wild and greasy, and in his black shirt he now looked more like a gangster than an academic hipster. He leaned on the bookcase and tilted up the handgun with his forefinger and thumb.

He exhaled. "There is a structure to things. There is a way that you climb the ladder. Like Jacob. The usurper. He snatched everything he could take and found the gateway to heaven." He crossed his arms, the gun pointing out from under his bicep.

I couldn't be taken into custody. Who knew what other false accusations might arise? I gauged the distance between us. Could I charge him before he could aim the gun? It would be close, and risky.

"One must take what is his, Jonathan. Find the way to win. I am the master of my fate. The captain of my soul. Not anyone else."

"Who else is involved, Joseph?"

His cheek twitched.

He wasn't working alone.

He grinned. "'Under the bludgeoning of chance, my head is bloody, but unbowed.'"

A knock pounded on the office door. "UNR PD."

Kurtz glanced at his glasses on the desk. "Like I said. There is a way to go about things. And you, unfortunately, are not playing by the rules."

The doorknob clicked back and forth.

My eyebrows tightened. He had locked it when I came in.

"UNR PD. Open up."

I might not see freedom for months or longer. I thought of Eli and Naomi.

"Police. Unlock the door."

He reached out for his glasses and dropped the gun hand to his side. I saw my chance.

And sprang.

He shouted.

I drove him to the bookcase, catching his wrist above the pistol. The hutch tottered. He twisted and shifted, turning with me and ramming me back against it. He forced his gun hand into the air, sweeping in a broad arc to break my grasp. Books and plaques toppled and crashed. Shouts came from the other side of the door. I brought a foot up against the cabinet and pushed off.

I drove him backward. The air burst and the window shattered.

He struck his head on the sill and we hit the floor. My ears rang.

I cocked my fist.

But he lay there limp, unconscious.

My chest heaved.

The office door rattled and shook. Wood splintered.

I stood, heart pounding.

A two-story drop lay below the broken window. Less than ten feet if I hung from the sill.

The doorframe cracked.

I grabbed a book and scraped glass shards off the window frame. I climbed out of it—sharp pains digging into my palms, my shoes slipping against the brick veneer—and dangled over a narrow row of junipers.

A loud slam sounded with yelling and boot steps. I pushed off the building, dropped through a screen of scaled leaves, and landed on the grass with a gut-thumping impact.

I rolled, popped up, and dashed from the courtyard, shouts coming from the window above.

CHAPTER 34

Not since being chased by a pit bull as a kid do I remember running with the adrenaline-charged speed I managed then.

I flew through the university grounds—weaving between channels of foot traffic, hurtling hedges, and darting around corners. At Virginia Street near Eleventh I slowed to an inconspicuous walk, doing my best to blend in with other pedestrians.

My flight response waned, like lava into the sea. I rubbed sweat from my brow. A streak of blood stained my hand. Sirens echoed in the distance.

Reno wasn't an overly violent town. Shootings brought a gaggle of cops in short order. Eli's car sat on the south side of the campus, so I planned to head to Ninth, go east for a block, and then enter the parking lot there.

A horse-mounted RPD officer galloped up Virginia. I ran a hand through my hair and avoided eye contact. Radio traffic blared as she passed. Nothing I could make out. Farther south, between the high-rises downtown, emerged the red-and-blue flashes of patrol cars hooking turns up Virginia.

It occurred to me that they might shut down access and egress to the school. I quickened my pace—as fast as I could walk without drawing attention to myself. I pocketed my hands and kept my head down. Two RPD cars flew past.

The attention and bustle focused on the center of the university. A motorcycle cop raced by, followed by an Aprisa ambulance.

Ninth Street, in contrast, was deserted. I fought the urge to break into a jog. Going from a harried sprint to that methodical stride was painstaking and trying. It was no small relief to be leaving the sidewalks for the safety of Eli's Scout.

Base.

I slid the key into the lock.

A small engine slowed to an idle behind me, followed by an authoritative voice. "Hold it right there."

I stared at the door handle.

So close. I began lifting my hands and making a slow turn.

An obese parking attendant sat in a covered golf cart, forearm resting on the wheel.

I crossed my arms and cleared my throat. "Is something wrong?"

He shook his head with disdain. "You kids think you can park anywhere, don't you?" He barely looked old enough to grow a beard.

"I was actually just leaving."

He wiped his brow with a white handkerchief. "It don't matter if you're leaving or coming, bro. You still can't park here unless you have the sticker. And you don't have that, now, do you?"

I played along. "You're right. You nailed me. I thought I could park here for a few minutes and I—"

"Thought wrong. Didn't you?" So satisfied was he with his position of power.

I bowed my head in penitence. "I have no excuse. How much is the fine?"

He squinted, looked to the side, and then labored out of the golf cart. It tilted back to level. He scuffled up to me. "I'll tell you what. Don't let the boss find out, but I'm going to let you off. All right? Old Chuck will take care of you."

I let out a breath. "Thanks, Chuck."

He sniffed and ran a round hand beneath his nose. "Don't mention it, bud." He got back in the cart and waved. "You take care, now. Stay out of trouble."

If only.

I slid behind the wheel of the Scout. Now that I was on the lam, there were a few things I needed to pick up from home.

Tech savvy my father wasn't. Predictable, though? Without a doubt.

At this time in the afternoon he made a habit of visiting Tini's—a martini bar at the edge of downtown. I couldn't risk showing up at my house, and my dad didn't own a cell, so after I received no response on the home phone, I banked on the odds of his being there.

Part of me reasoned that I should go straight to pick up Eli from the morgue, but things had changed, and I was pretty sure I was going to be on the run for a while. I called Eli on his cell with no response and opted not to leave a message. In front of a curbside meter by Tini's, I scanned the surrounding street and businesses and dropped in a few quarters.

The dark bar made a stark contrast to the afternoon sunshine. Long and narrow, it reeked of cigarette smoke and salty nuts. Sure enough, my father sat at the far end, leaning on his forearms, watching the Giants game on an old television, a tall glass of amber beer in front of him.

I slid onto the stool beside him and glanced at the game. "Looks like Lincecum's on it today."

My dad nodded. "He's pitching a good one, all right." He turned. "Jonner."

"Hey, Dad."

"Strange to see you here."

"Yeah. I've run into some unusual circumstances."

"Buy you a drink?"

"No. Thanks."

I couldn't remember the last time I'd asked him for help. Maybe I didn't want to.

But I didn't know when I would see him again. And as inconvenient as it was right then, I knew I needed to try to make my peace.

For the first time since I was a child, I looked at my father without loathing or contempt. It was strange and sudden. "Dad, I want to tell you that I'm sorry."

He kept his eyes on the tube.

"I don't want to be bitter, or angry, or anything like that anymore. And I don't want to heap guilt on you."

He looked at his beer.

"We all make different choices, Dad. I don't want it to be that we can't have any real interaction. Actual conversation. I want to be able to relate with you."

The bartender strolled over.

I put a hand up. "Nothing right now. Thank you."

He meandered back down the bar.

My father removed his glasses and rubbed his eyes. He blinked away moisture. "Thank you for that, Jonner. I hope I can think that way about myself . . . someday." He grimaced.

I exhaled. "There's something else too. Another reason I'm here."

A crowd roared on TV. A high fly ball sailed over the center-field fence. Pablo Sandoval trotted around first.

"What is it?" he said.

"How are you to drive?"

"Barely touched my first."

"I need to get some things from the house. But it doesn't work for me to do it myself."

He eyed me. "You in trouble?"

"Yeah. Pretty big-time."

He looked down at the bar, then back at me. "What do you need?"

"Some clothes. My laptop. Cell phone charger."

He lifted a trembling cigarette to his lips and lit it. He took a drag and exhaled the smoke through his nostrils. "Okay."

"I wouldn't be doing you any favors by saying more."

He stood and patted me on the arm. "There's no need to."

The bar made an adequate interim hideout. I nursed a Sprite and watched the game. Eli called at the top of the ninth.

"Hey, Doc."

"How'd it go with Kurtz?"

"You mean before or after he fired his gun?"

"What happened?"

I gave him the details, covering my mouth as I spoke.

After a long quiet spell, he said, "This is getting worse by the minute."

"Yeah."

"Now you've got the bad guys *and* the good guys looking for you."

"Hard to tell who is who." I watched the bartender fill a glass at the tap.

"We need to change plans."

"Why?"

"RPD knows I'm here."

"How?"

"There was a murder-suicide domestic case on the north end of town last night. Two detectives met me at the morgue after you dropped me off."

"You think it's related?"

"Doesn't look that way."

I spread my forefinger and thumb across my brow. "Are you still coming up to—"

"Don't say it."

"You think we're being listened to?"

"Just in case. Hard to know anymore. But yes, I will. Later. I'll ride up with the other."

Naomi. She wouldn't get off until eight that evening. "All right. You want me to wait?"

He exhaled. "I don't know. It's probably best to stagger arrivals."

"Sure." Things were too hot for me in town anyway. "I should probably get going."

"Okay. That sounds best."

"See you later, then."

"God willing, son. Be safe."

"You too."

I pocketed my phone. The game ended and a teaser for the five o'clock news flashed on the screen. "Shots fired at UNR. A prominent staff member rushed to the hospital. Suspect at large." My Aprisa employee photo flashed on the screen. It was followed by a cutaway of armed officers staking out the grounds and clips of an ambulance leaving the scene. "Full story tonight at five."

The bar door opened. My father walked in, silhouetted by the outside light. I strode over and hugged him. He pulled away, a bit surprised.

I squeezed his shoulders. "You're just in time."

The drive to Tahoe felt long and eerie, the night before like a distant dream.

But Naomi and Eli were only a matter of hours behind me. Soon I'd be in the company of friends.

The lake stretched out beyond Tahoe City, sparkling and choppy with the late afternoon winds. The fuel gauge lingered at a quarter tank. I had fifty dollars cash. The only other money I had was squirreled away in traceable bank accounts. I hoped Eli kept another rainy day ammo box buried around the cabin somewhere.

My phone vibrated. A profile of Bones driving in the ambulance flashed on the screen.

"Hey."

"Jonathan. What is going on? Where are you at?"

"Not so free to say right now, bud."

"Did you have something to do with what went down at UNR today?"

"What makes you think that?"

"Jon-boy, come on."

"Are you working today?"

"I did a shift trade for somebody."

"Are you in the ambulance?"

"I'm at County." His voice lowered. "There are cops everywhere. I've already been taken aside for questioning. They want to know if I've ever seen you take narcs from the drug cabinet. Or if you ever came to work under the influence. Then they started asking other questions."

"Like what?"

"Like if I've ever seen you lie to a patient. Or if you've falsified facts on a chart. If you've seemed unhappy in your job."

"What'd you do?"

"I told them you were a tweaker with a propensity for fabrication."

"Great. Thanks, Bones."

"No problem."

Someone spoke in the background, and Bones said, "On my way. Hey, bro?"

"Yeah?"

"We're level zero again."

No ambulances available. "Imagine that."

"Wherever you are, be safe. And if you need anything—*anything*—just call. All right?"

"Thanks, Bones."

I spotted the turnoff and wound onto the sheltered dirt road that descended to the cabin. A short way in, a sky-blue Prius sat parked in a shallow turnout. Perhaps the least threatening car imaginable, yet my heart beat harder and my breathing quickened.

Could be some hikers or cyclists. I reached under the seat and found Eli's holstered revolver. I unbuttoned the strap and wrapped my hand around the wood-laminate handle. The words SMITH AND WESSON were stamped into the short barrel. I ran a finger along the cylinder. I couldn't remember the last time I'd touched a gun. I dislodged the cylinder to the left. All six chambers were still loaded. I clicked it back in place and set the weapon between the gearshifts.

Nothing more now but to go on.

I dropped the transmission in four low. The pistol rattled with the rocky descent. Shadows twitched at the roadsides. I picked up the gun and held it at the wheel.

Tire tracks in the dirt caught my eye. A set with the same tread. From our trip this morning, I reasoned. Until I saw another pair with a differing pattern.

I skidded to a stop.

The new tracks split off from the others for a brief section. It looked as if someone had been trying to follow the previous tire tread and veered off.

I ran my thumbs along the steering wheel. I didn't want to push on if there was a better option. Go back to Reno and meet up with Eli? Drive back up the road and intercept Eli and Naomi before they got to the turnoff?

I dropped the Scout back in gear and pressed on, my palm sweating around the revolver handle.

Several turns later I came upon two hikers in the middle of the road. One was a grimacing heavyset man, about thirty, sitting with his leg in a two-foot-deep hole. The second was a woman of similar age with a water backpack and hat and a worried expression.

I set the emergency brake and left the engine running.

I opened the door and stood sideways behind it, the way I'd seen cops do, keeping the firearm hidden by my leg. "Who are you?"

CHAPTER 36

The woman's brow furrowed. "He's hurt badly."

The man gripped his leg with both hands and tucked his chin to his chest.

I glanced at the edges of the road. "Why are you here?"

She put her hands on her head, looking about to cry. "We were hiking. Can't you help us? Please."

I looked closer at the hole. It was more like a trench, about four feet long and three feet wide. Two rows of iron spikes, at least eight of them, protruded from the bottom. A different pattern and color to the dirt traced along a line where it looked as if the ditch might extend across the whole road.

The woman paced away.

"Stop!" I put up a hand. "Don't move!"

She froze midstep, hovering over the odd-colored ground.

"Look down."

She brought her foot back and turned toward me.

I sidestepped out from behind the door, inching forward, keeping my head on a swivel. I put both hands in the air, still holding the gun.

Her eyes grew wide.

At the edge of the different-colored dirt, I poked the ground with the gun barrel. Dust shook on a thin layer of cardboard. I pushed harder and it slid into the trench, revealing another set of iron spikes.

The woman stumbled back. "What is all this?"

Two seconds more and I would have driven the Scout right into it.

I searched the roadsides. The surrounding foliage spun into a mass of green, brown, and gray. Someone could be out there, just feet away, and I wouldn't be able to see them.

The obese male hiker looked on, pale face twisted in anguish, his lower calf pierced through with a spike. Blood soaked through his sock. Nothing fake-looking about the injury.

They'd simply had the misfortune of stumbling upon a trap set for me.

The spike may have severed the man's popliteal artery. I tucked the gun in my belt. "I'm a paramedic. I'm going to check him out. Okay?" I knelt by the trench and reached out for his wrist. "Hey. What's your name?"

"James."

His pulse felt thready and rapid—compensating shock from the bleeding. Removing his calf from the spike could worsen the blood loss. I felt around the lower leg. The tibia and fibula bones seemed intact. With care I removed his hiking boot and checked for a dorsalis pedis pulse at the arch of his foot. I shifted my fingers around but couldn't feel anything.

Eli had a shed behind the cabin. I reasoned I might be able to find something there to cut through the spike. James needed a surgeon and a way out of there. An ambulance wouldn't make it down the road. He needed the helicopter.

"Have you called for help yet?"

The woman shook her head. "No cell service here."

I pulled mine out. One bar. Worth a try. I dialed 9-1-1. The choppy sound of an intermittent ringer came through static. A female voice at the other end said something about dispatch.

"Yes, hello? I'm in Emerald Bay, near the south side shoreline with a hiker who has a traumatic injury to his lower leg."

"Sir, you—very broken. I understand you—leg—ald Bay?"

"Yes. Emerald Bay. We'll need a helicopter."

"Underst— On way."

The line disconnected. I called back twice with no success. The hikers looked on with expectation and concern.

"They're on their way. The medical helicopter is."

If it was AprisEvac, Naomi would be with it.

James tilted his head. "I'm so thirsty."

The woman came up to him and placed the rubber tube from her water backpack in his mouth. "Here. Here you go, babe."

I shut off the engine in the Scout and found a box of road flares in the back. I took four to set up a landing zone for the helicopter by the shore. Flight time for the bird would be about fifteen minutes, plus seven minutes or so warm-up time on the pad at County. I'd strike the flares in twenty. Sooner if I heard them coming.

I leapt over the trench. "James, I'm afraid you'll lose too much blood if we pull your leg off the spike."

He nodded, as if in agreement. They had probably come to that conclusion on their own.

"I'm going to see if I can find a hacksaw by the cabin down this road. We'll cut the spike and secure it until you get to the hospital, where they can remove it safely."

"Do what you need to."

I pulled the revolver from my belt and jogged down the road—the gun swinging in my fist still seeming odd and out of place. Eli's cabin came into view a couple hundred feet ahead. I slowed and moved to the side of the road.

A hiker might be hurt, but I wasn't going to do him any good if I got killed trying to help him. I brought the hand that held the flares up in front of me and rested the gun across my forearm. I moved steady and deliberate, with as little noise as possible.

Wind rustled the pine trees. A mountain bluebird flapped and squawked from a nearby branch.

A thud hit the forest duff.

I pointed the pistol at a squirrel skittering toward a fallen pinecone. He went to work stripping out the seeds. I wondered if I would have even hit the tree behind him had I fired.

I turned my attention back toward the cabin and the shed behind it.

A hundred feet to go.

I could hear the lake now, a subtle lapping of wind-driven waves.

I decided to clear the house before entering the toolshed. I didn't want any more surprises.

Whoever set the spike trap wanted the Scout incapacitated. Were they hanging around to apprehend me as well?

I sidestepped in a broad arc around the cabin, squeezing closer in a descending orbit.

At the porch steps I stopped and listened, gun pointed at the front door.

I crouched, set down the flares, and eased up the board that covered the ammo box with the door key. As I lifted the box, I noticed the combination lock hanging on the front latch.

Thinking Eli may have left the door unlocked, I shifted to the side of it, held the revolver across my chest, and tested the doorknob with my free hand.

It clicked. With a slight push the door creaked inward.

At the end of the hallway a shadow moved.

CHAPTER 37

I slammed back against the log wall, gripping the revolver with two hands.

Perspiration dropped from my temples.

Inching to the edge of the doorframe, I peeked in. A rectangle of light stretched along one wall.

I wrangled down my breathing to listen.

Nothing.

My eyes darted to the outside corners of the house.

I rubbed my brow with a forearm and threw another glance inside.

Hallway. Light.

And the shadow again.

I drew back and shouted, "Who's there?"

No response.

With another glance I saw the same shadow.

Something wasn't right. It was making the same motion.

I stared down the hallway.

Sure enough, I saw the shadow again, moving up and down like a blacksmith hammering a hot iron. But it didn't have quite the right shape to be a fist holding a hammer. Or even an arm for that matter.

A fluttering sounded overhead. A large falcon flew away from the cabin with a chipmunk in its beak. Inside, the shadow's motion diminished, and I realized that it resembled a tree limb—one that swayed with the weight of a bird of prey.

I firmed my resolve and stepped inside, arms in front with the pistol in hand. I checked the kitchen and living room and kept moving at a slow but steady pace down the hall, clearing both back bedrooms.

I walked back to the entry, muted light shining through the half-open doorway. I lowered the gun and leaned on the wall. Cold black soot lay in the fireplace, couch pillows still askew. The blanket we'd slept under lay folded over an armrest.

The threshold creaked. A gun-wielding hand froze in the doorway.

I drove my shoulder against the door. It slammed on the wrist, and the handgun dropped. I threw open the door to see a slim-built man with a navy blue ski mask. I raised my gun, but his fist crashed against my face, knocking me to the floor. A boot kicked my pistol hand, knocking the gun free and flaring pain through my fingers. I swiped at his knees and scampered backward.

He bent for the gun, and I launched into him, driving him to the floor. He grabbed at my face and yanked at my hair. I shoved my palm into his nostrils and swung my fist against his ear. He swiped at my arms. Grabbing his collar, I shoved him to the floor and yanked off his hood.

We stopped for a split second—me in recognition of his face, he in realizing I had.

Trent Matley.

He lurched sideways. Locked like steers, we struggled to our feet. He broke free a fist and drove it to my abdomen. Breath burst from my lungs.

We whipped around and tumbled over the couch. I sprang from

the floor, toppling the coffee table, and fixed my hands in a boxing guard. Blows struck my forearms and flanks. I strafed back. My heel hit the hearth. I snatched the poker and whipped it toward his head. He ducked with an inch to spare. I swung again, and he jumped back, then hurdled the couch.

I pursued with the poker raised, only to see Trent rising from the floor, revolver in hand.

I swerved midstride—hot metal zinging past my flank—smacked the wall, and rolled into the hallway. Wood splintered. I dove into the back bedroom, locked the door, leapt over the bed, and squatted by the wall.

My heart hammered in my chest. Hot blood dripped from my nose.

A rectangular window stood over the bed, maybe four feet by two. I smashed the glass with the poker and scraped the frame free of shards.

I crouched and listened.

Still no sound at the room door.

Forget it. There was no way I was staying in the cabin. I tossed the poker outside and pulled myself up through the window, race-car style.

At a seated position in the frame, I heard pine needles crunch.

Around the cabin's corner, Trent leveled the revolver.

A shot fired. I dropped into the room, air singing. A bullet struck high on the bedroom wall. I scrambled low and unlocked the door. A third shot pinged. I scuffled into the hallway and shielded myself.

I counted the shots that had rung out. One in the living room. Two in the hallway. Three from outside.

If he only had Eli's gun, he'd be out of bullets.

I sprinted down the hall, slid into the front door and kicked it shut. I flipped the lock and scooted to the side, scanning the cabin floor for the other pistol.

Nothing.

Kitchen . . . Nothing.

Beneath the couch?

The circle of a matte black muzzle pointed at me from the shadowed floor. I tapped the barrel away and slid the gun out. An insignia on the grip read P. BERETTA with three upright arrows.

I ejected the magazine. Still full of bullets. Different shaped than Eli's. Longer. I palmed it in place and cocked the slide.

From the distance came the sound of a helicopter, blades chopping through the thin mountain air. I stood beside a window. No sight of Trent. Through the trees I saw AprisEvac, tracing over the bay like an insect.

I unlocked the front door and let it ease inward. The helicopter loudened. Moving along the outer walls, gun two-handed and angled toward the ground, I searched the perimeter of the cabin. I passed the room with the shattered window and came around the rear where the hawk had been on the tree limb. The shed stood a short ways off. A black jeep sat hidden just behind it.

I worked my way over, gun at the ready, throwing glances behind and to the sides. The Jeep was a soft top. A shovel and high-lift jack secured to the back. Fresh mud on the tires. Empty interior.

Trent had been lying in wait. But my showing up in the daylight and the injured hiker had thrown things off. Jacked up his plans.

I trekked back to the cabin and followed the opposite side back to the front door.

Had he bailed?

AprisEvac hovered over the bay. The flares lay on the porch

where I'd first set them down. I scanned the trees. Tucking the Beretta in my belt, I scooped up the flares and ran to the shoreline.

A clearing of hard-packed dirt and grass beyond the trees looked suitable for touching down. I struck the flares, sulfur bursts stinging my nostrils, and marked four corners of a landing zone.

AprisEvac circled like an eagle searching for a mouse. Then it dropped altitude, splitting the distance between the shoreline and Fannette Island. At about a hundred feet, a white-helmeted flight nurse opened a side door.

Naomi.

The pilot lowered the helicopter, the water waving outwards in concentric circles. She would soon put a foot out on the landing skid and lean out to make sure the tail rotor and boom were clear of any obstructions. She kept in communication with the pilot through the microphone attached to her flight helmet. I could even make out the extendable five-point harness she wore that would allow her to shift away from her seat. Just enough to do what she needed to.

I retreated to the tree line. They hovered for a bit, as though the pilot was reevaluating the landing site. Then the helicopter rose and arced away, curving over the teahouse. It returned and took a slow pass parallel to the shore. Angling around, it approached again—this time with a steady descent. Sand and dirt took flight. Water whipped through the air. I shielded my eyes, squinting through the barrage to again see Naomi.

She stepped out on the skid.

She turned to see the tail rotor.

But something was off. She was able to lean too far.

Before I could form a word, her harness snapped and she toppled headlong from the helicopter.

She plummeted toward the bay and crashed into the surface.

My world became a long narrow tunnel.

Naomi at one end and I fifty yards from her at the other.

I ran to the water's edge, stripped off my shoes, and tossed them behind. I hurtled forward until the water came up and around me. My feet escaped the lake floor.

The frigid cold stung through my clothing. I paddled freestyle with my head above the surface, kicking with the sagging weight of my pants. My lungs burned. I swallowed and hacked on a mouthful of water. I shifted to a breaststroke, not taking my eyes off her.

She floated at the surface, limp like a rag doll. I was sure she would sink, her body submerging to depths beyond my reach.

A strong wind beat against me. The water grew choppy and white-capped. AprisEvac hovered low by Naomi. Water pellets stung my eyes. I locked on to her white aviator helmet. Like a bobbing orb, it seemed to keep her afloat.

I swam but felt like I wasn't getting anywhere. Another flight nurse stood in the other open door of the helicopter, one foot on the skid, reaching out a hand. AprisEvac wasn't equipped with any pulleys or rescue gear. The pilot was taking a huge risk in hovering as close to water as he was.

The beating waves hampered my progress. "Pull up!" My voice blew behind me. "Pull up!"

I ducked underwater. Dropping beneath proved effective for pulling forward. In short order I'd halved the distance between us.

At twenty feet away the water smoothed and tightened. I kept to the surface now and pushed through the fire in my lungs, ignoring the oxygen-starved lightness in my head. I made eye contact with the flight nurse. She turned to the pilot, pointed, and brought both feet onto the landing skid. She crouched downward, holding onto the doorframe behind her, though her seat harness was still intact.

Another yard to Naomi.

Her eyes were shut, unfazed by the water lapping at her face.

I reached her and wrapped my arm over her shoulder. The fabric of her flight suit felt tight and coarse under my fingertips. I didn't feel any movement in her chest. I placed a thumb on her cheekbone and fingers behind her jaw to lift and open her airway. I rested my ear by her lips, and for a few seconds the coldness of the lake dissipated, the roaring of the helicopter faded.

I didn't breathe.

And then, like steam from a teacup, I felt a long, warm breath.

I leaned back, tilted up her torso. The helicopter inched closer, the pilot performing a maneuver that could kill us all with the slightest error.

The landing skid neared.

Five feet.

Two.

I reached for the tubular steel. My fingers, numb and cramping, caught it and then slipped off. We lost buoyancy and dunked below. I kicked to surface and gasped.

I stretched out my hand again. I kicked, straining with everything in me.

My palm met metal.

A hand grasped my wrist and the helicopter lifted. My chest

cleared the surface, the wind biting through my shirt. I propped Naomi higher with my legs. The flight nurse reached for her arm. But Naomi got heavier, as if the lake had anchored her.

She slipped downward. I let go of the skid, and we plunged to the water.

I brought my arms around Naomi's torso and leaned back. The helicopter lowered farther, to inches above the lake.

With the skid behind me, I shouted, "You get me. I'll get her."

The nurse let go of the doorframe and locked her hands around my chest like a railroad coupling, her full faith resting in that five-point harness.

With her as an anchor, I worked one foot up on the skid and shifted an arm under Naomi's legs. The helicopter lifted and tilted, giving me leverage. Gravity shifted us toward the cabin as we arced upward. The rotors overhead cut the air with blurring speed. I swung Naomi's legs over my shoulder and toward the inside, her body bent at the waist. I pushed backward on her shoulders, supporting her chest, and slid her body over the flight nurse and inside the cabin.

The nurse stood from her squat, her hands like a vise around my chest until I grabbed the edge of the cot and the doorframe and scampered inside, rolling over Naomi, who lay crumpled on the floor.

The flight nurse climbed in and the roaring engine and beating air dampened as she slid the door shut and slammed down the latch.

CHAPTER 39

Naomi coughed and hacked and spewed water on the floor.

The nurse grabbed her shoulder. "Keep her on her side." I made out her name from her flight suit—*Echo.* Gray hair tufted out from her helmet. "Disconnect the helmet strap."

I knelt beside Naomi and supported her head and neck, detaching the clasp at her chin. Echo slid off the helmet.

Naomi blinked, her face flushed, and eyebrows angled.

"Hey." I looked into her eyes. "It's me. We've got you."

"Where are—" She coughed. "We're in the helicopter?"

I nodded.

"How?" She winced, bringing a hand to her flank. "I think I cracked some ribs." Naomi coughed again, her face contorting with the pain. "What happened?"

Echo brushed Naomi's hair strands from her face. "What do you last remember?"

Naomi's expression switched to fear. "I . . . I fell."

"It's okay." I took her hand. "You're all right now."

"But, how?"

Echo shook her head. "Your seat harness tore."

"That can't happen."

"I know. I know, dear. But it did."

Tears shed to her hair. "How far?"

I glanced at Echo. "At least fifty feet."

She nodded. "Maybe sixty. Besides your ribs, where else do you hurt?"

Naomi's eyes flicked. "My ankle." She tried to move it and grimaced. "It might be broken."

Echo slid her hand behind Naomi's neck. "Any pain here?"

Naomi swallowed. "No."

"You're sure?"

She looked away. "Yes."

I glanced out the window. We hovered high above the bay. "That hiker is still trapped."

Echo looked at me. "How bad is he?"

"Impaled leg. Pale and shocky. Can you take both?"

She positioned the helmet microphone by her mouth. "We're okay to touch down for the original patient." She stared at the floor and nodded. Her eyes returned to me. "The pilot wants to know if you have an estimated weight for him."

I gritted my teeth. "He's big."

Echo spoke something into her microphone. The helicopter banked and descended. I held the side of a seat for balance.

We leveled, and Naomi tried to sit up. I moved behind her to help.

Echo took her arms. "Easy now. Watch her side."

Naomi sat up, shivering, her hand in mine, with fingers white and purple.

I looked at my own, pale and trembling. "Where do you keep your extra wool blankets?"

"Outside compartment." Echo reached back to the cot. "But we have this one." She unfolded it and wrapped it around Naomi's shoulders.

The pilot descended toward the flare-marked landing zone.

The skids soon rocked and settled on the ground. Echo slid the door open.

I climbed over the gurney and shouted by her helmet. "Stay with Naomi. I need to cut the rod he is impaled on and stabilize it."

"How're you going to get him back here?"

"You and me, the pilot, and the hiker's friend will all need to carry him out on the cot."

"How far?"

"Couple hundred yards, maybe."

Echo reached behind her seat and brought out a handheld radio. "Take this and our trauma bag. Let me know when you're ready to meet up."

"Okay." I dropped to the ground and hunched as I strode toward the tree line. I found the shoes I'd thrown off before I swam out for Naomi and pulled them on. My wet clothes pressed to my body. The gusts from the helicopter blades intensified the biting cold.

The engines whined down as I entered the forest. I made a beeline to Eli's shed. Two barn-style doors stood unlocked at its entrance. I pushed up an iron lever and pulled one side open. It was dank and smelled like sawdust and oil. A pegboard behind a painted workbench held an array of tools. A wood-handled hacksaw hung on the end. I snatched it and broke into a jog up the road, alternating hands with the tool so I could warm my fingers in a fist. I slowed to a stop at the spike trench and blew hot air into my hands.

The female hiker was red-faced and anxious. "Where've you been?"

I ignored her and went straight to James, who was nodding off. A quick pulse check confirmed my fears. I couldn't feel anything at his wrist and only a faint tapping at his neck. His blood pressure was tanking.

"James, I need to cut this bar off beneath your leg."

He grunted, eyelids hanging low.

"James?"

We didn't have long. I dropped the hacksaw and unzipped the helicopter medical bag. Inside I found a one-liter IV fluid bag and spiked it with tubing. I started a large bore IV in James's arm and ran the saline wide open.

"Here." I handed the bag to the female hiker. "Hold this up and squeeze it." I wound bandage dressings in an X pattern around James's leg with extra rolls beside the spike to stabilize it once I cut it free.

I gripped the spike under his calf and set the hacksaw to work.

The metal stripped loose in shavings. "Is he your boyfriend?"

"Husband."

I nodded. "How much would you say he weighs?"

"Does it matter?"

My forearm burned. "Yes. For the helicopter."

"Is he too heavy? After all this are they not going to take him?"

"How heavy?"

She stared at James. "I think he's around two-eighty."

Seventy pounds per person if we four-pointed the cot. It was going to be a painful walk back to the helicopter.

James began to slump his head forward. I enlisted his wife to support it and make sure he kept breathing.

Five minutes later I had the spike ready to sheer. I radioed for Echo and the pilot and made the final cut.

My fingers felt like they were going to fall off by the time we cleared the tree line. James's wife proved to be a good hand, as demanding of herself to carry her own corner as she had been toward me since I first came upon them. We'd stopped five times en route and now, with the bird in clear view, pressed on to our goal.

Naomi lay on the opposite end of the crew cabin, propped by the seat with the cut harness. We leveraged James up onto the lazy Susan–mounted cot, and Echo maneuvered him into the helicopter and locked it in place. She climbed into her seat, and the wife stepped up on the skid.

Echo put out a hand. "I'm afraid we won't be able to take you."

The engines screamed to life, followed by a deep rocket-engine roar. The rotors began a slow turn.

"Where are you taking him?"

"Washoe County Hospital in Reno."

The woman squeezed her husband's hand. "I'll be there soon, baby. I'll be there soon." She stepped down.

Echo grabbed the door handle. "Drive safe. Don't rush. We'll take good care of him."

She slid the door shut. The rotors became a translucent disc. The *chop-chop* sound of the blades increased. I led James's wife back to the tree line. She walked sideways, forearm by her face, watching. We found shelter in the trees and watched the bird lift about fifty feet off the ground—and then stutter and hover in midair.

Something wasn't right.

The helicopter jostled, then began a shaky descent toward the landing zone. Dirt and sand flew and it touched down. I told the wife to stay behind a tree and fought my way through the dust storm back to the helicopter. I glanced at the pilot, making sure I had the okay to approach. He gave a thumbs-up.

Echo opened her door and shouted, "We're too heavy. We'll need to take Naomi in and come back for James."

Naomi rose, shaking her head. "No. He's critical. Take him."

"Absolutely not. I'm not going to leave you here when you could have internal injuries."

Naomi's eyebrows tented. "This patient is bleeding out. I'll have Jonathan here."

Echo pushed her lips together. "Okay." She handed the spare trauma bag back to me. "She's your patient. We'll do a hot off-load at County and come back for her. Thirty minutes, tops."

"All right. I've got her." I walked around the nose of the helicopter and met up with Naomi, who already had her door open.

She held a hand around her belly and the other on the heavy blanket over her shoulders. She draped one foot toward the skid.

I extended my arms. "Here. I'll carry you."

She leaned toward me. I lifted, and she shrieked.

"You okay?"

Her eyes shut. "Just get me to where I can lie down."

I kept my head bowed, tromping with heavy legs away from the bird. Pellets sprayed my neck. James's wife came out from the trees and lent help carrying Naomi.

We set her down behind a thick tree, the helicopter blaring and rising over the bay behind us. Tear lines streaked her cheeks.

I rested my hands on my knees, breathing hard.

"What happened," the wife said.

"Too heavy. They'll be back for her."

I crouched next to Naomi. Her face tightened in pain. Her lips were a shade of purple, jaw shaking with the cold. The pulse at her wrist felt strong and regular, but rapid. Her breathing was labored.

James's wife stared up the hill. "My car . . ."

"Is that your Prius at the main road?" I said.

"Yes."

"It's a long drive. Be careful."

"Aren't you coming?"

I glanced at Naomi, her eyes shut and her teeth gritted. I shook my head. "The helicopter will be back before we'd even reach the hilltop. You go."

"Okay." She started, then turned. "Thank you."

I nodded, and she took off up the hill.

The last noise of the helicopter faded. I pulled the stethoscope from the trauma pack and listened to Naomi's lungs. Clear, but diminished bilaterally with her shallow breaths. Difficult to tell if she had a punctured lung. Her respiratory difficulty could have been stemming from the pain of the fractured ribs alone.

"Here." I hooked up an oxygen mask and strapped it on her face.

The sounds of the forest returned—the sway of pine needles in the breeze, the intermittent skitter of squirrels. The knocking of a woodpecker drummed in the distance.

What were the chances that Trent still lurked?

Dusk encroached. The trees formed a labyrinth of olive and russet. I felt around my belt for the Beretta.

Gone.

CHAPTER 40

Naomi shivered. "What is it?"

"I lost something in the lake."

"Hope it. Wasn't. Important."

"We need to get you out of those wet clothes."

"Bet you'd. Like that."

I smiled. "I won't lie to you. Come on. Let's get you in the cabin."

"Uh-uh."

"You're hypothermic, Naomi." I wasn't doing too well myself.

She shook her head. "Hurts too much to move."

"What if I carry you?"

She looked at me as if I had lost my mind.

Daylight. Was she still able to think clearly? For that matter, was I? "The temperature"—my voice vibrated—"is dropping by the minute. You're injured and we need to get you warm."

"I can't take moving that far."

I shifted my weight, searching for a solution. If I couldn't bring her to the cabin, I'd bring the cabin to her. "I'm going to get firewood and see if Eli has spare clothes." I drew the wool blanket together in front of her. "You going to be okay here?"

Her jaw quivered. "Yes."

I circled my hands behind her ears and kissed her. "I'll be right back."

I ran toward the cabin, unable to differentiate between my

feet and the ground, between my bare arms and the skin covered by my shirt.

Every shadow looked like Trent.

His gun had to be out of ammo. Mine was at the bottom of the lake. I had no choice but to focus on providing warmth. The helicopter would be back, but not before the temperature dropped below freezing.

The door to the cabin hung open, the inside dark. I found the kitchen drawer with the matches and lit the table lantern. The flame grew bright, a soft-cornered triangle. The slight warmth from it lifted my spirits. In the front closet I found two down jackets and beanies. I stripped off my wet T-shirt, buttoned up the jacket, and pulled a beanie to my ears. I tucked four logs from the fireplace hearth under my arm and from the front doorway squinted through the fading light to see Naomi. I could just make out her form sitting beside the tree.

I worked my way back to her, set the lamp and logs down, and fitted a beanie over her head. I held up the jacket.

She shook her head. "Fire first."

Using one of the logs I dug a shallow hole in the duff and then set the wood up in a crib with pine needles in the spaces. I lit pine needles and twigs with the lantern flame and at first created little more than thick gray smoke. But zephyrs blew in off the water, fed the incipient fire, and it flashed bright yellow. We drew close to it, warming our hands.

Night enveloped us. The cabin disappeared.

"It's okay," she said.

"What?"

"You don't have to go back to get anything. Just stay."

I wrapped the jacket over her blanketed shoulders. "How's this for now?"

"Good."

I heard water lapping but couldn't make out the lake through the trees. The landing zone was pitch-black.

"Naomi, I need to get more flares from Eli's car."

"What about the fire?"

"I'd have to build four separate ones. There's no guarantee they'll stay lit."

"Don't leave."

"The moon will be even thinner tonight."

She exhaled and stared into the darkness. "You're right. They won't land without it marked."

I picked up the oil lamp. "It's just up the hill. Couple minutes."

Not wanting to end up in the trench like James, I trekked up the middle of the dirt road with eyes fixed on the ground in front of me. My lamplight soon reflected off the chrome on the Scout. I scanned the dirt in front of it. A long shadow bent across the road, and my eyes adjusted and distinguished the shape of the trench.

I heard the strike of a car ignition and the muted rumble of an engine. I lifted the lantern and peered through the Scout's windshield.

Vacant.

No exhaust from the rear.

The engine sound grew louder with the sound of tires spinning over dirt.

Behind me.

I spun around. Headlights flipped on. Green halos danced. A Jeep barreled into view. The transmission shifted gears and roared head on.

I tossed the lantern at it and dove to the side. Glass crashed on metal with a burst of light. The Jeep skidded sideways and I rolled, the rear end swiping over my head. I collided with a boulder on the roadside. The Jeep rocked to a stop, half a foot from the trench, fire raging from the hood and the windshield. Knobby tires spun and engaged in reverse. I scrambled over the rock and jumped between trees. Metal struck the boulder behind me. Tires spun again. The Jeep reversed and took off down the road.

Naomi.

I darted between tree trunks and sprinted after it. No plan. I just chased the glow, running into the road, through a trail of smoke and exhaust and dirt.

Naomi screamed.

Metal crunched. The fire grew.

Helicopter blades beat overhead.

I came upon the scene, the Jeep mashed against a tree, its grill concave. Fire extended from the hood to the fabric top. Inside, the driver lay slumped over the wheel, flames spreading into the passenger compartment.

"Jonathan!"

Naomi lay in the dirt, sheltered on the opposite side of the tree. I ran and dropped beside her. "Are you hurt?"

She shook her head. "No. No. I'm okay."

I stood. "Hold on."

The fire became a blaze, the heat so intense I couldn't get close to the passenger door. I scuffled around to the driver's side, blocking my face, coughing through the smoke. The door looked jammed, folded in from the impact. I tried the latch without success, metal burning at my touch. I tripped back over a stone, crashing to the dirt. Fire reflected and shimmered in the driver's-door window.

I palmed the rock, made my feet, and smashed the glass. Smoke belched out. I lifted the driver's head off the wheel.

"Trent. Trent!"

The interior flashed into fire. I ducked low, scorching flames forcing me back.

The beating of the helicopter came from just beyond the tree line.

Echo appeared at the edge of the glow. "Naomi!"

"Over here," I led her to the tree.

Her eyes were frantic. "What happened?"

"Take her other side." I pulled Naomi's arm around my shoulder and lifted with Echo. "Let's just get out of here."

CHAPTER 41

AprisEvac descended on the rooftop of the Washoe County Medical Center.

Naomi, despite initial obstinance over not lying on the cot, acquiesced and rested her head back, falling asleep in minutes with a hanging IV bag tethered to her arm. I was sure that only a flight nurse could find repose like that in a helicopter.

Being a bit lighter than James, I found passage in the third jump seat, which sported an intact seatbelt harness. Had James been even thirty pounds lighter, Naomi could have ridden in on the first flight.

We neared the pad, and in the white roof lights I recognized two of three ER nurses standing with a gurney near the elevator vestibule—Sherri, a red-haired woman in her thirties, and Mitch, a bald man with a biker build and faded tats half hidden by his scrub sleeves. The third nurse was a skinny, bespectacled man with thinning black hair. The helicopter touched down. The pilot flipped switches and the engines shut off with a fading whistle. The nurses hunched over and approached.

Echo slid the door open by the cot. Sherri caught my eye with a look of surprise. I saw my reflection in the opposite door glass. Fat upper lip, soot marks across my cheeks, dried blood at my nostrils. Mitch glanced at me—an inquisitive expression on his face.

Naomi woke and groaned, returning a hand to her side. Spectacles and Mitch took one end of the cot. I helped Echo on the opposite side, stepping onto the skid with it and transferring Naomi onto their gurney.

She took my hand. I stroked her hair. "You'll be taken good care of."

They pushed her toward the vestibule and I lagged behind, feigning to search the helicopter cabin for something. The elevator doors opened and the four got in. With the gurney there wasn't much room for another.

I sidestepped to the nose of the helicopter, careful to stay away from the hot steel tube Naomi had showed me, and waved them on. "I'll get the next one."

Echo hit the button for the ER. Spectacles squinted at me. The steel doors drew together.

The pilot wrote on a clipboard in the cockpit. I stood there, unsure what to do next, my legs bone cold with the rooftop breeze. Digital numbers flipped in descending order above the elevator doors.

Naomi would be cared for. But I was a wanted man.

Security cameras angled from the rooftop corners. I brought a hand to my brow and walked to the vestibule. Hospital security would likely want to visit with me.

The helicopter rotors turned at merry-go-round speed. The pilot got out and rummaged through a rear compartment on the tail boom. I scratched my neck.

Now where?

I hit the call button for the elevator and patted my thighs.

In the original County Hospital—the old brick-and-mortar structure now overshadowed by the modern steel-and-glass towers—Dr. Eli kept a small office in the basement, one that had been designated decades ago for use by the mortician. It was tiny and so removed within the hospital that administration had kept it for the medical examiner's use. But Eli, reclusive lab dweller that he was, rarely made it over, preferring to work in the glass-walled office adjacent to the morgue examination area.

If I could get to the old building, I'd have a place to hide.

The elevator dinged. I stepped inside and pushed the button for the Operating Room floor. If I was going to make it to Eli's office, I would need a new outfit.

Anesthesiologist Dr. Flynn had been a great asset in my education, permitting me to practice intubations on patients down in the operating room. It was through him that I'd years ago acquired the elevator code for the OR, secured my own locker in the doctors' shower facility, and had easy access to surgical scrubs.

I strapped on a pale blue surgical cap and a face mask, complementing the scrubs I'd found. I exited the locker room and walked down the hallway between the operating rooms. Wearing a face mask in the hall was a bit unconventional but not outrageous. To be safe I snatched a clipboard from a break room and moved at a brisk pace, feigning a summons by the severity of information found on the clipboard paperwork. In reality, it told me that the seventeenth annual orthopedic luncheon would be hosted downtown next week. But people made way for me and the assumed authority I possessed.

The clipboard, mightier than the sword.

I progressed to the elevator, made the first floor, and snaked my way uninhibited through the narrowing corridors that led to the old hospital. I descended to the cool cellar that Eli had showed me years back, almost as a novelty. I remembered following his tour with the curiosity of one visiting the Winchester Mystery House in San Jose. Painted white plumbing hung low from the ceiling. HVAC ducting required one to bend beneath it. There were no security cameras. Dim-wattage incandescent bulbs lit the corridors. At the end of one hall stood a white door with a thin black plaque. I wiped a layer of dust from its title—*Coroner*.

The corridor remained empty. I tried the knob.

Locked.

Remembering Eli's comment about keeping a key near places he didn't go to regularly, I felt the molding above the door and found one. I blew the dust off and slipped it into the lock.

I pulled the brass chain on Eli's desk lamp and closed the door behind me. Three bookshelf-lined walls stood in the lampshade's green pall. I slumped back in the chair and tossed my surgical mask and cap on the desk. The room smelled of old plaster and stale air.

Trent had to have been working with Kurtz. They knew about the cabin. They knew we were going there. But more than that. Somehow they knew that Naomi was connected to me. Had Trent sabotaged her seat harness? She would've been killed had she been anywhere but over the water.

I pulled out my phone to dial Eli, pushed the on button twice, and groaned. Apparently it wasn't waterproof. A Touch-Tone phone sat on the table. I dialed Eli's cell from memory and waited.

It went to voice mail.

I hung up and tried again, with the same result. "Call me" was all I said on the message, forgetting until after hanging up that he would not be able to reach me.

What about Naomi? What made me think she'd be safe even in the hospital? We needed more answers.

I rested my neck on the chair back. I needed to find a way to get Naomi out of the ER once she was treated. I'd found a place of short respite. A hole in the ground. But I couldn't stay.

I grabbed my forehead.

If I met up with Naomi, assuming she was well enough to move, I could get her a wheelchair and we could leave together and find a way to meet up with Eli.

It would look too strange to walk around with a full face mask in the ER. Instead, I strapped it on my chin and stood with clipboard in hand.

Off to the lion's den.

Activity buzzed in the emergency room—EKG techs pushing carts, phlebotomists with trays of blood-draw vials, a host of nurses I knew too well. If I was going to be recognized anywhere in the hospital, this was the place. I remained deliberate in my movements, using the clipboard to shield my face. I examined the room-assignment board and searched for Naomi by her last name, Foster.

Farmer. Fenell. Foust.

No Naomi.

Sherri pushed a cart into a patient room. Mitch wrote on a chart at a counter. I needed to find out where she had been moved.

I turned and bumped into a nurse.

Spectacles.

I looked down. "Excuse me. Sorry." I strode for the exit, only glancing back when I'd made the door.

Spectacles stared at me, a phone already at his ear.

CHAPTER 42

I found myself in the ambulance entrance breezeway—a narrow corridor with a stash of backboards leaning against one wall and a door to a small room with a desk for charting by paramedics. Behind me were the sliding doors to the emergency room, in front, the automatic doors to the ambulance parking.

I'd been marked in the scrubs I now wore. Inside the hospital I'd show up on every corridor security camera. The outside grounds and parking lots were too wide open.

"Jonathan."

My muscles tightened.

Out of the corner of my eye I saw Bones emerge from the charting room.

"Bones."

"What are you doing here?"

I escorted him back to the room.

"Hey, Jonathan. What's going on?"

My heart drummed. I locked the door behind us.

He shook loose and sat on the desk. "Nice scrubs."

"Give me your uniform."

"What?"

I pulled off my shirt. "Just do it."

He laughed, shaking his head. "I know I said if you ever need anything . . . But I kind of need this outfit right now. I'm on until midnight."

I kicked off my shoes and dropped my pants, shoving the scrubs in his chest. "Tell dispatch you're out of service for biohazard. You had a call with a ton of blood and emesis, and you need to swing by Aprisa to retrieve another uniform from your locker."

"You're serious."

"Never been more."

"And now what? Where are you going?"

"I have to find Naomi. Then Dr. Eli."

"I actually just saw her."

"Where?"

"A guy from transport was wheeling her out of the ER."

"Do you know where to?"

"Yeah." He looked down and to the side. "Yeah. I said hi and asked her if she was all right and what happened. She said it was a long story but that she'd be okay." He looked up. "She said they were taking her to the floor for overnight observation."

"Third or fourth level?"

"Not sure."

"Okay. Great. Now take off your clothes."

He started unbuttoning his uniform shirt. "I've had nightmares about this. Only we're in the ambulance and you have a Swedish acc—"

"Shh." I put a finger to my lips. Conversation carried in from the hallway and then dissipated.

He tossed me his shirt and I squeezed into it. His brass name badge showed his last name only.

He unbuckled his pants and paused. "You know, if it ever gets out about us being in here like this, I—"

"Bones, would you just—"

"Okay. All right." He pulled out his wallet, keys, and cell phone.

I eyed the phone.

"What?" His shoulders slumped. "You want my cell too, don't you?" He stood in his tighty-whities, hands on his hips, and stared at the ceiling. He looked the diving figure in Mousetrap. He handed me his cell phone and two twenties from his wallet.

"You're a true friend, Bones."

I tucked in the shirt but had to leave the pants unbuttoned and secured with the belt. I turned the doorknob. "Hey, Bones?"

"Yeah?"

"Do you have your Aprisa ball cap?"

"Sure. Back in the rig."

"In your backpack, front-side compartment?"

"That's it."

"Thanks again."

He waved a hand, still in his underwear. "Ah, don't mention it."

I walked with head bowed out to the ambulance, opened the compartment door, and retrieved the hat from Bones's bag. I seated it low on my brow and reentered the hospital through a different set of doors, ones that led through the patient waiting area.

I avoided eye contact and kept my hands pocketed, bypassing the elevator and opting for the stairs. At the third floor I exited and approached a nurses' station, where a blond-haired woman in scrubs sat with her back to me, sorting through files.

I stepped to the counter. "Excuse me. I'm looking for a patient named Naomi Foster." The nurse spun around, and I recognized her at once. "Bobbi?"

"Hey!"

"Hi. I thought you—"

"Worked at Saint Mary's? I still do. But I was offered a good per diem gig here. It's floor nursing, but hey, easy money, right?"

"Right." I adjusted the ballcap.

"What about you? You must've cleared up all that trouble with Aprisa and everything."

"Yes. Yeah. All that."

"That was fast."

I nodded. "Yeah."

"I never believed it. Just didn't sound like you, you know?"

"I do."

She leaned back and played with a pencil. "I bet you didn't just come here to chat with me, did you? Who'd you want to see again?"

"Naomi Foster."

She rolled the chair back and shuffled through files behind her. "She just come in?"

"Had to've been within the last hour or so."

Bobbi shook her head. "I'm not seeing her. You sure she's on the third floor?"

"Could be upstairs."

"Hold on, let me check." She typed on a keyboard and hunched her shoulders. "There she is. Room 424."

"Excellent." I checked the corridors and lowered my voice. "And hey, Bobbi?"

"What's up?"

"My supervisor doesn't know I came up here to check on a patient, and they've been super strict lately. So . . . if anyone asks . . ."

"I never even saw you." She grinned.

I tapped the counter and backed away. "Thanks so much."

"Sure thing." She glanced at my name badge, paused, and then smirked. "Good talking with you . . . Mr. McCoy."

I froze midstep, remembering that I had Bones's uniform on. My mouth hung open, not sure what to say.

"Go." She waved a hand. "I don't even want to know."

CHAPTER 43

A hive of security officers buzzed around the fourth-floor elevator lobby.

It made sense that, since I arrived with Naomi, they'd expect me to try to visit her. I took a second glance through the window in the stairwell door. There was no way to get through that without being stung.

I wanted to punch the wall, to break something.

I descended in a slow simmer, each flight adding to my anger. If Naomi couldn't be reached, then I'd have to meet up with Eli on my own. Perhaps he could get her discharged.

I crossed the parking lot and descended the morgue stairs. I remembered the code thanks to Eli's gallows humor. Standard casket dimensions—eighty-four inches by twenty-eight inches.

A metal click coincided with a green light. I pressed against the door and took a last look up the stairs that led to the parking lot. Most spaces up there were empty, office employees gone for the night, brightness from the light standards washed out the evening sky.

Shadows filled the basement hallway. A single fluorescent security light shone in the middle of the exam room. Through the glass wall the space looked deserted, sterile, and cold. I opened the steel-framed door. The air inside was quite different than I expected.

Hot.

Oven hot.

I stepped in, letting the door ease shut. "Eli?"

The exam tables were empty, Eli's office dark and decorated by small glowing lights of computer peripherals.

Something tapped.

I shot a glance at the wall of body drawers.

"Hello?"

I heard it again. Like a pebble in a dryer.

My throat was parched. I couldn't swallow.

Where was the light switch?

The entry wall was all glass. I couldn't make out a switch on the others.

I shouted. "Eli?"

The tapping stopped.

I froze.

It started again.

I leaned my ear to it, trying to isolate it.

Tap. Tap. Tap.

The refrigeration drawers mocked me. Stacked four high, five wide. Carcasses waiting for examination.

All dead bodies.

Tap. Tap. Tap.

I moved closer.

Tap. Tap. Tap.

Past the exam tables.

Up to the drawer wall. I put my hand on it. "Eli?"

The sound ceased.

I looked around, searching for anything out of place. Any sign of struggle, any clue.

The tapping came again. A glint caught my eye.

At the far end of the exam room. By the crematory oven.

On the floor.

I inched toward it, away from the drawers. The sound grew louder. The object was small, metallic, and if I turned my head just right, it reflected the security light.

Tap. Tap. Tap.

I didn't realize what it was until I picked it up and held it in my palm.

I brought a shaking hand to my mouth and stared at a brass pendant with singed and discolored edges—the etched type still legible. . . .

Do No Harm.

"Eli!"

I spun toward the crematory oven, now comprehending the tapping and knocking to be coming from it, like a car engine cooling down in a garage. I seized the lever for the oven doors and cranked open its steel jaws. Heat dispersed. And through the waving glow within I saw a flat body tray on the rollers. A long pile of ashen remains lay upon it.

I squeezed my fist tight. The pendant dug into my palm. Breath escaped me. My head became light. I stumbled backward, catching myself on an exam table.

My grip loosened, blood trickling from my hand.

Murderers!

CHAPTER 44

I collapsed as if someone had struck me in the gut.

What now?

Focus.

Think.

I strode to Eli's office and shoved through the door. My fingers found a light switch.

Computer, microscopes, a specimen fridge, a small safe. He'd said he was on to something, that he was nearing a conclusion. That he needed to be *sure.*

I forced myself to concentrate and sat down at the keyboard. I tapped the space bar. A log-in screen materialized. Wiggling fingers over the keys, I thought of obvious passwords.

eli123

elipetrov123

His deceased wife—*Maureen*

maureen123

Casket dimensions—*8428*

No luck. I could be there all night and still not get it. Even if I was close with any of my attempts, the variations alone . . .

I tilted my head back on the chair. Eli's pendant twin fell into my sternal notch. I lifted it up—brilliant brass, its edges unmarred. The Hippocratic Oath.

Maybe . . . .

I typed *hippocrates* into the password field.

The entry screen flicked with a start-up tune. A desktop image of Eli and Maureen appeared. They held glasses in toast—their fortieth anniversary. It had been a great party.

Icons appeared. The third folder down read *Poisoning Analysis*. It held dozens of files. Many were filled with lab values and data. But one was entitled *Letell_Conclusions*. It had the current date. I opened it and skimmed to the end. The last sentence said it all.

> Therefore, based on the poisoning data collected and evaluated from Simon Letell's liver and kidneys, there can be little doubt that the primary cause of death was secondary to morphine sulfate overdose.

Morphine.

Of course.

When I first worked on Letell, I'd injected just enough Narcan to reverse the opiate effects and illicit consciousness, however brief.

I scrolled down, expecting to see more. But that was it. The end of the report. I closed it out.

One more file stood out, simply titled *JT_NF*.

I let the cursor rest atop it. Jonathan Trestle and Naomi Foster? I double-clicked. Gone were any semblances of legal format and data documentation. This was a personal note.

> Dearest Jonathan and Naomi,
>
> If you're reading this, then we've likely been separated and the situation further devolved.
>
> Time runs thin. There's much to explain, but understand this— the murders happened by means of morphine sulfate overdose. After all my searching for some complex and obscure poison, it turned out to be a common opiate. The evidence suggests that it

was injected—I've found points of insertion at jugular veins in two of the bodies, though I'm sure an intramuscular injection of the same massive quantities would prove just as lethal.

As a precaution I've locked two vials of the antidote Narcan in the lab safe—one for each of you. The safe code is 5–12–9, the alphabetical-numeric equivalent to my name.

The note ended there, as though he intended to write more but had been cut off. I walked over to the safe, spun Eli's code, and pushed down the lever. Inside were two vials of Narcan next to two needled syringes. I held one of the small containers up to the light.

In the back of the safe lay a handwritten note.

J and N,

I leave these with the hope that they'll never be needed.

A scream shot down the stairs.

Scuffling, and the sound of footsteps. A muffled cry.

I flicked off the office light and scampered down behind Eli's desk. I pulled back on the syringe plunger, uncapped the needle, and held a vial of Narcan over it. My hands trembled so hard I couldn't land the sharp on the rubber membrane. I poked my hand twice before inserting the needle into the vial.

A muted scream.

A man's voice.

I injected air in the vial and drew up the liquid.

The exam room door slammed open. Feet shuffled.

I capped the needle and palmed it like a knife. From the desk's edge I peered out.

Dr. Kurtz cupped a hand over Naomi's mouth. In his other

hand he held a needled syringe by her neck. He jerked Naomi into the exam room. She hobbled, eyes wide and frightened.

Kurtz tightened his grip on her face. He forced her head back, exposing her neck. "It's not that big of a morgue, Jonathan."

He stopped out of sight near the center of the exam room. "It may help you to know that I have a rather sharp object pointed at a cohort of yours."

Naomi yelled.

"Pipe down."

Scuffling.

"Stop. Now."

She quieted.

I slipped the Narcan syringe into the side pocket of Bones's medic pants and stood in the doorway to Eli's office. "Here."

Kurtz smiled, hair hanging wild, his round glasses stained with dried sweat spots around the edges. A vein bulged at the side of his forehead. "Jo-ha-nathan. There you are. Took you a bit." A scarlet trail trickled down Naomi's neck.

I locked eyes with her. "What're you doing, Kurtz?"

"It isn't obvious by now? I honestly expected more from you. Maybe you really did cheat on your MCATs."

His focus shifted to Eli's computer screen in the office. A flash of concern broke his air of confidence. He sidestepped with Naomi, positioning himself between me and the exit. "Been doing some reading, have you, Jonny-boy? Like a good med student? Catching up on a little research?"

Naomi torqued the pinky finger of the hand covering her mouth.

Kurtz shouted.

"Jonathan!" she said. "He's going to kill us both. Don't—"

Kurtz jerked her back by the hair and kicked behind her knees. She hit the floor. I lunged forward.

He waved the syringe. "Back off. Off!"

I took two slow steps backward.

"Farther."

I took two more. He stepped on Naomi's calves and kept a violent grip on her hair. Her neck craned, forcing her to stare at the ceiling.

His face shook, covered with sweat. "It was working."

"What was?"

"Aprisa. All of it. Half a dozen cities all lined out."

"What are you talking about?"

He grinned. "Who do you think made Aprisa everything it is?"

"So being medical director was a front."

"A bonus. The company has to look like a community endeavor, not a corporate one. It benefits the many."

"You've been lying about the true costs."

"I do more with less. That's good business."

"You mean it's lucrative."

"And going nationwide, Jonathan. The public loves it. It's cheap, not tax subsidized, and an ambulance will always be there."

"Eventually."

"Doesn't matter."

"Tell that to Letell. Who'd you bribe to get the county to sign off on it, Kurtz?"

He jutted his lower jaw.

I walked to an exam table. "You have a business model that could make you a fortune, but with one hiccup—you have to cover up the fact that it doesn't actually work."

"There's no turning back. Didn't we talk about this? About what it takes to succeed? You were on your way. You had it all laid out. But you just couldn't shut up."

"Is it just the hope of riches, Kurtz?"

His eyes squinted.

I ran my fingers over the cool flat metal. "No. No, you need the money now, don't you? You owe somebody."

He huffed. "Some folks are not very forgiving of their debtors."

"I used to look up to you. I thought you cared about people, but what you cared about was buying your way into power. Is that how you became the med school's youngest dean?"

"Don't pontificate to me. Self-interest drives us all." He yanked Naomi's hair. "The shrewd will always rule the ignorant."

"You bribed and borrowed, and now your plans are falling apart. That's it, isn't it? Took a fat loan from some shady characters, and now your neck is on the line. How were you going to repay it, Kurtz?"

He shifted his head and swallowed.

Sweat rolled down my spine. "You're siphoning off Aprisa profits to pay the man. Easy money when you can doctor the response times."

He shook his head. "I was wrong." He raised his eyebrows. "I was wrong, Jonathan. You actually are a bright fellow." He cracked his neck.

"You've lied and murdered. How much did Trent get paid, only to sacrifice his own life?"

Kurtz pulled a syringe from his shirt pocket and slid it on the floor toward me. "You know, it's been *so* pleasant chatting like this. But what you need to do now, if you want your girlfriend to live, is uncap that needle and shoot yourself up with its contents. No questions asked."

An air bubble floated near the plunger. "What is it?"

"Ah, ah. No questions."

"You expect me to inject myself with this? Why should I believe that you won't kill Naomi?"

"A narc-popping paramedic suicide is easy to establish. You're a criminal now. Who's going to question your death?" He twisted his grip on Naomi. "As for this one, I've taken persuasive measures with her family to make sure she stays quiet, indefinitely."

I brushed my hand over the pants pocket with the Narcan. I had to hope Kurtz's syringe held only morphine.

"It's simple, Jonathan. If you want her to live."

Naomi jerked and shoved his hand away. "He's lying. He'll kill us b—"

He jabbed the needle into her neck.

"No." I threw out my hands.

He set his thumb on the plunger. "Do it." He started depressing the syringe. "Pick. It. Up."

"Okay. Stop. Okay. I'll do what you say."

I reached for the needle on the floor.

CHAPTER 45

I stood with the syringe.

The muscles in Naomi's throat shifted when she swallowed.

Playing chess with Eli, at times I had been filled with the utmost of confidence—the game was mine and nothing foreseen could bring me down.

And I was right. Nothing I predicted ever did lose the game for me.

It was the unseen mistake that had damned me, bearing its ill-tasting fruit half a dozen moves later.

I couldn't see any other way.

I uncapped the needle and placed it at a rounded vein in my forearm. I broke my skin with the beveled tip, blood shooting into the liquid chamber in a twisted cloud of crimson.

I fixed my gaze on him. "Now take the needle from her neck."

He scoffed.

"I'm doing what you said. Just let me remember her face, when it's not in pain. Please. Just take away the needle for a moment and let me at least say good-bye."

The skin around his eyes tightened. "Why not?" He pulled the needle out and loosened his grip on her hair.

She lowered her chin. Her pupils were large.

My breathing quickened. "Good-bye, Naomi."

Tears raced down her cheeks. She shook her head. "Don't do it."

"It's the only choice."

Kurtz blinked.

I sprang, yanking the needle from my arm.

He shifted and swung at Naomi. My hand met his wrist, but the force was too great, knocking my fingers away and driving the needle deep into the base of her neck.

We collided and toppled over, crashing to the floor behind her. He latched a grip on my hand that held the other syringe. I clenched his throat. He clawed at my face. I forced the needle closer to him, and he pushed against me.

He maneuvered his feet and leveraged his weight. I skidded up against the wall to bring myself up. He focused his momentum on the syringe, spinning me back toward an exam table. He drove my hand toward the sharp metal corner.

I shouted and dropped the needle, blood spilling from a jagged gash on my hand. A fist drove into my jaw and knocked me from my feet. I struck my head on the tile and the room blackened.

Vision returned in blurry backlit images. Three of Kurtz staggered toward me. I pushed to my feet and swung in vain. My knuckles grazed a shirt button. His form focused, hazy at the edges.

I tackled him, driving toward the table. He hit the edge and arced backward. Lifting his legs, I flipped him onto it. He flailed to roll off, but I caught him by the shoulders and pinned him supine. I drove a salvo of face punches, gripping his collar in the other fist. A spider web of blood streaked across his cheeks.

I struck him.

Again and again and again.

Until the skin sheared from my knuckles and his face became a swollen mass of purple and red.

His arms went limp.

I brought my fist in the air. With shaking realization, I wondered if I'd killed him.

Beyond the foot of the table, Naomi lay unconscious on the floor, hair fanned over the tile, arms draped out.

A sharp sting burned my neck.

I brought my fingers up to find a syringe dangling like a half-broken branch. From the table, Kurtz bared his bloody teeth.

I yanked out the empty syringe and staggered with the sickening realization.

Kurtz burro-kicked me in the chest. I stumbled backward but stayed on my feet. He charged, driving me into the vestibule wall.

The glass shattered. A steel cross member caught my legs below the knees. I struck the ground. A dozen sharp points sent pain across my back. My head clouded. I couldn't focus. Kurtz stood at the other side of the wall, hands at his sides, shoulders heaving.

His voice sounded distant and muffled. "This ends now."

He yanked Naomi up by the shoulders and dragged her across the room.

Past the exam table. Past Eli's office.

Toward the crematory oven.

The world spun and blurred, and feeling left my limbs.

CHAPTER 46

Numbing casts encircled my arms.

I forced a hand to the side pocket in my pants, blinking through the blur to plunge my fingers inside, using more shoulder than anything. I managed a semi-fist and withdrew my hand. The end of the Narcan syringe lay wedged between two fingers. It hung up at the lip of the pocket and fell to the floor.

Respirations became labored. I fought for deeper breaths but found no relief. The room rotated. I shook my head. Haze encroached at the edges of my vision.

I dragged a hand along the floor to the Narcan syringe and captured it in my palm. I bent my elbow and heaved my torso, propping on my side.

If ever I needed to nail an IV, this was it.

I bit down on the plastic needle cover and pulled the syringe free. Sweat drops blurred my eyes. I wiped them with my upper arm.

The room grew hotter.

A cannon of a vein snaked through the crook of one arm—my best shot.

My stomach flip-flopped. Bile coated my throat. I saw two syringes, then three, four. I tried to breathe but was out of breath.

I plopped a hand on my forearm, aimed at the vein, and drove the needle like a diver into a pool.

Shadowed burgundy flashed into the catheter hub.

I set my thumb on the plunger but couldn't depress it. Shifting my hand to get the heel of my palm against it, I cupped the flanges of the syringe and pushed it in.

No finesse about it. I didn't ease it in over two minutes, the way they taught in paramedic school. High-dose Narcan would hit my bloodstream like cold water on a scalding pan.

I tilted my head, waiting in fearful anticipation of what was to come. At best, it would block the action of the morphine long enough for me to have a chance to stop Kurtz. At worst, it could hurtle me into intractable seizures.

This isn't going to feel good.

It screamed in like an eighteen-wheeler—blaring horn and headlights and all.

There was no way to dodge. My mind and body divided through the front grill. A deluge of needles, raining white-hot, pierced my limbs and torso, pinning me to the floor.

It raged and crescendoed.

And ceased.

The world lay silent and barren, a vast desert plain. Then something opened in the sky, a swirling mass of clouds. It spun with violence and descended in a corkscrewing funnel. Raging wind forced into my mouth, down my trachea, expanding my lungs.

I lifted from the ground and the wind turned to rain. Volumes of cold, drenching rain. It dropped me to my knees, the downpour coating my back and neck, my clothes and hair soaked through.

I saw her in front of me.

My mother, lying in the mud.

Life infused her cheeks. Her fingers extended, eyes blinked. She reached out and touched my face.

"Jonathan." Her eyes crinkled at the sides.

A clank echoed.

My mother vanished.

Clarity met my mind. Shattered glass littered the floor. The exam room sweltered, and the rattling of a conveyor began.

I palmed a glass shard and stood, primed like a defib in high whine.

CHAPTER 47

I stepped over the window supports and broken glass wall and strode toward the oven.

Kurtz shielded his face at the opening, guiding Naomi feet-first into the burning gullet. Her body vibrated on the roller tray.

I broke into a sprint and slammed Kurtz to the floor. I jerked the lever knob back, forcing the conveyor to a sudden halt. Heat raged. I grabbed Naomi beneath her arms.

Kurtz shouted. He grabbed my chin and twisted. I thrust an elbow in his chest. His grip loosened.

I pivoted. His fist struck me in the face, knocking me to the floor.

Light refracted in blurry halos.

The conveyor clanked into motion.

I shut both eyes and opened them, my vision clearing enough to see Kurtz bent over the lever, his face maniacal. He shifted position and began pushing Naomi's tray toward the oven himself.

A hammer pounded in my head. I propped myself up, my fingers feeling a jagged edge of broken glass.

I heard Eli. *"Knowing your anatomy will save you."*

I gripped the shard and lunged for Kurtz's legs. He kicked, fists beating at my head. I bear-hugged his thighs and drove the dagger deep behind a knee, slicing through his popliteal artery. I yanked it out and incised the other.

He flailed his arms around his legs, wobbled, then collapsed.

I seized Naomi and heaved away from the tray, tumbling with her to the floor.

Kurtz slumped in a burgeoning pool of blood. He slipped on his elbows, trying and failing repeatedly to get up. He fell back, trembling, his skin pale like rice paper.

I dragged Naomi to the middle of the room.

She wasn't breathing.

I spun. Frantic.

The other Narcan vial. I stumbled into the office and snatched the second syringe and medication from the safe. I drew it up and scuttled to Naomi's side.

She lay with no movement in her chest. Cyanosis encircled her lips.

I stretched out her arm and whipped off my belt, tying it tight around her bicep. I patted the skin in the crook of her arm and prayed for a vein.

A blood vessel emerged. Barely visible. Hardly palpable. But it was all I needed. I inserted the needle and a flash of blood shot back in the chamber.

I fed the Narcan into her vein. And when the needle was dry, I pulled it from her arm and threw it across the room. I tilted her head back, placed my mouth over hers, and breathed.

Her chest rose and relaxed.

I breathed again, her chest inflating and falling—but with no rise of its own. I checked her carotid pulse and felt a faint tapping.

Bones's cell phone sat in my pocket. I pulled it out to dial 9-1-1.

No signal.

We had to get out of the basement. I propped her over my shoulder in a fireman's carry and listed toward the door, broken glass crunching underfoot.

My thighs burned climbing the stairs. I pushed upward, new hope in movement, like we were escaping the hold of a sinking ship.

I staggered through the darkened reception area, banging off a desk, guided only by the streetlights' glow through the front-door glass.

I pushed the bar handle with my hip and struggled onto the front walkway, two patches of lawn on either side of it. I fell to my knees on the grass and laid Naomi on a layer of thin evening frost.

I dialed 9-1-1 and felt again for a pulse at her neck.

No heartbeat.

The phone rang.

I repositioned my fingertips on the side of her throat.

The line picked up. "Nine-one-one dispatch. Please state the nature of your emergency: fire, medical, or police."

"Medical." My voice sounded hoarse, foreign. "I'm on the front lawn of the—"

"Please hold while I transfer you to the medical dispatcher."

Still no pulse.

I traced Naomi's rib cage to the base of her sternum, placed the heel of my palm on her breastbone, and began chest compressions. Her shoulders and head jerked.

Rushing emotion met a dam in my mind. My eyes ran hot and blurry. Streetlamps turned to glaring stars too close to earth.

Heaven upon us.

Hell beneath.

Eighty-four by twenty-eight.

My left brain counted. *One and two and three and four and—*

Dispatch picked up the line. "Please state your medical emergency."

"I'm on the lawn of the morgue at County Hospital with an adult female in full arrest."

"I understand, sir. An ambulance is on its way. Have you checked for a pulse?"

I chucked the phone and shifted to her head, opening the airway and delivering two more breaths. I scooted back and resumed chest compressions.

God, let her live.

The tiny voice of the dispatcher came from the other side of the walkway.

"Sir? Sir, are you there?"

A siren stabbed the night. An air horn blared. Fire whirled in the light bar of an ambulance turning at the end of the block. It raced down the street, engine revving high.

I moved again to Naomi's head.

And for a moment, all the furious efforts of the physical and the closing grasp of the spiritual—all of it shifted.

It was no longer Reno, or evening. My hands became another's— shining like the sun. I felt myself lean beside her, my lips upon hers, and an energy not my own flowed out from me and filled her chest.

Night returned. Dew soaked through to my knees.

A siren shut off. Bones jumped out of the ambulance.

And she drew a breath.

Her eyes flashed opened, pupils dilating.

"Naomi."

I lifted her to my chest.
She brought a hand to my face and mouthed my name.
I shook my head in disbelief. In awe.
In utter desperate awe and gratitude.

CHAPTER 48

I slept so hard I forgot I was in jail.

The thinness of the mattress, the air temperature several degrees too cool, the smell of ammonia—none of it mattered. A valley and a mountain had been traversed in my life. In one day, over two decades, however one measured it.

I had at once the peace of gazing over a ripe field of wheat, the sun low and golden, and the earth uninterrupted on the horizon, mixed with the bitter gall and haunting ache of a loved one departed too soon.

So it was with a sense of newness and empty tomb excitement that I saw my father standing at the door to my cell.

"Hey, Jonner." He was clean-shaven, his hair combed to the side, hovering light and dry with a hair-spray hold. His eyes were clear. He wore an alligator polo and pleated slacks.

I rolled off the bed and walked to the barred door. I stuck my hand through, and he took it, locking thumbs with a clasp.

I was quiet for a moment, then said, "Eli's dead . . . And Kurtz."

He nodded and squeezed my hand, patting it with his other.

"I heard. I am so sorry, Jonathan." He let go of my hand. "Eli was a great man. He was . . . He was always there when you needed him. I really am so sorry." He took a deep breath. "But not for myself anymore."

Voices echoed around the corner.

He took off his glasses. "I had made guilt my home. Ignored you and your life." He looked at the floor. "When you came to the bar, I realized that I still had something to offer. Somewhere along the way, I convinced myself that I'd forfeited that right." He lifted his chin. "I wronged your mother, and I wronged you. Lord knows I can't change that. But you are my son. You are still my son."

Bad Moon stepped behind the guard desk. A mechanical buzz rang from the door. "I'd recommend pulling out your arm lest you want to leave it here when you go."

I moved back.

Detective Humbolt rounded the corner. My dad wiped his eyes and replaced his glasses. Humbolt motioned for me to step out.

I nodded. "Detective."

"Mr. Trestle." He held a manila folder. The edges of eight-by-ten black-and-white glossies poked out from a stack of papers and a couple DVDs in plastic holders. He held it up. "It would appear that sufficient evidence has surfaced to allow your release."

I glanced at my father. He watched Humbolt.

The detective continued. "I know this is a hard subject. But we have security video of Dr. Petrov's murder. And we also have video of Kurtz's killing." He brought his lips together. "The circumstances he created inevitably would have led to another murder, had you not intervened."

He thumbed through the file folder. "A man named Shintao has been arrested on charges relating to the crimes at hand." He closed it. "I personally don't believe that self-defense and the protection of the innocent are any reasons to keep a man jailed. And it would appear that the judge agrees. Per his orders, you're free to go under two conditions—don't leave town until the arraignment, and keep daily contact with your court-designated chaperone."

"Who's that?"

Humbolt stretched an open palm toward my father. My dad smiled. The detective offered his hand to me.

I looked at it, studied his face, then gripped his hand and shook. "Well, all right, then."

My dad drove us home. Sitting in his old Ford Tempo, looking at his profile, I saw a dim reflection of Eli in the lines of his face. I saw myself in the shape of his jawline, the angle of his nose, and the curve of his cheekbones.

I shifted in my seat, my back sore from healing glass cuts. "Have you heard how Naomi is?"

"Her parents called. And someone from Aprisa. Dale . . . ?"

"Spitzer?"

"That's it. She's doing well. They're watching her in the cardiac unit, but the prognosis is very positive."

"So no complications?"

"A little memory loss surrounding the event."

"That's probably a good thing."

"She has some broken ribs."

Probably from the CPR. That and the fall from the helicopter. But she was alive. Not only living, but well. My heart ached to see her.

I touched the pendant around my neck. I traced the etched words, hearing them in my mind.

I would become a doctor.

And Eli would live on for me in a physician's words over a millennia old.

We crossed the Truckee River at the Arlington Bridge, making our way into Old Southwest.

My dad stopped at a crosswalk and ran a hand along his chin. "Humbolt did a little digging into Kurtz's finances."

"Yeah?"

"Sounded like Kurtz was leveraged to the hilt, including a couple big loans from some not-so-reputable sources."

I nodded. "He was trying to grow Aprisa into something bigger. But it was all based on a business model that didn't really work."

"Why didn't he cut his losses and quit?"

"He said he already had deals on the table to go nationwide. I guess he just needed the stats to back it all up. Fortune and fame at his fingertips. Just had to tweak a few run times, make the big contracts, pay off the bad guys, and all would be good."

"But this guy, Letell, found out about the time changes?"

"Yeah. And when he started making noise about it, Kurtz resorted to murder to cover things up."

"But not just he alone."

"No. He hired at least one thug to do some of the dirty work. And there's Shintao. He oversaw the accounting department. My guess is that Kurtz paid him well to keep things on the down-low."

We turned onto a narrow residential street.

I gazed at sidewalks that arched over bulging tree roots. I stared at my hands, incredulous that they'd taken a life. "If Eli hadn't discovered the cause of death and provided the antidote . . ."

My dad pulled into the driveway. "It's an incredible gift. For you. For me. Naomi. No one can ever take that fact away." He put his hand on my shoulder.

I grabbed his wrist and blinked through the moisture in my eyes. "It's great to have you back, Dad."

CHAPTER 49

I stopped chasing.

I learned to run a race of endurance, my goal and destination lying on the not-too-distant horizon, in a home unbound by time or death.

Now we see in a mirror dimly.

Almond shoots and cherry blossoms burst forth from stem tips on the university grounds. The temperate May afternoon lent blue skies populated by voluminous white barges. They pasted ethereal, like an aged ceiling mural.

The crowd din and rhythmic repetition of the master of ceremonies simmered in the back of my mind. The full green grass around the old buildings, the warmth of sunbaked bricks, and the special outdoor ceremony for the graduating med school class—it all contributed to filling my heart with a sense of culmination.

But none birthed greater joy than the sight of Naomi, standing in her spring maternity dress, the fullness of the third trimester ensconcing our child. Sunlight sparkled off the modest engagement diamond and wedding band I'd slipped on her finger three years before.

Her mother stood alongside, new life in her strengthened frame, the last vestiges of sickness far from her countenance. Her father stood proud. By him was Bones, still slight as a flagpole, smiling, arm in arm with his beaming and slightly heavyset fiancée. From the day he first worked up the courage to talk to her in dispatch, they'd become inseparable.

Bookending the lineup, looking ten years younger though four had passed, stood my father. His chin pushed up and chest filled with air—the pathophysiology of pride in his son, and the evidence of life discovered anew.

I felt the small brass pendant that hung outside my gown.

Thank you, Eli.

"Doctor Jonathan Trestle, summa cum laude."

My row of supporters clapped with exuberance. I strode with confidence, a grin uncontainable in my cheeks. I clasped hands with the present med school director, Dr. Thomas Wheatland. The sun glistened off his copper brow, an approving look in his eyes.

I took in my other hand the passing of a baton, the summation of my work in a paper tube bound with red ribbon.

I supped of that moment, satiated with joy, knowing our lives to be but a breath.

For tomorrow we die.

"If only for this life we have hope in Christ, we are to be pitied more than all men.

But Christ has indeed been raised from the dead, the firstfruits of those who have fallen asleep. For since death came through a man, the resurrection of the dead comes also through a man. For as in Adam all die, so in Christ all will be made alive."

—Paul the apostle

ACKNOWLEDGMENTS

To the Logos, God from the beginning, who became flesh and made His dwelling among us.

To my wife, Sarah Beth, for her unceasing support and help. To our children, who light up our home—Daniel, Claire, and Noah.

To my mom, who showed me Jesus from as early as I can remember.

To all my extended family, both near and far, and to my friends, both distant and close-by, for your encouragement and excitement for this book.

To my editor, Karen Schurrer, and the fantastic team at Bethany House Publishers.

To my agent, Janet Grant, for your wisdom.

To Mike Berrier, Katie Cushman, Carrie Padgett, and all my kinsmen in the written word.

To all the underpaid, overworked, and underappreciated paramedics and EMTs out there—God bless and Godspeed in your endeavors.

ABOUT THE AUTHOR

SHAWN GRADY has served for more than a decade as a fire-fighter and paramedic in Reno, Nevada, where he lives with his wife and three children. He was named "Most Promising New Writer" at the 2008 Mount Hermon Writers Conference and is the author of *Through the Fire*.